# 228

by

David E. Weischadle

Published by:

DW Global Strategies, Inc.
P.O. Box 8137
Princeton, New Jersey 08543-8137

ISBN 978-0-6159-4022-9

For more information on the book and the author, go to www.228thenovel.com

## ACKNOWLEDGEMENTS

No book reaches fruition without many hands helping out. I am particularly grateful to Granary Way Media LLC. Granary Way is comprised of two young men, Douglas and David Weischadle, my sons. They took my book, gave the author a new view of it, and helped me to publish it.

I must acknowledge the work of Doug Weischadle, who proved to be a stern taskmaster for his father. He made me re-think each chapter, and then re-create and re-write major sections of the book. His ideas and suggestions proved inspiring and challenging, and if the book is any good, it is because he worked so damned hard on it.

I have to thank my wife, Mary Ann, who has always been a mainstay in my life. She resurrected the book and told Doug and Dave about it. From there, it became a real family project.

# PROLOGUE

The morning was already going bad. Charles E. Custard, Captain, Signal Corps, US Army, holding the paper at arm's length, was regretting his stop at the 21st Signal Group headquarter's tent. After a search for his glasses failed, he finally got the orders focused by stretching his arm out in front of him. Now he could read it. It read:

Department of the Army
Headquarters, 21st Signal Group
APO 96312

Special Orders             5 September 1966
Number 079

1.     On or about 1 September 1966, commanding officer, Site 7, 5th Special Forces, reported that the following enlisted man was killed (KIA) as a result of enemy action:

BURGESS, Andrew NMI, SSG E5, 228 Signal Co., 022139, Asg. To: 5th Special Forces, Detachment 5, Duc My, RVN.

2.     Upon receipt of this order, Commanding Officer, 228 Signal Co., will assign an officer to visit site of incident and issue an official report on all events related to this KIA.

3.     All notes and written report will be forwarded to this headquarters as soon as possible, but no later than 30 September 1966.

FOR THE COMMANDER:     Oswald. D. Harris
                                   CPT, SigC
                                   Adjutant

For Custard, the Vietnam War was pretty much summed up by the order. Orders were given, and orders were taken. His contact with the war for the most part was second handed. He did what he was told.

He already knew about troubles at Duc My, a site that was about 20 clicks north of Nha Trang. Much of it had been personnel issues. The wrong people were sent to do the wrong jobs. Then, there were reports of disagreements among the troops there. However, this issue seemed a little different.

Who was he going to assign the job of dealing with the killing? He needed someone he could control. He was expecting a new officer. He received a promise from Group that a new lieutenant would be assigned from the next batch of replacements. "That's my pigeon," said Custard almost out loud.

With that problem solved, Custard moved to his next problem - where to have breakfast. Grabbing a two-week old issue of *Stars and Stripes*, he headed to his jeep and to the MACV Officers Club and some peace and quiet with a stop on the beach.

# CHAPTER 1

Unlike the soldiers in all the movies he had seen, David Whitehead had no weapon or helmet. He was in khakis, probably the only soldier not in olive green of some sort. He was in the coastal lowland region of Vietnam, getting combat pay and not knowing what to do to earn it.

After leaving Travis Air Force Base, he suffered through the longest ordeal of his life--a plane ride lasting seventeen hours with an hour stopover in Guam. There was also a drunken stopover in Hawaii, but he could only remember sitting near a palm tree. If you can't remember what went on, it doesn't count.

Sitting next to Whitehead on the plane was Ralph Cook, a not-so-young looking, dark-haired first lieutenant. Like Whitehead, Cook was assigned to the 228 Signal Company.

"When do we get to Guam?" Whitehead was trying to make conversation.

"In about six hours!"

Whitehead sat up and asked, "How do you know that? You seem pretty sure."

"I am. I was there a few years ago. Took some training there," Cook said with a yawn and a sigh. He rubbed his blue eyes and slapped his hollow cheeks, trying to sober up.

"How long have you been in the Army?" Whitehead asked after a few moments of silence.

Cook hedged a little and finally said he had been a civilian working for the government for a few years. He joined the Army only a year ago and went through OCS at Fort Gordon.

"I helped set that program up and taught there," said Whitehead. "Don't remember you. I thought I would recognize everyone who went through."

"I think I remember seeing your name," Cook

replied, looking at Whitehead's name tag. "I didn't have you in class."

"I guess that could happen."

Both men were only two of nine officers on the plane assigned to the 228 Signal Company in Nha Trang. No one knew anything about the unit or why it needed nine new officers. One of the other officers assigned to the company thought it was because the unit had seen heavy action and lost all its officers. No way, hoped Whitehead.

The night was clear. The temperature was near 60 degrees, nothing like the heat he felt all day. But the humidity was still oppressive.

Now in the city of Nha Trang, Whitehead could just barely remember the conversation coming out of Hawaii. He was trying to remember who paid the bill at the bar. Afraid to look in his wallet, he hoped it wasn't him.

*

His mind took him back to Ton Son Nhut Air Base. Dawn. The Saigon sun was seeking to shine through a morning haze as Whitehead boarded an Air Force bus for the trip to Ben Hoa. Replacements arriving in-country went to Camp Alpha at nearby Ben Hoa for assignment to units up-country. Camp Alpha was not a shithole. It was a mud hole; the mud reached ankle level and just smelled like shit. Whitehead couldn't believe that this was an Army base of any sort, but it was.

After about three hours of whining to himself and others, Whitehead heard his name over a public address system.

He was perplexed about answering the call and how he would leave his two bags in the open for anyone to steal. Stealing was a popular past-time and was the first thing that everyone warned you about.

"Fuck it!" growled Whitehead. "Let'em take anything

4

they want." Deep down, he hoped someone would steal his belongings. Maybe the Army would send him home to get new clothes.

At a screened-in wooden box, Whitehead identified himself and was told to report back in thirty minutes. Back in only five minutes, he asked what was happening. The NCO at the public address system said someone was picking him up for assignment.

In another ten minutes, two lieutenants who looked vaguely familiar came to claim Whitehead. Looking them over closely, he recognized them from Fort Gordon.

"Well, well, well, if it isn't our old instructor from Fort Gordon! Look! He's a first lieutenant now. They'll promote anybody." Speaking was a tall blond officer from New York, John Gorshen, who was serving in the personnel section of the First Signal Brigade. "Couldn't let you rot in Camp Alpha. Meet George Connolly."

Gorshen and Connolly signed some paper, grabbed Whitehead's bags and led him to a well-washed jeep. After starting the jeep, Gorshen began driving with a recklessness that scared the shit out of Whitehead. Whipping past old shacks and rickety buildings, Gorshen's guided tour comments were lost in the wind. The muddy roads soon turned to asphalt of some sort and the buildings got better. They were less ugly now, but still dirty and decrepit.

The Vietnamese people walking in the streets seemed to ignore the swift moving jeeps. The old Poppa-sans called out obscenities when the jeep actually bumped them. Finally, the streets widened and the character of Saigon as a city started to appear. Sure enough, in true guidebook form, Connolly called Saigon "the Paris of the Orient." Perhaps the crowds, and the wide streets, and maybe the buildings, but not the smell.

"Do you guys smell something?" asked Whitehead.

"It's the food. Those little sidewalk stands and the restaurants give off that smell."

"On purpose?" Whitehead was asking seriously.

Both personnel officers laughed and promised Whitehead that he'd get use to it. In his mind, Whitehead was asking himself what could possibly happen to him that would enable him to get use to that smell.

The jeep suddenly slid to a stop in front of a building with the letters MACV underneath a red shield with a sword. "Military Assistance Command, Vietnam," was stenciled in black letters. Connolly leaned back and asked for a copy of Whitehead's orders. Taking a copy, he jumped out and headed for a door. Meantime, Gorshen threw the jeep into reverse.

"I'll take you to the villa," said Gorshen, flooring the pedal and taking the corner on less than four wheels.

Hanging on to the seat and edges of the jeep, Whitehead was getting self conscious about the fact he was the only person in a khaki uniform. He also was getting concerned about the VC. Where were they? Time Magazine, CBS, NBC, and ABC said they were all over Saigon, blowing up one building or another. In the mean time, Gorshen was driving like a New York City cab driver and bragging about avoiding the trouble spots. Only once did he stop for a few seconds at an intersection. There, Whitehead was propositioned twice, offered four wristwatches, and had one of his bags almost stolen.

The villa turned out to be a three-story house. It was clay colored and had shutters instead of windows. While telling Whitehead that it was built by the French, Gorshen took a bag and led Whitehead upstairs to a second story room which looked over the street. It was a very attractive room and, according to Gorshen, no one else would be sharing it with Whitehead.

Gorshen said to call the Momma-san if he needed anything and he would drop by later to discuss dinner.

"You'll be here a couple of days until we can secure some transportation for you to go up North," said Gorshen.

"What's the 228 like?" asked Whitehead.

"Who knows!   I think every officer coming into the country is assigned to the 228.   Most never make it; they get sent to other units."

Whitehead asked about the other officers who came with him on the plane.

"They left already.   They were all junior to you, except Cook.   I don't know where he went; I think he had special orders."   Gorshen seemed to know what he was talking about, leaving Whitehead with some uneasy feelings about his friend, Cook.

Shutting the door behind Gorshen's parting remarks, Whitehead surveyed the room.   "So this is what war is like?" he mulled.   He laid down on the bed and awoke the next morning at 7 am.   "What happened to dinner?" he mumbled to himself.

*

Three more days of waiting and eating, separated by walking tours, Saigon began to take on a vacation atmosphere.   Then, that Wednesday, a bomb exploded just off To-do Street adding new meaning to the exotic nature of Saigon.

Whitehead had just entered a plaza and could see panic.   People were running and crouching behind benches. He walked toward the center of activity, but stopped when he slipped on something wet.   Catching himself, he looked down and saw the blood.   Looking right he saw the body.

Repelled and sickened, he tried to wipe his sneaker clean.   It wasn't working, so he gave up.   Wanting to look again at the body, he held his breath, felt sick, and looked for the way home.

Moving quickly away from the area and back to the villa, Whitehead found his thoughts locked on the very real dangers of Saigon.   He stood on the balcony of his room and looked down at the MP armed with an M16 in the cement bunker. His mind visualized how easy it would be for a cab loaded with explosives to run into the building and blow it up. He then had an explosion in his head; that's why this room is empty. It's the room that is most vulnerable. "I may be a dead man, just waiting to die."

Before he collapsed, a knock at the door produced Gorshen from personnel. "You're flying out in five hours. Get your shit together. I'll pick you up and deliver you to the air field."

Whitehead nodded and thought about throwing up. Too late. He had to get packed. "Fuck it!" he said to no one. It just seemed the right thing to say.

*

At the airfield he got the initial flavor of the war. Everyone seemed to know what they were doing and ignored anyone who didn't.

Gorshen shook hands and wished him luck. Back in his jeep, Gorshen meshed the gears and stepped on it, out to make more deliveries Whitehead supposed.

"Drop and give me ten," the voice came out of nowhere. Whitehead reflexed into a bend at the waist but stopped when he remembered where he was. Turning, he saw Cook.

"Thought you had special orders," Whitehead said, more as a statement than a question.

"I do. How did you know that?"

Whitehead sensed he said the wrong thing. He responded vaguely that Gorshen or Connolly guessed he had. "What do I know!" joked Whitehead.

Cook changed the subject also. "We must be flying together. How do you rate this special treatment?"

"I thought I lost a lottery and got left with this shitass plane. I hope this isn't a special treat," moaned Whitehead.

"Listen-up everybody," shouted an Army pfc. Wearing a 45 Cal pistol under his arm in a shoulder holster, the GI was clearly in all his glory. "Grab a helmet and flak jacket, and when you get out, leave them on the airplane. We have one stop, and then straight on to Nha Trang. Any questions?" He paused and looked around. "No? Well, enjoy your flight."

Picking up helmets and jackets, both Cook and Whitehead got in the plane. Whitehead put his jacket on and held the helmet on his lap.

Someone had stored the luggage in the back of the plane. Doors were shut, motor started, and prayers said. They were in the air in minutes.

The noise was terrible. No one could possibly talk. A passenger could see only the person to the left or right. The six passenger seats were in two single rows along the windows. Cook sat across from Whitehead. Whitehead looked over and smiled at how Cook was sitting on his flak jacket and had his helmet between his legs. But Cook was deep in thought, reading some hand written notes. Whitehead looked away and out the window and could see American troops moving over the countryside. He then put his head back and fell asleep.

Whitehead awoke with a punch from Cook.

"Do you like the way your balls work?" Cook shouted over the roar of the engine. "If I were you, I'd sit on the jacket. No one in the plane is going to shoot you. The VC don't have any airplanes. But Charlie can aim his captured rifle up in the air and shoot you right in the balls. That's how low we are." Cook's good deed done, he fell back on the seat and dozed.

Not one to ignore good advice, Whitehead pulled the jacket off and jammed it under him and put the helmet under his thighs in front of the seat. He then started to think about a gun. No, he meant a "rifle." A "gun" is a cannon, a howitzer. Nobody would give him a cannon. A rifle, maybe. Jesus Christ, give me something.     He     looked over to Cook.     Where was his weapon?     He was just about to ask him when he noticed the ankle holster on Cook's crossed leg.     As each minute and hour went by, Cook seemed to be much more knowledgeable than his one year of service.

*

From Saigon, Whitehead made several attempts to call the 228 Signal Company in Nha Trang.   He only got through on the last attempt. He spoke to Norman Range, another lieutenant from Fort Gordon, who agreed to pick Whitehead up at the Long Van Air Base.

Rockets shot into the air.   Flares in all colors also went up.   Whitehead watched as the night sky filled with color wondering why Keyes never wrote about flares in the anthem.

Whitehead knew he had made a mistake coming to Vietnam.   It began with ROTC.   He had started out in the Air Force version, took the flight physical and passed it, but changed over to the Army because it required only two years of active duty.

At Rutgers, he majored in history and took education courses for teaching.   But he wasn't really sure he wanted to teach.   So he hedged with ROTC.   He lived home in New Jersey and really couldn't face not going in service, or so he thought.   As it turned out, no one in his family would have cared if he dodged the draft.   He thought everyone was really patriotic.   He only recently found out that the draft laws made everyone patriotic ex post facto.   4-F was good, too!

Like a lot of kids, he also listened to John Kennedy, not realizing he was a hero because he was a lousy navigator and a good swimmer.

It all worked out for awhile.   He went to graduate

school, got a masters and taught for a year. When he did go on active duty in 1965, he went to Fort Gordon for the officer basic course and then stayed to teach in that course and the new officer candidate school. They were looking for teachers and he was heading for Korea. A few questions and requests in what seemed the right places got Whitehead assigned to Fort Gordon. That reassignment eventually led to Vietnam. So much for the right moves. If he had left his orders alone, he'd be at Camp Casey in Korea waiting to go home in six months. From here, he may go home in a body bag.

Everyone told him the Signal Corps doesn't get shot at. Maybe a mine or mortar by mistake. He wasn't sure that was an advantage. In any case, he was here and he'd make the best of it.

Whitehead's thoughts went back to Cook. Getting off the plane, he had simply slapped Whitehead's back, smiled, and said I'll see you around. Cook literally disappeared in the sea of green uniforms all over the terminal.

Waiting was always fun, especially at night in a strange country at war, without any weapons, and dressed in khakis. He was looking for a lieutenant he vaguely remembered and wasn't sure he'd be recognized. But then he did, "Norm."

"Dave, how're you doing? I see you found Nha Trang. Like it so far?" Norm Range was about 5 foot ten, average build, and walked on his toes. His long face was little leaner than Whitehead remembered. Whitehead estimated that Range was about twenty-two years old.

"Yeah, it's great," Whitehead said sarcastically and added, "What do you do for fun?"

Norm confirmed what Whitehead feared: "This place is one big shit hole, except you landed in one that's not as bad as others. Just hope you stay here. No one else has!"

"You mean all those guys who were on my orders

are gone?"

"You bet! They've gone to places unknown. But you're a first lieutenant and we need one of them."

"I guess I should be happy. Why don't I feel that good?" asked Whitehead.

Norm changed subjects. "Let's get you settled in the villa; we have room. If you stay, you don't have to move. If they send you North, then kill a couple of days on the beach before the monsoons make it rough."

"What is this place, Seaside Park?"

Norm was from New Jersey, too. From a town near Rutgers. Sayreville. He also went to Rutgers, graduating three years after Whitehead. All this convinced Whitehead that he would be moving on also. Nobody would put people with the same backgrounds together and let them feel comfortable in this country. Norm was also a second lieutenant, needing only a few months for his promotion.

*

The company villa was a stucco bungalow without glass windows and surrounded completely by palm trees and an iron fence. A small Vietnamese teenager with a boy scout campaign hat opened the gate and waved Norm's jeep into a short driveway. He locked the gate and followed the two lieutenants onto the porch. Norm introduced the guard. He was one of many Vietnamese that Whitehead met that was named Nguyen.

Norm brought him to his room in the back and pointed to a bed and said sleep. It was ten-thirty at night, or 2230 hours. Norm said "good night." Neither officer had a warning that tomorrow would be a big day.

## CHAPTER 2

"Wake up; it's oh-seven-hundred!"

Whitehead snarled back, "Let me know when it's seven o'clock."

"Very funny. I think you'll have to see Colonel Duel today; first thing. He'll decide what to do with you."

"Will he send me home if he can't decide?"

Norm issued one of his many warnings. "Dave, that guy could send you to some pretty bad places. Be careful. He doesn't like the 228 Signal Company. Give him a good line of bullshit. My mistake was I told him that I was getting out after my two years were up. Tell him you want to go regular army."

"Christ, if I tell him I want to go regular army, he'll send me to the 101st Airborne and I'll get my ass shot off. Tell me exactly what you told him. If I use the same line, maybe he'll let me stay with you."

"Don't bet on it," replied Norm.

A shower, shave and a jeep ride later found Whitehead and Range eating breakfast in the officer's club at Group headquarters. Powdered eggs on a plate and coffee in a bowl. Whitehead asked about the bowl. Range said, "There are no cups in Nha Trang. We were only able to get bowls."

"That's strange," said Whitehead. "I bet some other group of bastards have all cups and no bowls. They're probably eating cereal out of a cup."

"I never thought about that," said a surprised Range. "Maybe I'll call a couple of units and see if they want to swap bowls for cups. I'm the company supply officer and can do things like that."

After a few seconds to sip coffee, Norm continued, "The old man said you should check into Group headquarters first thing and see the adjutant, Captain Harris. We better finish and get you there now. It's nearly

13

oh-eight-hundred."

"Does he have an x on his ass so I can be sure to kiss it correctly?"

"Don't joke, especially with Harris; he's a prick and a half. He, too, could send you to some bad places."

"Good luck," Norm said, heading for a tent with an orange decal that read "Decibel Devils, 228 Signal Company."

\*

Group headquarters was really only a tent stretched over wooden supports. The sides were built-up with plywood and had mosquito netting pulled down over it. Going in the tent, Whitehead walked to the first desk, came to attention, saluted, and handed the man behind the desk his orders, saying, "Lieutenant Whitehead reporting as ordered."

"Welcome to the 21st Signal Group, but I'm not Harris. I'm Private Hatrick. Use to be Sergeant Hatrick. I'll get Harris."

Shit, thought Whitehead, fly seventeen thousand miles and I report to a private.

"OK Whitehead, come this way and report to the Colonel. I'm Captain Harris."

"Yes, sir. Down the hall?"

Harris nodded.

The headquarters tent was pretty large inside, had a raised wooden floor, and was divided into four sections. Coming to the end of the tent, Whitehead turned smartly to his left and was about to report when he found he was facing no one. Colonel Duel was to his rear and he had made a complete jerk of himself. Again. He did an about face, saluted, and shouted, "Lieutenant Whitehead reporting as ordered."

"Stop shouting. Jesus H. Christ, everyone comes in shouting. Shut up and wait while I read this order I have to sign."

Whitehead stood at attention waiting for Duel to tell him to stand at ease. Duel didn't, and wouldn't. Duel, about 50 was a little heavy around the mid-section and looked short, even sitting down. He read the order and appeared to read it again. Signing it, he called Harris who came in and took the order for distribution.

"Sit down in that chair," commanded Duel. "Let me read your file. How did you get to be a first lieutenant in eight months?"

"I went to graduate school for a master's degree and then I taught school for a year," answered Whitehead in his strongest voice. He was petrified that this man would send him someplace that could get him killed. "It all counted for time and grade."

"You could be a captain in eight or nine months if you don't fuck up. Thought about staying in?"

"Yes sir," Whitehead lied. He didn't want to, but it seemed like the thing to do.

"Good," said Duel. "We'll keep you close by. Report to the 228 and make it your business to avoid the shitheads that are there now. It's one of the worst run outfits I got. Everything is fucked up. If I want someone, I have to go to the beach, or downtown. You watch your ass! I can still find a shithole for you. Now get out and get to work."

Standing up, he saluted and made a right turn, marching out of Duel's office and heading for the entrance. He was just about the leave the tent the same way he came in.

"Where the fuck are you going Whitehead?" The cry came from Captain Harris. Whitehead came back to his desk and stood. "Is that the way you report?"

Oh, shit, he thought, the honeymoon was over already? "I'm sorry, Captain. I was thinking about my assignment."

15

"You're not assigned yet. You have to go to Cam Ranh Bay and report to Lt Col Butler. He will assign you. Get your bags and report to the airfield for an air taxi down to Cam Ranh. Report to Butler, and if he agrees, come back on the next flight. Got that?" Harris seemed finished. "Do you have that, lieutenant? Give me an answer!"

Whitehead, thinking about the trip in another city, idly answered, "Yeah, I think I do."

"Who the hell do you think you're talking to?" Harris stood up behind his desk. "It's SIR! Do you hear me? It's 'yes sir'."

"Oh, sorry. I mean, sorry, sir."

Harris sat down and pointed to the door, "Get the fuck out and stay out of my way."

Not knowing what to do, Whitehead came to attention and saluted, and left, tripping over the netting hanging on the side of the tent covering the wooden structure.

Outside, he felt like throwing up again, and could only think to find Norman Range. He saw the tent with the decibel devil on it.

Pushing the flap of the supply tent aside, he called out, "Norm? Lieutenant Range? Are you in here?"

Jumping up from the desk, Specialist 4th class Charles Jumpers leaped to attention, and then shouted, "At-tent-shun!"

Whitehead did what he was told, he came to attention. Norm came up behind him and whispered, "At ease."

Passing Whitehead in the entrance, Norm told Jumpers to sit down. "Come in, Dave. You have to get used to Jumpers. He wants to go airborne, but I won't let him go. I need him here because only he knows where all the equipment is. This is his second twelve-month tour."

"Hello, Jumpers," said Whitehead. "I guess you

have the right name for airborne."

Jumpers looked confused and replied, "Charlie is a pretty ordinary name. Nothing airborne about that, sir."

"I meant Jumpers."

"Oh, yeah, I guess it does sound airborne. Never thought about that."

"Norm, I have to go to Cam Ranh Bay and report to a Colonel Butler. I'm coming to the 228 if he says yes. But I have to get my bags and fly there today."

"Same old game. You think they'd stop playing this game. Come on, I'll get the jeep and collect your things. We can make the airport in time. No problem with flights to Cam Ranh. Could probably get an artillery spotter to fly you there also. Want to see some action? You sit behind the pilot while he calls in artillery fire on Charlie. How about it?"

"Norm, I just want to get to Cam Ranh Bay. I'll check out the war later. Just get me to the airfield and let me get on one of those big planes. I had enough of that Otter I flew up to Nha Trang in."

Back in the jeep and after a stop at the villa for the bags, Range and Whitehead were heading for the airfield. Whitehead couldn't believe how Range took everything in stride. Must be his survival technique.

Coming up to the entrance of Long Van Air Base, Norm had to weave around the Vietnamese nationals going and coming through the gate.

"Norm, where do all these Vietnamese come from? What do they do here at the base?"

"You'll see. They're all over the place. No one is worried about security. GIs take pictures of everything and then give them to the Vietnamese shops to develop them. It's perfect for espionage activity. The company has a couple who do typing of one sort or another. They could be typing top-secret documents all over this base."

Long Van was a pretty well developed air base.

Most of the buildings were permanent, made of corrugated tin or prefabricated material. The Air Force knows how to live right.

There were many wooden buildings, apparently constructed with local labor. Driving through the base almost made you feel at home. Base chapel, library, PX, and all the other amenities were waiting for use by the airmen, and apparently everyone else as well.

There were as many GIs as airmen, but there were certainly more Vietnamese than anyone else, which brought the subject of the Vietcong to Whitehead's mind. He was just going to ask Norm where the VC were when Norm stopped the jeep and pointed to the terminal.

"Let's get you on board. You could be back by tonight. Call me at the villa and I'll come out to get you."

"God, when you get back to civilian life, you'll be able to drive a taxi in New Brunswick, Norm. You've learned a trade!"

"Don't mention home to me, Dave. I want to go there too bad."

Whitehead checked in at the terminal desk and got authorization for Cam Ranh. Bags in hand and moving toward the plane, Whitehead said, "OK, Norm, thanks for the ride. I'll call you later, unless the gods send me somewhere else. I guess that's still possible."

*

The plane landed as swiftly as it took off. Whitehead got up and met a sergeant at the ramp who was throwing the luggage onto the tarmac. He used no care or tact with the luggage or the passengers. "Those of you getting off, get off quick. Those of you getting on, get on quick. Otherwise, stay the fuck away from the aircraft." Nicely phrased, thought Whitehead.

Whitehead picked up his luggage and looked for the

terminal. Seeing it, he carried and dragged his two bags and reported to the desk.

"Where do I find the 79th Signal Battalion?" asked Whitehead.

"Lieutenant, I may look smart, but I don't have any idea where any battalion is. I'm just a plane dispatcher. I can get you to Danang, Hue, An Khe, and Da Lat. But I don't know no battalions." The army staff sergeant suggested Whitehead go to the telephone and ask for information.

Whitehead took his suggestion and was surprised to find that it worked. A PFC serving as company clerk answered the phone for the battalion and said he would send transportation to the terminal. But it could be some time before it got there. The PFC took his name and said he'd have him paged at the terminal.

Realizing it was nearly noon, Whitehead looked for food. He found a snack bar, ordered a can of soda and a wrapped sandwich. The soda was great, the sandwich was sick. He got another soda and returned to his bags which were still where he dropped them by the phone. He found a chair, sat down and began his wait. He dozed and awoke to find somebody shaking him.

"Are you Lieutenant Washington?" The kid may have been eighteen, more like twelve. He repeated, "Are you Lieutenant Whittington?"

"How about Lieutenant Whitehead?" Whitehead asked.

"That's close enough for me, sir. You suppos' to go to the 79th?"

"Yep, that's me!" said Whitehead. "What's my new name?"

"I'm sorry sir. They scribbled your name on a paper and I can't find it. I was working on the latrine and they pulled me off it to get you."

"Private, I'm glad they have a sense of priorities in

your outfit," Whitehead joked as he picked up the bags, handing one to the kid.

"What's your name, son?" Whitehead could say that because he was twenty-four and a lot older.

"Brackett."

They walked to the jeep but said nothing. Brackett got in behind the wheel, started the motor, and almost got it in gear. Stalling, he got the jeep started again and jerked away down the road.

"Driving long, Brackett?"

"No, just started. I never drove a stick shift before I got in the Army. Never drove a car even."

"You're doing fine," assured Whitehead. "Try third gear now that we're moving."

Before the conversation could develop, they reached the battalion area.

"I'll bring your bags, sir"

Whitehead nodded a thanks, looked around for no reason, and then entered another tent-like building. He saw a captain sitting at a desk, making sure he eyeballed the captain tracks on his collar. He wasn't going to report to a pfc again. He proceeded to the desk, came roughly near attention, saluted and announced he was reporting as ordered.

"Whitehead?" The captain, whose name tag read Russo, scratched his balding head and tried to organize what few thoughts he was capable of. "Do you have orders or something to tell me what I'm supposed to do with you?"

"Yes sir. I'm here to talk to Colonel Butler. I talked with Colonel Duel earlier today and he has assigned me to the 228."

"You're going to be assigned to the 228? Impossible. No one gets assigned to the 228; no one goes to the 228. Duel said you were going there? Take a seat."

Russo turned to the phone, gave a number, and waited a few seconds, and then said. "Sir, this is Russo.

I've a lieutenant here who said that Col. Duel assigned him to the 228. Thought you liked to know. Ok, sir. We'll be expecting you."

"OK, Whitehead. Keep sitting there, Butler's on his way over to make the appropriate noises."

About fifteen minutes went by with neither Russo nor Whitehead saying a word to each other. When Russo finally did move behind his desk, a Louis Lamour novel fell off his lap. He apparently forgot about it during the conversation. Must be a tough war for Russo, too. When Butler did arrive, Russo was very officious and acted in the ways adjutants are supposed to act.

Butler was tall, well over six feet. He looked down at Whitehead and told him to come to the rear of the tent where he had his office. "When did you see Duel?" he asked while sitting down and motioning Whitehead to stay in front of the desk. Apparently, Russo knew enough to stay with them.

"This morning, sir. I arrived from Saigon yesterday morning."

"You mean Ben Hoa," probed Butler.

"No sir," answered Whitehead as flatly as he could. "I was picked up at Ben Hoa on Saturday by personnel people and brought to a villa where I stayed for three days."

Butler looked at Russo. "Nice treatment. Who was responsible for that?"

"I taught at the Signal School in Gordon. I met most if not all the new lieutenants coming into service over a nine-month period. All of them seem to be over here."

"Any reason why Duel decided to assign you to Nha Trang?"

"None that I know of. I didn't ask." Whitehead was beginning to worry. The reaction he felt here was a little strange.

"OK, Russo will cut orders assigning you to the 228. Be back in about an hour to pick them up and we'll get you a lift to the airfield."

Whitehead straightened a little, saluted, and was about to leave. "Whitehead, remember, you're in this battalion, not the 21st Signal Group. Orders come from here." It was clearly a warning from Butler.

"Yes, sir." Whitehead moved to the front of the tent and waited for Russo who was still talking to Butler.

What the fuck am I getting into, thought Whitehead. These guys are paranoid about something. They must think I'm somebody's illegitimate son.

Russo came out of his conference.

"The officer's club is up the hill about a mile. Take a walk up there, get something to eat, and then get back here for your orders."

"Ok, will do."

"OK, will do what?"

Oh shit, he did it again, "Ok, will do sir." Whitehead corrected himself and said, "Sorry."

Russo, in true military fashion, shouted, "Don't be sorry! Get the fuck out and don't be late."

Whitehead left and moved toward the club. Going cross-county to the club meant walking in sand. No grass or dirt existed here. Boards had been laid on the ground as walkways. Fuck it, he thought. The sand will feel like Point Pleasant. The ocean can't be far away.

Whitehead retraced his steps back to the battalion and reached it there well before an hour had passed. Russo greeted him.

"What took you so long? Your orders were ready a half hour ago. Just talked to Harris at Group. He can't figure your assignment either. You must have one line of bullshit."

Brackett appeared from around the tent and put Whitehead's bags in the back of another jeep. Whitehead got in the jeep and saluted Russo who waved a return of sorts. Bracket pulled away, grinding all the gears he used.

The ride to the airfield was quiet.    Whitehead was in total thought about the assignment.    What the fuck was he getting into?

*

He started thinking about his experiences in Cam Ranh Bay, but the plane dipped for landing before he could even put a couple events together.    The landing was terrible, but better than crashing.

At the terminal phone, he gave the GI operator Norm's number.    After Jumpers answered with the official unit designation, Whitehead asked for Norm.    Norm came on, "Did you survive?    Are you still with us?"

"Yes, but I had to tell Butler I was Duel's illegitimate son.    What the hell is going on?    This assignment is taking on very mysterious overtones.    You must be sitting on gold in Nha Trang.    No one wanted to know shit about me, except how I wrangled the assignment."

"Dave, you'll like it here.    Go where I met you the other night.    I'll be there in fifteen minutes."

Whitehead did what he was told.    Norm was there in ten minutes.    "Let's go to the Air Force club.    I'm done for the day.    We'll put your bags at the desk for safe keeping."

In five minutes, they were in front of the club, an unimpressive permanent building of little apparent importance.    Inside, the appearance changed.    It was decorated in Air Force motif, propellers, pictures of airplanes from all the wars, and wall-to-wall bodies of guys drinking themselves into oblivion.

"The drinks are cheap and the food is good," said Norm.    "Come with me. I have chits."

"Did you say you have the shits?" joked Whitehead, knowing full well what chits were.

"No, but I did have them yesterday.    You may have

them tomorrow.   I have chits -- C-H-I-T-S", he spelled. "You need them to spend any money in the clubs.   You buy them in a book.   You can do that tomorrow.   I'll buy tonight; then you buy tomorrow night."

"Can I afford you, Norm?"

"Yeah, I'm cheap.   Everything is cheap in Vietnam."

"Go ahead, say the next line, Norm.   Life is cheap here, too."

"Just watch your ass.   CYA, remember that," primed Norm.

"Cover Your Ass.   No truer words e'er spoken. Poetry to one's ears."

After a couple of drinks, Norm suggested a view of the beach.

"Oh, god, yes, my day would be incomplete without a view of the beach which everyone tells me is beautiful."

Norm thought a bit, trying to figure out if Whitehead was serious. Giving up, he answered, "It's the best beach outside of New Jersey.   It use to be a resort town, like Asbury Park.   Now it's supposed to be an R&R center for the VC.   Nha Trang and Vung Tau are favorite seaside resorts for the VC.   No one bothers them, and they don't bother the Americans."

"Pretty nice deal for everyone," added Whitehead, hoping it was true.

*

Norm spoke in true travel guide fashion, "I do believe we are near the water.   Ahead is Beach Road which runs along the entire stretch of sand and ocean."

At the corner, Norm didn't turn.   He went straight, hopping a little curb and driving out onto the beach.   Norm stopped the jeep and shut off the motor. Right and left for a half mile was the Nha Trang beach.

Everyone was right. It was beautiful. There were very few people at this time of day. Whitehead's watch was reading almost six-thirty. They got out of the jeep and stood in front. A couple of Vietnamese walked by, looked but said nothing.

"Feels like Island Beach," said Whitehead, recalling how that Jersey beach was isolated and wild. He looked around and felt removed from his near week long experience in this strange, new country.

Norm resumed his tour guide, "Those buildings are beach restaurants. The locals eat there; some GIs do, too. I stay away. When I first got here, a couple of soldiers were killed by VC who sold pineapples on the beach. They had hand grenades inside them. The GIs opened them to eat and blew themselves up. That's why, smart people warn you not to let the beach lure you into a false sense of security."

"Beautiful harbor," said Whitehead, mulling what Norm just told him.

"The harbor was mined not too long ago. The VC sank a couple of oil tankers and shot at some guards on those barges that are out there. Some of that shooting you heard the night you came in was probably retaliation for something. If the VC does something, the Americans and South Vietnamese do something in return. Or the reverse occurs. If each side remains quiet, nothing happens. That's what I'm told." Norm added, "Don't believe it; I think there are crazies on both sides."

"Norm, remember at Gordon? The RAs use to joke about Vietnam: It's not much of a war, but it's the only thing we got going! Everyone was anxious to get to `Nam and get a bronze star."

"Dave, I just want to get home."

"I'm beginning to feel a little guilty. I'm standing here enjoying a beach and watching people swimming. There are guys like you and me dying somewhere, not too far away. Duel could have sent me to some shit hole to die. Do we just take this assignment and shut up?"

"Hey, how about the guys in Canada? How about the guys home? How about the guy who takes your job? Why should we feel guilty?" Norm stopped but didn't seem convinced. "If I wasn't so scared, I would feel guilty."

"Thank God, I thought I was the only guy scared shitless," said Whitehead. "Everyone I run into is preoccupied with how I got assigned to the 228."

"Stay scared, Dave. One guy told me that being scared will get you through this place."

"You believe that, Norm?"

"I'm scared anyway. It seemed an easy thing to believe."

They both got quiet. Dust was turning into night. Finally, Norm said: "Let's go home!"

"Shit, I can't swim that far. New Jersey must be fifteen thousand miles away," Whitehead said. He then added, "But I'll give it a try."

They rode back to the villa and went to sleep with only a few words between them. Whitehead laid there for almost an hour, brooding about why he was in Vietnam and others weren't. The brooding turned to dreading as he gave into fears that the next 360 days were going to be the worst, if not last, of his life.

## CHAPTER 3

Friday morning arrived and found Whitehead and Range in the officers' club finishing breakfast. Range had been quiet all morning. Fascinated by the number of men in civilian clothes, Whitehead finally asked Norm who they were.

"Who the hell knows! They're either civilian contractors, consultants, reporters, or spooks."

"Spooks?" repeated Whitehead. "You mean like in black guys?"

"No, a `spook' is a CIA agent. They're like ghosts, they don't exist. Air America. Did you see those planes at Long Van?" Whitehead nodded yes, drank more coffee from his bowl, and looked at Norm as he continued his story. "The airline is run by the CIA. It was supposed to be a cover for them, but it's an open secret. They don't even deny it anymore."

"Pretty mysterious place when you know what's going on," mused Whitehead, hiding his fascination. He started to think about Cook. Maybe that's what he was, a spook. The man was pretty mysterious.

Range interrupted Whitehead's thoughts.

"Finished with your coffee?"

Whitehead nodded. "Let's go."

That morning, Whitehead was to report to Captain Custard, the company commander. Range told Whitehead what he knew of the C.O.'s history in the jeep on their way over. Born in Kansas, Custard graduated from West Point and came to Vietnam as a captain. His first two assignments were staff jobs which the man did not like. As a result of several bad judgment calls, Custard was assigned to the 228 still looking for a promotion to major. According to Range, no one left 'Nam the same rank he came with unless he was a fuck-up.

After parking the jeep near the supply tent, the two

men approached the orderly room. It was one of a series of four narrow buildings each having screened windows and going back about a hundred feet.

"This is the orderly room and operations center. Custard's office is to the left as we enter; Lt. Dancer has a desk in the back. You may like Dancer, Dave. I find him generally cold and self-serving, but he opens up at times and seems real human. He's smart and knows how to get a job done. Those three other buildings are barracks for the troops. The NCOs live in villas like we do. Good luck, Dave, and, as always, watch what you say."

Dancer was already coming out of the back as they entered the building. "Hello, Norm. What have you got for us? New blood?" Putting his hand out, he said to Whitehead, "Hi, I'm Jim Dancer, operations officer. The old man will be right back. Then maybe we'll all go in and talk about assignments."

The lanky, sandy-haired Dancer had on a set of jungle fatigues. They were dark green, having never been washed. He had pinned his metal brass on, not having had a chance to bring them to the tailors next door to have the cloth emblems sewed on.

They all moved to the back into the operations area. On the walls in the operations area were several maps with circles on them. Whitehead began scanning the maps. Dancer noticed his interest and began an explanation.

"The circles are our isolated sites. We have two just north of here that are very important. A team at Nimh Hoa supports the Koreans. Another at Duc My provides communications for a special forces ranger outpost. There seems to be some personnel trouble at Duc My. I asked Sgt Boggs to go up there tomorrow. Maybe you'll be able to go with him."

Dancer stopped when he heard movement toward the front of the building. "I think that's the old man coming back. Let's go meet him."

Dancer spoke up, "Sir, this is Lieutenant Whitehead."

"Good to meet you, Whitehead. Welcome to the company." The welcome was said coldly and without any warmth. "Did Lieutenant Dancer tell you about us? Or maybe Range did? In any case, we'll talk once you get settled."

"I'm looking forward to it, sir," answered Whitehead, thinking it sounded like the right thing to say.

"Really, you mean that?" Custard's words stopped everyone. They seemed to wait for the next words from the company's senior officer. "Never mind that question." Custard was obviously trying to recover.

Custard's office was bare. In it was an Army wooden desk with an almost standard name stand. To the left of his name were signal flags; to the right were captain tracks. No pens or pencils were in sight. In front of the desk was one chair.

The four officers were now standing and waiting for Custard to begin the meeting.

"Dancer, what's the trouble at Duc My?"

"Captain, it seems that Burgess went off the deep end and is fighting with everyone. I told Boggs to plan a visit tomorrow and be prepared to straighten the situation out. Lieutenant Whitehead might want to go with him to see the site and get a feel for the country up there."

"Good idea. Get settled in today. Range will get you what you need for tomorrow." Custard seemed pleased with getting rid of Whitehead. "Has Dancer talked to you about assignments?"

"No, sir."

"Okay." Custard sat silent for a few moments. "Lieutenant Whitehead, you'll be site commander at Goldfinch. They need some leadership down there."

"Yes, sir." Whitehead responded.

Turning to Whitehead, Dancer said: "Sergeant Boggs will be your platoon sergeant. The trip tomorrow will be to one of the sites you now have responsibility for."

Turning back to Custard who was already thinking something else and staring out the window at the next building, Dancer interrupted his thoughts. "Is there anything else, sir?"

Turning to Dancer, he quietly replied, "No, no! Dismissed."

All three officers said, "Thank you, sir." They saluted and then left.

Returning to the operations center, Dancer spoke to Norm. "Leave Whitehead with me for the morning. Get him any gear he might need for tomorrow. They can use my jeep and a truck from the motor pool. Around noon, go down to Goldfinch and get Whitehead so you two can go to payroll and personnel for all the paperwork."

"OK, Jim. Dave, I'll see you later." Norm turned and left the tent for his supply duties.

"Dave, I'll call Boggs and tell him you're coming. McCready will drive you down to Goldfinch to meet Boggs and some of the other NCOs. Stay there this morning and learn what you can about what the company is doing. Then, this afternoon, you better check into the area personnel office and get your pay records organized."

Putting his hand out again to shake, Dancer once again welcomed Whitehead and wished him luck.

*

The 228 Signal Company was not a "strac" outfit. In other words, it neither looked good nor performed well. Its equipment was old. The 2 1/2 ton trucks were left over from the Korean War. Generators were always breaking down. The unit seemed a target for problems since its creation.

Activated in December 1941 in the Philippines, it was captured by the Japanese three months later.

Deactivated after the war, it was again brought to life for Vietnam. By the time Whitehead reached Nha Trang, the 228 was providing radio relay connections between Field Forces V headquarters in the city and American and Korean combat troops to the North.

Besides installing telephones, laying wire, and operating the main switchboard, called Goldfinch, the company had teams and equipment attached to combat and special forces units throughout the central coastal plain surrounding Nha Trang. These teams required frequent visits by the officers and NCOs of the 228 Signal Company causing the unit to become more frazzled than it should have been.

It was a classic case of too much being asked of too few. Never did its manpower grow beyond 120 enlisted men, 15 noncommissioned officers, and three commissioned officers. Whitehead, en route to Goldfinch the next day, became the fourth officer.

Goldfinch was both a place and a process. Located across from the 8th Field hospital, it bordered the South Vietnamese section of Long Van Air Force base. Also, on one side was the hospital's medivac helicopter landing zone.

Goldfinch serviced all of Nha Trang as a switchboard. A two-man team installed the nearly 500 phones while a six-man team from the 701st strung the wire. The switchboard itself was old and, in the eyes of the members of the company, should never have been brought to Vietnam. It worked, but just barely. A new long distance switchboard sat by the airfield in two big trailers waiting for someone who knew how to operate it to arrive.

Accompanied to Goldfinch by the company's acting first sergeant McCready, Whitehead found sergeant Boggs in the process of setting up two new radio antennas. The two antennas looked more like big flyswatters to Whitehead. Upon seeing the man, Whitehead thought immediately that Boggs was Abraham Lincoln reincarnated. Boggs, tall and skinny, was stripped to his waist and sweating. He was giving directions and working at the same time.

Without getting too close to the work, McCready called to Boggs, "Hey, Boggs, when you get done playing with your troops, I've got someone here for you to meet."

"I'm a little indisposed right at the moment. Should I drop what I'm doing?"

Boggs was indeed in a tough spot. He was grasping what looked to be a pretty heavy post holding the antennae and taking directions from someone in a hut mounted on the back of a two and a half ton truck. "Hey, sarge. We got it. We're getting the signal five bye."

Boggs let out a sigh of relief. "Finally! Ok, McCready, I'm all done and all yours. Kilmer, plant this pole and don't lose the signal."

Kilmer looked pleased at the opportunity. Whitehead couldn't believe that anyone could get that excited about filling a hole.

"Thanks, sarge. You really know you're stuff."

"Boggs, this is Lieutenant Whitehead, your new platoon leader. Take good care of him. I'm going back to the company."

Both Whitehead and Boggs watched as Sgt. McCready turned, got back in the jeep, and sped down the road and away from Goldfinch.

"Boggs, I understand we're taking a trip tomorrow," Whitehead said, turning back to Boggs.

"Yes, sir. I thought we'd stop at Ninh Hoa and then go to Duc My. Duc My is where the trouble is. Did the old man tell you what it was?"

"Sergeant, he didn't tell me anything." Whitehead found himself looking up to Boggs. He had to be over six-four. Whitehead was at best five foot eight. "As a matter of fact, Sarge, I'll confess to you right now, I don't know much about anything. No. I take that back. I know that Nha Trang is a great place for beaches, booze and broads.    I know that because everyone told me so from Saigon to Cam Ranh Bay."

"Well, I can't attest to all that.    I've only been here three weeks.    I understand the first sergeant, when he comes back, can tell us a lot about all three; he's a specialist in anything that makes money."

Boggs had his fatigue top back on and had motioned for them to walk back to what seemed to be the center of the site.

"Are you an engineer, sir?"    Boggs asked.

"I use to teach social studies in the 8th grade in New Jersey.    For the last 12 months I was at Fort Gordon teaching military law and combat logistics in the officer course at the OCS.    I have absolutely no technical training."

Having said all that, Whitehead could see a haze of disappointment on Boggs' face.    "However, I had an earth science minor in college and know a lot about dust and mud."

Boggs didn't know what to say.    He smiled, and then smiled again.    After smiling again, he asked, "Coffee?"

"No, thanks anyway. I know from your face you were looking for someone who knew what was going on. But I don't.    I hope to in a little while; I'll try like hell. One thing I don't want, it's to get anyone killed.    So, if you see I'm doing something wrong, tell me.    I don't want to screw things up any more than you do.    I'm a reserve officer, out of ROTC, but I respect that this is your career."

Before Boggs could say anything, Whitehead added, "Sergeant, Lieutenant Range is going to pick me up around noon for chow and then take me to personnel.    Why don't you go ahead with your regular routine for today. Tomorrow we can talk some more.    Then, maybe we can spend the next few days working together on what you see as urgent."

"That sounds good, sir.    You going to draw a rifle

and flack jacket from supply?"

"Hadn't thought about it," admitted Whitehead.

"Well, I'll see Jumpers later today and tell him to have it ready for you at 0800. We'll leave right after seeing the old man. Sergeant Southland will come with us in our jeep. I think we're using Lieutenant Dancer's. Fritz from the motor pool will drive a deuce and a half behind us with some new generators."

"Sounds good to me. I thought I would spend some time just roaming around and seeing what's happening here. Think that's alright?"

"Sir, this is all yours now. Everyone will know who you are. Ask any question you want. I'll see you tomorrow." Boggs gave a quick salute that was natural and nice. Whitehead hadn't expected it and recovered to return as good a salute as he could remember.

*

The next day, Range picked up Whitehead a little before noon and after parking the jeep nearby, the two men headed to the Officer's club. The club was packed. The bar was closed, but the building was air conditioned. Norm and Whitehead folded their caps and looked for seats.

They moved to the cafeteria line passing some pleasantries as they went. Whitehead had a tray in his hands and, not knowing what to do with it while waiting for his turn at the food, held it behind his back. He felt it hit someone and turned to apologize. "I'm sorry. I didn't -- Cook?!" But then he looked carefully. It looked like Cook, but the name tag read "Benson" and the oak leaf on the collar meant "major."

"Excuse me, I thought I knew you, sir. I apologize for hitting you with my tray." The words came out but the meaning was pro forma.

The man behind Whitehead looked like Cook.

34

Whitehead was sure it was Cook. But the man insisted he wasn't.

"It's OK, lieutenant. Just be careful with the tray." The voice was almost like Cook's, but there was no sign of recognition from "Major Benson."

He couldn't look back. Whitehead felt stupid. But he couldn't help feeling it was Cook standing behind him. Finally, he turned around and was going to try again. But neither Cook nor Benson was there. An Air Force colonel was and he said, "Lieutenant, how about paying for your food and moving along."

"Oh, sorry sir."

Paying his chits for both Norm and himself, Whitehead continued to look all over the club. No sign of Cook or Benson, or whoever it was. Cook began as a mystery, and remained one.

Sitting down, Norm asked, "What's wrong, Dave? You look a little white. What did that major say to you?"

"Norm, I could've sworn that the major behind me was Lieutenant Cook. He said he wasn't or, at least, didn't accept my identification. What the fuck is going on? I'm here a week and I'm losing my fucking marbles."

"Hey, Dave, everyone in uniform starts to look alike. That's why they put name tags on the fatigues. Look around, you'll see a dozen guys who look like Crook."

"Not Crook. His name was Cook."

"Eat," ordered Norm. It was the only time he ever heard Norm issue an order. Whitehead followed it.

Lunch was followed by a ride to the beach then a short nap at the villa. Around two o'clock, the two men headed to the personnel office where Whitehead spent the afternoon completing forms for his personnel file. Two hours later, Norm was driving Whitehead to the Special Forces Club. The club opened at 1600 hours for drinks and 1700 hours for dinner.

The food was good. On their way out, they

considered another drink, but decided against it. They considered a movie, but each said tomorrow was a long day. Heading toward the jeep, they would be satisfied with some letter writing and sleep.

From somewhere behind, a voice called out: "Dave, Dave Whitehead."

Both Norm and Whitehead turned; it was Ralph Cook. "Remember me? Ralph Cook. I just got in from up North. I saw you leaving the mess hall."

"Yeah, I saw you this afternoon, too," said Whitehead.

"Not this afternoon. I flew in on a chopper at 1600 hours and hitched a ride over here. You must have mistaken someone else for me."

"Yeah, that's what a Major Benson said, too."

Whitehead didn't pursue it further. Obviously, Cook had something in mind here. Whitehead kept the game going by introducing Norm. "Good to meet you, Norm. Dave and I came over together."

Cook seemed a little uneasy and finally said, "Dave, could I see you a minute." Looking at Norm, he added, "Alone."

Norm picked up the clue. "I'll wait at the jeep, Dave. Nice meeting you, Cook."

Cook watched Norm go and then said to Whitehead, "Dave, could you hold something for me? I'm going to be traveling a little up and down the country for my unit. I've got something in my bag that's very valuable to me and I don't want to lose it. Would you mind holding it for a time? Maybe a month. I'll be back in Nha Trang then and will get it from you."

"Gee, I don't know. What is it?"

Cook reached into the duffel bag he had and took out a carbine, M1 type, which was used in the Korean War extensively by officers. In Vietnam, the carbine had some renewed interest because it was light and easy to handle.

Many people carried their own private weapons, so the market for carbines and even weapons like a Thompson sub-machine gun was quite good. The carbine that Cook had was worth about $150.

Cook handed it to Whitehead.

"Just hold onto it. Keep it for me."

Whitehead noticed that Cook looked around from time to time, making him feel like he was participating in an illegal act. "Well, I don't know."

"Hey, I guarantee you this is not an illegal weapon or anything like that. You're just doing me a favor. I like the carbine and don't want to lose it. Please hold it for me."

"OK, I guess I can do that. Are you sure that wasn't you in the officers club?"

"No, it wasn't me." Cook smiled. "And thanks for holding the carbine. I'll see you in a month. Take care."

Cook and Whitehead shook hands and both turned walking away from each other. Whitehead stopped and turned around. Cook was gone again. Whitehead looked and walked to the opening between the buildings, but Cook was gone. He turned and went to the jeep.

Norm saw the carbine.

"What the hell is that?"

"Cook asked me to hold it for him. Think I made a mistake?"

"Who knows. I got one just like it behind my bed. Let's get to the villa. It's dark and we're close to the edge of the town."

*

The ride to the villa took only ten minutes, but it was a little scary because of the darkness. The villa, too, was dark and the two lieutenants moved quietly to their room. Once again, little was said. Whitehead put the carbine in the corner next to his bed and then laid down. He began to think about Cook but fell asleep, finding himself being shaken by Norm at 0700 hours.

Both Norm and Whitehead rushed to the club for breakfast and got to the company area by 0800. The jeep to carry Whitehead and the others to Ninh Hoa was nowhere around. Jumpers had a helmet, flak jacket, and M14 for Whitehead. He asked Whitehead to sign a hand receipt, saying that if the lieutenant got killed, he wanted to be covered. Sergeant Boggs, carrying his gear, appeared saying he was looking for Sergeant Southland.

Before too much could be said, Custard came out of the orderly room and spoke to the group. Most of the group saluted him, and he waved a similar salute, "OK, cut the bullshit, no side trips to anywhere. Lt. Whitehead, get to Duc My as soon as you can. Conditions have changed. Burgess isn't causing trouble anymore. He's dead."

## CHAPTER 4

Southland arrived a little after 0800 to pick up Whitehead and Boggs. Pulling into the company area, he was met by the two men. Whitehead stood with flack jacket, helmet and rifle in hand. Boggs looked at the jeep and began swearing.

"Southland, get in the back seat. Lieutenant, please, get in." Boggs jumped in the driver's seat and backed around with the speed of a hundred horses.

Throwing it in first, he burned rubber and raced to the motor pool. Once at the motor pool, Boggs took a second wind.

"What the fuck did you drink last night?" Boggs screamed. "You must be crazy! I have never seen anything like what you did to this jeep."

The jeep that Boggs was upset about looked like a tank. Southland had spent the early morning filling sandbags and laying them on the hood, fenders, floor, and under the seats. The jeep was laying low on its springs and, during the drive to the motor pool, badly strained the four cylinder motor. To drive it, you had to look over a sandbag barrier.

Southland brought up a drunken conversation with a Ranger sergeant the night before at the NCO club. The sandbags offered protection from mines and hand grenades rolling under the jeep. In its retelling, Southland started to get the feeling that he over-reacted. It didn't seem to sound as good an idea as it sounded the night before. Boggs added to the feeling.

"You know, if anyone's seen this wild-ass scheme of yours, we're done for it. They'd laugh their asses off. Get these bags off before Van Rankin comes in and we have that asshole on our case for the next ten months."

"Hey, I'm sorry Sarge." Boggs, Whitehead, and Southland pulled the bags off in about five minutes. It had taken Southland two hours to fill them and put them on.

"Sergeant Southland," Boggs began, "the next time you decide to go whoring, please, go whoring. You're too dangerous when you go drinking. Shit, here comes Kelley and Fritz. The lieutenant and I just saved your ass."

Whitehead had remained strangely silent during all this. He took his lead from Boggs. He had thought the sandbags might be a pretty good idea. However, now, he understood what Boggs was talking about.

Fritz and Kelley came over and saluted Whitehead, and immediately began, "What's all the sandbags for? Someone going to attack the motor pool?"

Boggs stopped the questions, "Stop laughing and throw those sandbags on your truck. You'll need them to keep the generators from bouncing around. Sergeant Southland saved you a lot of work by picking them up this morning."

Whitehead looked at Boggs and gave him a knowing look. Southland was trying to say something like thank you, but Boggs wouldn't let him.

"Come on, let's get going."

*

The little convoy of two trucks moved through the city of Nha Trang. Boggs drove the jeep, leading the big deuce and a half driven by Fritz and Kelly. Whitehead noticed that the truck had only single rear tires instead of the required dual wheels.

Nha Trang was a small version of Saigon -- tiny cafes, street vendors, and cyclos. Peddie cabs were fewer, but motorbikes were all over the place, driven by young men in and out of uniform. Young and old women were dressed in Vietnamese costume, which later Whitehead found out was called an daio. Some were all white; others had multi-colored tops and bottoms. The people were very thin and gentle looking.

"Let's show the lieutenant 100 `Pee' alley." Southland called from the back seat of the jeep.

"I told you, no more ideas, Southland," Boggs said with a straight face.

Whitehead said nothing, sensing that Boggs had softened his anger toward Southland.

"Next time, OK lieutenant?"

Whitehead shifted his eyes off the surroundings, and looked at both men, "Anything you say. Just don't get me killed."

Southland responded: "Don't worry, sir, you're safe with us."

Boggs, still driving, but turning in his seat, said, "Southland, shut up, just shut up. Don't say another word to me or the lieutenant until I tell you."

For the next ten minutes the drive was quiet. The city was a mess compared to American cities, but seemed a little better than Whitehead expected. Boggs fell into a line of traffic which led to a one lane bridge. Apparently, a VC mine had blown a hole in the right side of the structure but left enough room for vehicles to pass.

While waiting in line, Vietnamese children went from vehicle to vehicle begging for gum, cigarettes, and money.

One kid pulled at Whitehead's sleeve and said, "Hey, lieutenant, you number one, me number ten."

Boggs saw that the lieutenant was wondering what the kid meant. He clarified, "He means you're rich and he's poor; you're lucky and he's not. Number one means good."

Whitehead listened to Boggs. He looked at the kid again, and said, "I'm number ten, you number one. You got any gum for me."

The kid looked at Whitehead, "No! You number one, I'm number ten."

"No, you number one," Whitehead pointed at the kid.

41

"You number one, lieutenant number ten."

The kid, upset and angered, stamped away.   Boggs laughed and said, "I thought he was going to offer you his sister until you started back at him.   He looked a little pissed at you."

Boggs pointed out into the river which the bridge crossed.   There were rocks which the Vietnamese fishermen used for a shrine.   He also pointed out an old stone monastery on the other side that was a tourist site.   He was going to describe more, but the traffic started moving. Boggs put the jeep in gear and drove over the bridge.   Once over the bridge, the traffic thinned out and the two vehicles started making good time.

Looking back over the bridge, Whitehead saw why the outside tires were off the deuce and a half.   The bridge wasn't wide enough to hold the truck with two tires on each side.   GI ingenuity at work.   He'd see a lot of that over the next eleven months.

A half hour of driving through pretty lush countryside, pleasantly green and cool, followed.   Neither Boggs nor Whitehead spoke, until Boggs slowed and stopped at an intersection.   He got out and walked back to the deuce and a half.   Coming back to the jeep, he turned and waved to Fritz and Kelley who made a left turn onto a dirt road.

"They're going to the Ninh Hoa site.   We'll stop there on the way back," Boggs volunteered to both Whitehead and Southland.   Before starting again, Boggs turned around to Southland and asked, "What are you so quiet about?"

Southland barked, "Shit, sarge, you said don't talk unless you talked to me first."

"God, you took me serious!"

Southland continued.   "No, I knew you were fooling.   I was checking out my new midget camera. Look, it's smaller than a pack of cigarettes.   I got it from

Sergeant James for $5. I've got real fast film in it so I don't need a flash when I'm inside."

"Well, you're outside now, so put it away." Boggs looked around the jeep and made sure the weapons and flak jackets were handy.

After a few miles of silence, Southland spoke. "Hey, this guy last night told me never drive through piles of buffalo shit on the road. The VC hid grenades or mines in them. When the jeep hits them, they explode."

Boggs made a noise and then drove through a pile of shit in the road. He leaned back on his seat and said to Southland, "I liked it better when you said nothing."

"Hey, sarge, I'm just trying to make conversation."

"Southland?"

"Yeah, sarge?"

"Shut up!"

With Southland turning quiet again, Whitehead watched the passing scenery. Water buffalo roamed without any shackles; several came to the road and waddled in the muddy ditches along side. Every few miles there were shrines to local gods which travelers could pray to for protection. Several times they passed marching ARVN - Army of the Republic of Vietnam - units. In no real sense were they marching; they were simply walking along the road together in a bunch. Most had removed their GI boots and had put on shower thongs or sandals. They all waved and smiled in spite of threats from their officers and NCOs.

Whitehead couldn't help remarking with chagrin. "Some army they have! To think, we taught them everything they know."

"Sir, these may be their best men. They're training to be Vietnamese Rangers. That's what the Special Forces group up here is doing. There's the entrance ahead."

As the jeep approached the entrance, Whitehead looked at the huge statue on the right. It consisted of three Vietnamese soldiers in fighting stance, each appearing more heroic and noble than the other.    He noticed they all had their boots on.

Boggs slowed the jeep as it entered the compound. Standing near what appeared to be the headquarters building was a Special Forces sergeant who, when seeing the jeep, turned and called to someone in the building.    Out came a major in jungle fatigues and beret.    Both men were about six foot tall and appeared to be made from the same mold.

When the jeep stopped, they quickly walked over to Whitehead.    Whitehead saluted the major and shook hands with both. He then introduced Boggs and Southland.    Major Thomas Lakeland and Sergeant Major Emory Harris guided the 228 contingent into the messhall and provided a lunch not unlike their colleagues served in Nha Trang in the open messes.    Crisp salad and seasonal fruits and a meaty stew followed by a rich coffee with fresh cream and sugar.

All during lunch, not one word emerged about Burgess.    Talk about the weather and the Vietnamese Rangers kept everyone busy.    Whitehead caught Boggs discreetly checking out the uniforms and decorations worn by the two Green Berets.    Of course, they had the US jump wings and Combat Infantrymen Badges or CIBs on the left breast.    On the right, they had the Vietnamese versions. Sleeves were rolled up, revealing only a small portion of the star on Harris' chevron.    The chevron, like Lakeland's oak leave and US insignia, were embroidered in black.    Also in black outline on the left shoulder was the Special Forces patch with a semicircle RANGER patch above it. Whitehead, Boggs, and Southland had all the colors of the rainbow on their uniform, giving them some feelings of foolishness.

*

When lunch was completed, Lakeland asked Whitehead to come to his office.    He suggested that Boggs

44

go with Harris and that Southland remain with the jeep.

In his office, Lakeland began the story: "When I called your company commander this morning, I was a little hesitant to say what happened, because we didn't know all the details. Now, we are fairly sure that the evidence shows that Burgess was killed by VC.

"Just after I called, our people found a hole in the perimeter fence which allowed the perpetrator to enter, sneak up to Burgess's hootch, and shoot him. I think he was surprised to find Burgess in the hootch. He panicked and shot our radioman. The VC then ran back to the fence and escaped through the hole.

"One of our patrols last night did shoot a VC coming from the direction of the compound. We just checked his weapon and it appears to have been the weapon that killed Burgess."

"As a result, we are calling the death a KIA (killed in action). We will complete a battle report and list Burgess as a casualty. In effect, you and your commanding officer need do nothing except write a letter to the soldier's mother, wife, or sweetheart, or all three."

Whitehead had taken notes during the telling of the story. "Could you fill me in on times and places?" Whitehead made a mental note to say "sir" the next time he asked a question.

"I think so. Burgess was shot at 0200 this morning. The patrol reported killing the VC around 0330 and bringing the body in around 0600."

"Sir, who found the body? Who led the patrol?" asked Whitehead.

"Harris. Harris found Burgess and, since he was scheduled to do so anyway, Harris led the patrol."

"Anyone else in camp?"

"Strangely enough, the post was empty except for a dozen ranger recruits. All our personnel were out on maneuvers and training. Harris called me and I secured the area."

Lakeland sat waiting for the next question.

Whitehead didn't really know what to ask. He had served as trial counsel and defense counsel for Courts and Boards at Fort Gordon and was struggling to recall the kind of pertinent information needed to make some judgment about what occurred.

Finally, he said, "Could I see Burgess's living quarters where he was shot, and then, could I see the body?"

"Do you think it's necessary? After all, we are going to deal with it as a combat casualty. He'll receive a Purple Heart to go with his campaign ribbons." Lakeland seemed annoyed at Whitehead's request.

"Yes, sir, I think I better touch all the bases for your sake and mine. I served on Courts and Boards at Fort Gordon and saw some Army lawyers seek to reprimand officers for failing to do complete jobs. What have we got to lose?"

"Okay, come this way, lieutenant." He rose and put his beret on, leading Whitehead to a row of motel-like structures.

\*

Arriving at a door that was barely recognizable as a door, he pushed it open and allowed Whitehead to enter. It was obviously a scene of death.

Dried blood was all over the floor by the door. Whitehead almost stepped in it. The back wall, like the door, was chewed up by automatic weapon fire. Maybe twenty or thirty rounds. Whitehead had stepped over the blood spot and saw some blood outside the room on the landing. The bedding and personal gear of Burgess was all very orderly and neatly put together.

Remaining quiet too long, Lakeland volunteered that Burgess's body was found where the blood was, near the door.   Harris had to push the door open with his shoulder to get inside.   Burgess was already dead.   Harris left the scene and got Lakeland right away.   As he was ending this brief description, a young uniformed Vietnamese approached Lakeland, saluted, and said he was wanted on the phone.   It was Lakeland's commanding officer at 5th Special Forces in Nha Trang.

Lakeland asked Whitehead to accompany him back to his office. Whitehead said he wanted to remain a few minutes.   Lakeland seemed on the verge of insisting that the lieutenant come with him, but finally said he would be right back.   He left, doing double time across the compound.

Whitehead didn't know why he asked to stay at the site of Burgess' demise.   He poked at some personal effects and was going to lift the bedding when Southland appeared at the door. "What a mess!"

Somewhere in Whitehead's brain a bell rang.

"Do you have your little camera?"

"Yes, sir."   Southland seemed a little confused by the question.

"Come in and take some pictures all around.   I'm going to stand at the door and if I tell you to stop, hide the camera right away."

Taking pictures, Southland asked, "How many do you want?   There's 24 on this roll."

"Take an even dozen," replied Whitehead.   "Then, when no one is watching, go out to the fenced area and take a picture of the opening.   Okay, stop, here comes Lakeland."

When Lakeland arrived, he was visibly disturbed by Southland's presence.

"Lieutenant, we can't have everybody walking through the hootch."

"Sorry, major, but Southland was a friend of Burgess and felt he wanted to see to the personal effects.   He just asked me if he could take them, and I said that you would have to release them, probably at a later date."

"Yes, that's right."

"Could we see the fence and then the body, major?"

"This way." Lakeland showed Whitehead the fence. Nothing unusual. Apparently, someone used wire clippers to cut through the fence.

The body was a little different story. Still in uniform, fatigue bottoms and white tee shirt, Burgess was not a pretty sight. The body seemed to be swelling due to the heat. His shirt was blood soaked, showing several bullet holes.

At that moment, Boggs came in with Harris. Whitehead and Boggs looked at Burgess' body together, neither of them knowing what to look for. Boggs lifted the bottom part of the sheet, revealing that Burgess still had his boots on and pants bloused in GI fashion.

Feeling queasy, Whitehead signaled he had enough. The fresh air was the only thing that stopped Whitehead from throwing up. He asked, "Sergeant Boggs, do you have any questions?"

"No, sir, I've had a full run down from Sergeant Major Harris and I made some notes."

"Ok, I guess we can hit the road back to Nha Trang. Major Lakeland, thank you for your indulgence and willingness to go over the details. Will you let us know what we have to do in terms of paperwork? You're making the battle report, so we'll wait for information from you."

The major nodded. "Sergeant Harris will send the 228 a carbon copy of the report. You may not have to do anything as I said before. Good luck, lieutenant. Good to meet you, Boggs." Lakeland turned and walked to his office. Harris made similar statements to Whitehead and Boggs, and then to Southland who showed up at the jeep saying he just used the latrine.

*

Boggs again drove and pulled carefully out of the compound back onto the road to Ninh Hoa.  No one spoke for nearly a mile.  Then Whitehead touched Boggs and motioned for him to pull over and stop.

Boggs pulled over and shut the motor off.  He then turned to Whitehead, "What's the matter Lieutenant?"

"Something's wrong with the story.  I don't know what it is, but something is wrong."  Whitehead recounted the story that Lakeland gave him.

"Well, their stories check out.  That's exactly what Harris told me.  It's almost word for . . ."

Boggs had stopped before he finished the sentence.

"Go ahead, Boggs, say it. Their stories are almost word for word."  Whitehead continued, "The hooch was in perfect order except for the blood.  Burgess was shot at 0200 and had his boots on and pants bloused.  Why wasn't he dressed for bed?

"Wouldn't automatic weapon fire knock him back against the back wall and leave blood there?  All the blood was by the door.  Some was outside.  Maybe all those things could be explained, and maybe they couldn't.  Everything was just too pat."

From the rear, Southland spoke. "Lieutenant, Harris saw the camera.  He didn't say anything, but he saw it.  I was out by the fence and had it cupped in my hand.  I didn't use it then.  Later, when the four of you were looking at the body, I went over and took some pictures of the fence."

"What the hell is going on?"  Boggs asked looking at Whitehead.

"I don't know," Whitehead answered.  "When we get to Ninh Hoa, I'll call the old man and tell him their story.  As it stands right now, I buy their story.  What choice do we have?"  The sergeants nodded.

Boggs turned around in the seat and started the jeep.

49

Before he could pull out, another jeep was barreling down the road. Boggs let the jeep and its three passengers go by.

Losing sight of the jeep, Boggs drove at about 35 mph. The three remained silent and reviewed their thoughts. Their silence was broken by a loud explosion ahead of them. Boggs slowed while Whitehead and Southland readied their M14s.

Loading a clip of ammo and taking the rifles off safety, they approached the explosion area.

Turned on its side was a jeep. Three GIs were laying on the ground. Boggs took command. "Lieutenant watch your side for VC; Sergeant Southland watch the other. Shoot if you see VC."

Boggs stopped his jeep, but left the motor running. He got out and walked with his rifle to the damaged jeep and checked the GIs. Coming back, he said, "They're all alive. We better send the jeep back to Duc My for help. Southland and I will stay here. Lieutenant, would you take the jeep and get help?"

Whitehead was moving over to the driver seat, when Southland motioned to the North side of the road. Dark figures were coming out of the thicket in squad combat formation. Boggs turned to look back toward Duc My and could see a vehicle speeding toward them. It slid to a stop behind the 228 vehicle. It was Lakeland and Harris.

Lakeland jumped out with an M16 in his hand, telling Whitehead, Boggs, and Southland to get down along side of the jeep and stay low.

"Let the teams scout the road a little bit," Lakeland ordered. "We've called a chopper in already. A medic is checking to see if first aid will help those three men."

From the tree line, a Green Beret waved. Lakeland stood up and motioned for the rest to do the same. "God, you guys were lucky." Harris walked over and joined them.

Harris spoke out, "They made the mistake of running

through buffalo dung. Charlie hid a mine in a pile of it over there.   Sir, we can handle this, if Lieutenant Whitehead wants to get back to Nha Trang."

"Good idea, lieutenant," said Lakeland.   "Get your jeep started and get on the road.   Watch out for buffalo shit!"

The three did just that. They got in and didn't stop the jeep until they got to Ninh Hoa.

*

At Ninh Hoa, Fritz and Kelly had the generators in place and were bullshiting with the team stationed there.   In the radio tent, Whitehead informed Captain Custard of the story offered by Lakeland and Harris while Boggs and Southland listened.   Custard's only response was that he was glad that the Green Berets were going to do the paperwork.

Afterwards, Whitehead's thoughts turned to the other jeep.   Boggs and the others led him into a tent that held supplies and spare parts.   When Boggs turned and looked at Whitehead, the young lieutenant threw up.

Whitehead excused himself and walked to the jeep. Leaving the foul smelling tent, the two sergeants busied themselves with the generators and the signal site, leaving Whitehead to sit in the jeep.

They finally joined Whitehead and prepared for the trip back.   "Are you OK, lieutenant?" asked Southland. He beat Boggs to that question by moments.

"Sorry to make a mess of that tent."   Whitehead paused, then looking at the two men said, "Do you two know what made me throw up?"

"I thought it was the viewing of the body and the heat," offered Boggs.

"I was fine until I realized that the jeep that blew up in front of us was really supposed to be us.   That jeep was our clone.   It was dusty and dirty and it had three passengers.   Had we not stopped and had our conference, we'd be laying on the ground up near Duc My."

The questions came quickly from Whitehead. "How did the Green Berets get there so fast?   How did Lakeland and Harris know what was going on?   I'm beginning to feel that we were set up; that we were supposed to hit that mine." Whitehead stopped, because he was scaring himself shitless.

"I can't believe our own people would set us up," said Boggs.

Sitting in the back, Southland leaned forward, "Sir, I meant to tell you before.   But after the excitement, I looked for my camera.   It's gone.   I left it on the seat of the jeep when we were crouched on the ground."

Whitehead, feeling sick again, said, "I bet I know who has it."   Both Boggs and Southland knew who had it, too. Now all three were sick.

Back at the jeep, Whitehead, Boggs and Southland simply looked at each other.   Without speaking a word, the three got in the jeep.   Boggs started the jeep and drove to Nha Trang.

## CHAPTER 5

It was Sunday in Nha Trang. For most GIs, it was a day off. The city ran a six-day war, leaving the GIs a day to read, swim, pray, sin, or drink. Some probably did all of the above.

For Whitehead it was a chance to think. While shaving, he used the time to think of his decision about the Duc My affair. Burgess was shot in combat. A KIA. That was their story and, for now, it was the only one. Yeah, and the cow jumped over the moon, thought Whitehead.

Boggs and Southland arrived and, after filling the jeep with gas, drove Whitehead to the company area. Custard was coming out of the orderly room when the three men pulled up in the jeep.

"Lieutenant, I was just going to send someone to look for you. I have some news regarding Duc My."

"Sir?"

"I just got off the phone with Major Lakeland. He told me about Burgess and the jeep incident. I think the Burgess affair is closed. They'll take care of the paperwork and writing to his next of kin. You move on to other things."

With that, Custard turned and got in his jeep. Pulling away he returned Whitehead's limp salute.

Boggs and Southland heard the whole conversation. Boggs offered his conclusion. "So much for our concerns. We almost get killed and he's ready to accept a cock and bull story. He's really doing us a favor. OK, lieutenant, we'll see you soon. Come on, Southland."

As they walked away, Whitehead called them. "Boggs? Southland?"

Boggs turned, "Yes sir?"

"Thanks, both of you. If either of you hear anything, let me know. I'll do the same." Whitehead was going to stop, but then added, "Neither of you know me too well, so I can understand any hesitancy you may have in talking to me.    But be sure to tell each other, and think about letting me know, too."

Whitehead returned to the villa and found Norm awake.   They decided on breakfast and a ride so that Range could show Whitehead a giant statue of Buddha.   Powdered eggs and a ten story buddha.    Just a good old fashion American Sunday.

*

After eating, the two men drove through areas of Nha Trang that were congested with Vietnamese venders and farmers. The smells ranged from rancid garbage to sweet gardenia.   Up a steep hill, Range maneuvered the jeep to a clearing; the Buddha seemed to rise out of nowhere.

The Buddha was huge, over a hundred feet high and probably fifty feet around.    It sat on a broad table that you could walk around.

Norm had a new Pentak camera and began taking pictures while walking around the Buddha.    As the two lieutenants moved away from the jeep, a group of little kids moved closer.    Finally, they just rushed up and asked for money.   Beggars.   Whitehead was looking for change, but finally gave each of them a 100P bill, about a dollar each.

Norm walked around the statue again snapping more pictures as he moved.    Alone, Whitehead drifted off and leaned against a tree.

"Lieutenant Whitehead!   Dave!   Hey, how're you doing?"

The words came from a young blond haired American.    "Remember me?    I came with you on the airplane with Ralph Cook.   Pete Laskin."

"Hi, Pete."    Whitehead searched his memory, but still couldn't remember this guy.

"I saw Cook not long ago. He said he gave you something. When he found out I was going to Nha Trang and would see him again on Friday, he said to look you up and get it."

"You mean the carbine?"

"Yeah, yeah, the carbine. You don't have it with you? No, you couldn't. Well, I have to go to Long Van and fly out right away. I'll let him get his own carbine. Hey, it was good to see you again. Take care. Don't get your ass shot."

"Ok." Whitehead wanted to ask him where Cook was, but Laskin was gone as fast as he appeared.

Finished taking pictures, Range appeared and the two men began walking back to the jeep.

"Dave, are you alright?"

"I was just standing here and a guy comes up to me, knows my name, and said Cook wanted his carbine. What do you make of that?"

"You're a well known guy."

"Fuck, let's get out of here."

\*

Norm parked the jeep in the driveway locking the gate behind him. It was about 1600 and both lieutenants planned to nap before dinner.

But when they entered the room, they found it in total disarray. The beds were pulled apart and clothes were thrown all over. No one had seen or heard anything while the men were away.

Setting things straight, they found that nothing was missing. Norm had his new camera. Whitehead's watch was on the floor and loose change was on both night tables. More importantly, Whitehead's notes were on the table untouched.

"I can't figure out who did it or what they wanted." It

was Norm speaking. Whitehead was quiet but thinking the same thing. His mind went to Duc My, but it didn't make any sense. They had Southland's camera.

"The carbine. That's what they wanted." Whitehead looked behind his bed. "It's not here. They wanted Cook's carbine and couldn't figure out which one it was, so they took both."

"I don't think so. Maybe they were here. It would explain why nothing was taken. But the carbines weren't here anyway."

"What? Why not?" Whitehead tried to remember seeing the carbine.

"I brought the carbines to Jumpers yesterday so he could field strip and clean them," Norm explained. "He didn't have time to finish so he locked them in a connex, one of those square shipping containers."

"Shit, I hate this spy crap."

They thought about calling the MPs but what good would it do. They straightened out the remaining mess in a few minutes and laid down on the bunks. Strangely enough, they relaxed and dozed off.

*

When they awoke, Range suggested dinner at Le Fregat, an old colonial restaurant in Nha Trang.

"It's a holdover from the old French presence," Norm stated in true tour guide fashion. Upon seeing the building, Whitehead found little to argue with the description.

A one story summer home appeared to have been lifted from southern France and dropped in this coastal city in Southeast Asia. The entrance was shaded by palm trees and lush arching greenery. Inside was a handsome, wood grained bar where Range and Whitehead stopped for a cocktail. Range had a gin and tonic, Whitehead a white wine.

They took their drinks to a table and ordered shrimp. Whitehead was surprised, the shrimp were the size of lobsters.

As they finished with a dessert of lime ice, the waiter approached and said in near perfect English, "Is one of you Lieutenant Whitehead?"

The two men looked at each other before Whitehead answered.

"Would you please come with me, sir?"

Whitehead looked at Norm as if to seek guidance. Not getting any, he said, "Yes." Turning again to Norm, "I'll be right back. Something must be wrong at Goldfinch."

The waiter walked ahead, passing to the right of the bar. He came to a door, opened it, and said, "This is the manager's office. A gentlemen wishes to speak to you in private."

"Thank you," Whitehead said, entering another impressive room of teak and mahogany.

The gentlemen was Cook. He was in civilian clothes and seemed to be familiar with the office. "Surprised to see me, Dave? I won't keep you long, then you can rejoin your friend. How are you doing?"

Whitehead adopted the friendly tone of Cook's and said, "Fine. I'm getting use to Vietnam. It's full of surprises. You're one of the biggest I've run into."

Cook's face made some expression of sympathy but soon turned to wonderment when Whitehead told him about this afternoon. "What the fuck is going on with you? Are you Army or CIA or CID or the man in the moon? Who's this guy Pete Laskin who wanted the carbine?"

"Yeah, I'm one of them," Cook admitted. He didn't say which. "Look, Dave, I don't know a Pete Laskin. But, don't worry. You don't have to deny you know me to anyone. Just tell the truth, that you know nothing about the work I do."

"Do you want the carbine?"

"No, hold it in a safe place. I'll pick it up later. If I do send anyone, I'll give them the serial number of the carbine. You can give it up then. OK? I just wanted to thank you for your help. Don't keep your friend waiting. Thanks again. And sorry about the room."

Cook got up and shook hands with Whitehead and led him out to the bar. Cook waved at the bartender and left.

Whitehead watched Cook leave the restaurant and then went back to his table, asking the waiter for another wine. Norm asked him what happened. He told Norm the whole story of the meeting. Norm shook his head and tried to think of something to say. In the end, he just shook his head again.

A pianist was now making music as evening came upon the diners at Le Fregat. The waiter returned to the table and asked about another round of drinks.

Receiving a negative answer, he said the check had already been paid. He wished the lieutenants a good evening and departed for his other customers.

Norm and Whitehead were looking at each other again. Norm asked, "Cook?"

They finished their drinks.

"I guess so," Whitehead said as he got up. "Let's go."

## CHAPTER 6

The next few days were pretty routine for Whitehead. He spent much of his time at Goldfinch getting familiar with the overall operations of the switchboard, the radio relay equipment and his other assignments. He also spent a lot of time watching the 8th Field Hospital Landing Zone.

Choppers were making regular runs with wounded who had not dined at Le Fregat or enjoyed the Nha Trang beach. He had often tried to visualize how he would react in combat or in dangerous situations. Whitehead didn't hold out for heroics; he expected the worst of himself. Fear is a powerful determinant of action.

On Wednesday around 1100, Sergeant Franklin found Whitehead by the edge of the site near the runway. "Lieutenant Whitehead, there's a call for you from Lieutenant Dancer."

"Thanks, Franklin. " Walking back to the operations hut, Whitehead asked Franklin if he knew what was in the silver tanks.

"Yes, sir, the Air force said it was Agent Orange, a herbicide for clearing jungles. It's safe. They said don't worry about it."

Whitehead noticed that everyone used the tanks to sit and lay on during their breaks. It was a good view of the airplanes taking off. He wondered if they were really safe. Maybe he would try to get the tanks moved.

Picking up the phone, he said. "Whitehead here."

"Dave, can you come up to the orderly room for a few minutes?" It was Dancer.

Franklin had Boggs' three quarter truck. He drove Whitehead up to the company headquarters. Coming in the orderly room, he noticed McCready was still there and that another sergeant was milling about. McCready introduced him. "Sir, this is Sergeant Grace, our operations NCO.

He works for Lieutenant Dancer."

"Howdy, sergeant. I've come to see your boss."

"He's expecting you in the back." The young NCO walked quickly in front of Whitehead and looked to be the kind of physical specimen the Army put on its recruiting poster.

Dancer was leaning against his desk, smoking a cigarette. "Dave, thanks for coming up. I just want to fill you in on some things that have to be done. I've already talked to Boggs and Southland because I saw them first. I didn't mean to by-pass you."

"Don't worry about me. I'm still trying to find which end is up. What do you need and what do you want me to do?"

"Sergeant Southland is taking a radio relay team on temporary duty with the 4th Infantry Division near Phan Rang. He'll take the spare Mickey 6 and Mark 54 at Goldfinch. Make sure he takes our newest trucks.

"Also, sergeant Boggs needs to bring a replacement to Duc My for Burgess and maybe stay a couple of days to make sure that site is operational. The two men are running 12-hour shifts; they really need an NCO up there. Talk to Boggs and Southland; help them get these two jobs done." Dancer stopped, apparently trying to think if he forgot anything. "Any questions?"

Whitehead shook his head no, but he really had a thousand questions. They were all stupid so he decided to hold them. "OK, I'll get with them and see what help I can be. Take care."

"Before you go," Dancer added, "take a look in those two trailers at the rear of Goldfinch. They're a long distance switchboard which we will probably have to install. You'll probably get that job. See if you can find an NCO who can honcho the job for you. You'll need to construct the site and then set up the wiring. But that's about a month away."

"Ok, will do."

*

At Goldfinch, Boggs was waiting and told Whitehead his version of the two little jobs dropped on them by Dancer. Having listened carefully, Whitehead said, "Make sure Southland gets what he needs. You and him work out who is to go. I'll rubber stamp it. Same with the equipment. Have you checked out the two vans?"

"Yes sir, and that's a problem. We used part of the spare MARC 54 for the rig that shoots to Ninh Hoa. Maintenance is working on that unit that was redlined. Lieutenant Range has control over maintenance. Maybe you can ask him to speed up repairs."

Whitehead picked up the phone and gave the number for supply. Jumpers answered. Whitehead asked for Range. "Yeah, Dave, what do you need?"

"I need a part of a Mark 54 that's in repair. We're sending Southland with a Mickey 6 and a Mark 54 to the 4th Infantry Division on temporary duty. We need those two units and the trucks checked out for that job. Can you help out?"

"Your wish is my command. I guess you need it done yesterday?"

"No, Norm, I need it done last week. OK?"

Hanging up, he asked Boggs about Duc My. "I think I'll bring Staff Sergeant Polanski and a new kid up there. That should make it a more stable team. One veteran and one rookie. I've given them no instructions. I figure I'll let them be innocent and unsuspecting."

"OK. You want me to come with you?"

"No, we'll hold you in the bullpen. If there's trouble, then someone knows what's going on."

*

Norm was busy at supply, so Whitehead had lunch at the Air Force club alone.

Inside, the club was cool from the air conditioning. The chow line was long, but he had plenty of time. Paying his bill, he saw an empty table. Walking toward it, he passed Cook. He was going to stop and thank him for dinner, but he saw it was Major Benson instead. He simply nodded.

Benson's presence, or was its Cook's presence, one of them, ruined his lunch. It was a great day until he saw Benson or Cook. He changed seats, facing the other direction, to avoid looking at the Air Force major. A good five minutes went by; he turned around, but Benson or Cook was gone.

He scanned the club, looking for Benson or Cook. Gone. No sign of the man anywhere. Giving up on lunch, he went to the telephone and called Franklin to come get him.

Whitehead spent the afternoon at Goldfinch then stopped by supply to see Norm. Range suggested taking a ride into downtown Nha Trang and walk around, a suggestion with which Whitehead agreed. A quick stop at the villa to change into shorts and pullovers and the lieutenants were city bound.

*

Nha Trang city was only two or three streets of shops and bars. Over the shops and bars were whore houses.

It was nearly dark and the lights in the shops and bars were just coming on. The two men visited a couple of shops. Norm bought his wife an daio. Whitehead picked a ring which the clerk insisted was jade. It wasn't, but it was cheap. He bought a pendant and some other things. He planned on sending them to his mother and the girl from

Trenton he'd met before leaving the States.

With their packages, Norm and Whitehead walked along, weaving through street vendors and pimps and kids with sisters to sell to the rich GIs.

Across the street, Norm saw someone waving his arms. Elbowing Whitehead, he asked, "Dave, do you know that guy? I think he's waving to us."

Looking in that direction, Whitehead recognized Sergeant Major Harris from Duc My. Harris began crossing the street. Traffic was not heavy, only a three quarter truck was posing any difficulty.

Whitehead didn't realize the truck was picking up speed. Norm did.

"Dave!" Norm shouted. "The three quarter!"

The truck began to weave.

His eyes on Whitehead, Harris raised his arm again and called, "Lieutenant Whitehead."

The truck hit Harris slowly. First the front wheel, then the back wheel rolled over the body. The truck took off, turned left and disappeared.

Range and Whitehead ran to Harris. He mumbled a few words and then died. An MP jeep pulled up and cleared the crowd. From Range and Whitehead they got the details of the hit and run.

"Do either of you know him?" asked one of the MPs.

Whitehead answered. "Yes, he's a sergeant major in the Special Forces. His name is Harris."

The other MP who had been going through the dead man's pockets had a wallet. He looked up at Whitehead and said. "ID says he is Major Benson, US Air Force, stationed here at Long Van. You must have the wrong man."

The MPs asked Whitehead and Range a few more questions before dismissing them.

"Thanks Lieutenant, we'll take it from here. We have your names and unit if we need more information."

Walking back to the jeep, Norm grabbed Whitehead's arm. "Dave, he called out your name. He knew you. You were right. He must have had a phony ID."

"Or he was a phony Green Beret." Benson, Harris, Cook. Who was who, thought Whitehead. And why all this cloak and dagger routine. He told Norm about Benson-Cook that afternoon at the Air Force officers club.

"Well, it looks like one of them won't be playing Benson anymore," joked Range. Neither one laughed. "Let's get back to the villa. Maybe we can find Boggs and see if he knows something we don't."

Back at the villa, Whitehead tried to reach Boggs by telephone. No one knew where Boggs was. Whitehead kept trying till 2300 and then gave up and went to bed, but didn't sleep. Sleep and answers were hard to find lately.

## CHAPTER 7

Vietnam was an important event for the professional soldier. It had to do with rank, decorations, and retirement. For most soldiers in the enlisted ranks, it meant at least one promotion. For officers, it meant having Vietnam on your personnel form.

Everyone got some ribbons and medals; some got more than others. For many, this Southeast Asian war meant an improved retirement plan. It even saved some from retirement. Few NCOs and officers were being passed over; even fewer were being forced into civilian life. The need was just too great.

The real danger was doing the wrong thing and being held responsible for it. Every rank was concerned about that. With nearly enough time to retire, Boggs had only one tour in Vietnam. When done here, he could go to Germany and finish his career. He just had to be careful. Southland understood that. Only time would tell what Whitehead knew.

Boggs arrived at Duc My a little after eight the next morning accompanied by Polanski and Hernandez, the replacements. Inside the camp's headquarters, Boggs was told the Burgess affair was being handled by the 5th Special Forces, not the 228. Also, Major Lakeland and Sergeant Major Harris were both gone. Boggs decided to call Goldfinch and tell Southland what he had discovered.

*

Whitehead was next to the switchboard operator when Boggs' call came in.

"Boggs, this is Lieutenant Whitehead. Is everything OK up there?"

"Yes, sir."

Before Boggs could say anything, Whitehead began

again. "I tried to call you last night.   No one could find you. Listen, closely.   Harris is dead.   Killed last night in Nha Trang.   He was crossing the street to talk to me.   A hit and run, but maybe something more."

Boggs said nothing. Whitehead spoke again. "Sergeant Boggs, are you still there?"

"Yes, sir.   Major Lakeland's not here.   I was calling to tell you that Lakeland and Harris were gone. Now you tell me that Harris is dead.   I guess it's a whole new ball game up here."

"Sergeant Boggs, the KIA story for Burgess holds. Let it rest for now.   Until we know something more, we have to live with the official version.   Have you said anything to Southland?"

"No, sir, I got you first."

"Tell Southland when you see him today," said Whitehead. "I expect to be back early this evening.   I'll meet you at Goldfinch if you want."

"We'll see you later."

Whitehead hung up the receiver. Walking back to operations, he pondered the news about Lakeland.   Not knowing what to do, he took his own advice.   He shifted his attention to Southland's mission with the 4th Infantry Division.

*

Before he could really get into Southland's mission, he found Franklin waiting for him.   "The old man wants to see you, Lieutenant.   It sounded urgent."

Arriving at the orderly room, Whitehead kicked some dust off his trousers and entered.   He was ushered into Custard's office before he had said a word.   Custard was sitting behind his desk as Whitehead walked into the room.

"At ease, Lieutenant." Custard said.   The captain's

eyes never left the desk.

Looking up finally and then out the window, he resumed his conversation with the world outside, never once looking Whitehead in the eye. "Spec 4 Wilson. Know him?"

"I don't think so. Boggs takes care of the details and assigns the men. I may know him."

"You will know him, Whitehead, because he's yours, now and forever. Whatever he does wrong, he will pay the consequences, and so will you. Let me tell you what this evil little son of a bitch did."

"While joyriding in my jeep yesterday, Wilson fucked up royally. First, he let someone else drive my jeep and, while he sat in the passenger seat, he did an obscene thing to a young Vietnamese girl. Not only did he do an obscene thing to a young girl, he did it at a stop light with Colonel Duel sitting in a jeep behind him. Duel thought this jerk was me. He thought I was doing this obscene thing.

"You are to take this little bastard and make an example of him for all your troops. I will not tolerate a soldier in my unit who performs lewd sex acts. Understand, Lieutenant? You will report to me tomorrow what you intend to do with Wilson. Dismissed."

Whitehead turned, and then stopped, and tried to ask something, namely, what did this guy do that was so bad. Custard must have sensed it. "Don't say a word to me Lieutenant. Get out and get that little bastard."

"Yes sir."

By now the orderly room was empty. Chow time.

He walked over to the supply tent and found Norm talking with Jumpers. "Hello, gentlemen," said Whitehead, falling into Jumpers empty seat behind one of the two desks in the tent. "What keeps you fellows busy today?"

"The old man's car. I just got reamed out because the car hasn't come in yet. He really thinks he's going to get it.   He can't even use it if he does get it.   Hell, he doesn't even go anywhere outside of his office and the latrine.   You going to eat today?"

"Yeah, I guess so, but I have to beat the shit out of one of my soldiers.   He's in a lot of hot water, and I think he's pulled me in after him, or with him."

Jumpers listening, asked the question.   "Who's in trouble, sir?"

"A young stud by the name of Wilson," answered Whitehead.

Jumpers began laughing and coughing.   "You'll have to excuse me, I'm going to chow, sirs."   With those words and more laughing, he left.

"Norm, take me to Goldfinch.   I have to talk briefly to Wilson, if he's there, and then we can lunch."

"OK, but let me lock up.   Jumpers just left me with the job."

Range and Whitehead rode with little conversation, listening to cannon fire off to the west.

"Sounds like someone is seeing some action today. Glad it's not us."

Whitehead nodded as Norm made the turn into Goldfinch.

Stopping the jeep and getting out, the two officers moved toward the communications hut.   Franklin was standing by the door and turned when he heard the jeep pull up.   He met Range and Whitehead half way.   "Are you looking for Wilson, Lieutenant Whitehead?"

"I'm afraid so.   You got him here?"

"Yes, sir, He's in the hut.   He's scared shitless, sir. Could you be a little easy on him?   You don't know Wilson," said Franklin.

"I'm going to know him."

The conversation had gone on while walking to the hut.   When Whitehead got to the door, he looked in and found Spec 4 Woody Allen looking at him.

Allen, alias Wilson, jumped up to salute only to smash his head against the metal roof.   His hand on its way up to salute, passed salute and went directly to rub.

Rubbing his head and now beginning to weep a little, Wilson was hardly the sex fiend described to Whitehead in Custard's office.   Whitehead now knew what Jumpers was laughing about. Wilson was hardly the type to perform lewd sex acts.

"Sit down, Wilson, before you knock the shit out of yourself.   I'm under orders to do that for you.   Don't do my job.   Once your head stops ringing, tell me what you did."

A few minutes went by.   Norm was standing in the door looking at Wilson and Whitehead.   Whitehead was sitting on the desk, Wilson in a chair at the rear of the hut.

Finally, Wilson seemed ready to talk.   "Lieutenant, I didn't mean any harm."

"I'm sure you didn't.   Al Capone never meant any harm.   His mother thought he was a wonderful child.   Just misdirected.   Tell me what happened."

"The old man told me to get his jeep washed.   I did."   Wilson stopped.

"Wilson, the old man isn't pissed at you for washing his jeep," Whitehead said.

"Well, I picked up my friend and we went down to the city of Nha Trang.   At a stoplight, I reached out and patted a Vietnamese girl on her rear end."   Wilson stopped again.

"And?" asked Whitehead while looking at Range.

"That's it, sir.   Oh, yes, Colonel Duel was in the jeep behind me."

"I know that.   Tell me the serious part."

"I'm sorry, sir.   That's it."

"You mean that Custard is going bananas because you touched a Vietnamese girl on the ass?!"   Whitehead looked at Range.   "Is he that crazy?"

Looking at Wilson, Whitehead asked again.   "Is that

all? If you're lying to me, I'll pat your ass up and down Beach Road with a two by four."

"I swear Lieutenant, that's all I did."

"Franklin!" Whitehead shouted.

"I'm here, sir."

"Did you hear Wilson's story?"

"Yes sir."

"Is it true?" asked Whitehead.

"Yes, sir. But Wilson didn't tell you one other thing." Franklin got very serious and quiet. "His friend driving was me."

"No wonder you're so concerned. I suppose you thought it was pretty funny what this young man did?"

"Well, sir, I told him to do it. He didn't want to, but I egged him on. He finally did it and now he's in trouble because of me." Franklin was totally upset. "I'll go to the old man and tell him."

"Hell, don't either one of you go to the old man. He'll have you court-martialled and busted. Don't do anything until I tell you."

"Be here at 2 o'clock, I mean 1400. Both of you. If either of you talk to anybody about this, I'll personally kick the shit out of you. If you see Boggs or Southland, tell them to be here, too. OK, Norm, let's go."

*

Lunch at the Air Force club was terrible. Whitehead kept thinking about Wilson and Custard. When not doing that, he was looking for Cook or whatever his name was. He had to come up with something for the Wilson affair. He couldn't punish the kid for what really was a kind of nice innocent little gesture of growing up.

Driving back to Goldfinch, Whitehead came to a decision. The Wilson problem could be solved by getting Wilson out of the way.

As Range and he pulled into the site, they saw that Sergeant Southland had already arrived. At that moment his decision took full bloom. Wilson had to be sent away and Southland was going away. They would go together.

"Good to see you Southland. Are you getting all the equipment you need?"

"Yes sir. The trucks will have new tires and the radio gear will be in the rigs tonight. I'll be ready tomorrow at 0800."

"Good, you'll have an extra man with you. Follow me and I'll introduce you to him."

Southland had started to make a face and say something, but he didn't know Whitehead well enough to object. He knew something was in the wind. He followed Whitehead past Franklin who also looked a little uneasy.

Inside the hut with Whitehead was Wilson, Southland said aloud, "Oh, no! Not Wilson. He's trouble. He's double trouble. You can't do this to me, Lieutenant."

"Southland, it's all settled. The old man said OK also," lied Whitehead. "It gets Wilson out of Duel's sight and it's for a good cause. Tell Wilson what he needs to bring and he'll be ready tomorrow at 0800. You can give him the shittiest job you got. Right, Wilson?"

Wilson didn't know what to say so he sat right there not saying anything.

"What about Sergeant Boggs? Does he know this?"

"No," answered Whitehead. "Sergeant Southland, this is your problem. Deal with it."

*

The next morning, just walking into the orderly room resulted in disaster.

"Lieutenant Whitehead, just the man I want to see." It was Blutik speaking. "Here's the duty roster, the KP assignments, the pay vouchers, and all my other jobs. As long as the lieutenant is assigning men and sending them on missions, he may as well do my other jobs."

"Thanks for the offer, sergeant, but you can keep the jobs."   Whitehead kept a straight face and avoided any sarcasm in his voice.

"Well, why the fuck did you send Wilson with Southland?"

Whitehead let the profanity go.   "He's assigned to my section.   I can send him where I want."

From out of nowhere, came a loud, almost uncontrolled voice.

"Whitehead!"

Blutik began smiling.   "Maybe you should tell the old man what you just told me."

Custard was at the door.   "Whitehead, you better have one good explanation for doing what you did.   You were supposed to punish Wilson, not send him on a vacation."

"Sir, I believe the assignment will do him good. It's my understanding that the assignment was not an easy one. Maybe it will straighten him out."   Whitehead was hoping he was right, but was having difficulty even thinking that could be the case.

"Young man, never, I say again, never, do something like that again.   Or," Custard stopped, and looked into Whitehead's face with his bad breath, "you and Wilson will be sleeping with Charlie in some shithole you never heard of.   Now get the fuck out of my life."   Custard turned and left Whitehead with Blutik.

Whitehead walked into the operations hut without a word.   Dancer, standing at his desk, saw Whitehead and offered his opinion.

"You fucked up, you really fucked up.   You fucked up everything."

Whitehead looked at Dancer and said, "Hey, I really would like to stay and talk about this some more, but I have some things I need to get done. Take care, I'll see you later." He waved and left.

*

"The word out is: Whitehead fucked up! That's a quote by the way." Norm was smiling. Jumpers was laughing.

Whitehead, looking for someone to take out his anger on, yelled at Jumpers. "Jumpers, go get me that carbine of mine."

"Hey, lieutenant, you ain't gonna' shoot somebody?" He was giggling now.

"I'll use it on you, Jumpers, if you don't shut up and get the goddamn carbine." Whitehead was pissed, mostly at himself. He should have let Wilson burn for his stupidity.

Whitehead got up, walked into the next room and found Jumpers in a connex looking at five carbines.

"Hey, Lieutenant, which of these carbines is yours?"

"Shit, Jumpers, you can't remember the serial number? I think Lieutenant Range has it. Check with him."

Jumpers squeezed by and left Whitehead with the carbines. Whitehead looked them over and picked up the carbine which looked like the one that Cook gave him. However, Jumpers came back, looked at the number and shook his head. He looked down at the others and picked another, "Here it is."

Whitehead looked at it and said, "It looks different."

"It may be," said Jumpers. "I field stripped them all last week and put them back together. They should look a lot cleaner."

"You put them back the same way you took them apart?"

"Sure. They all work."

Whitehead understood Jumpers, but added. "Are you sure you put the stocks back on the same metal parts?"

"Hey, lieutenant, I was in a hurry. I put them back the right way." He hesitated. "Pretty sure, anyway."

"Show me how to field strip one."

Jumpers and Whitehead went to a table outside the connex. The young black soldier went through the steps and showed Whitehead how to do it. Whitehead took a second carbine and walked through it with Jumpers.

"OK, Jumpers, go back to Lieutenant Range and help him. I just want to tinker with the other carbines. If I need help, then I'll call you. Thanks."

A short while later, Whitehead came back out to the front room.

"Dave, this just came." Range handed Whitehead a piece of paper.

"It's from Cook. He wants me to call him ASAP."

"You going to call him?" asked Range.

"Not right now." Whitehead looked at Jumpers. "If anyone comes for the carbines, you don't know where they are. Keep them locked up and let no one touch them until we know which one is Cooks' stock. OK? Cook will have my ass if we lose it."

"If it's OK with Lieutenant Range, it's OK with me."

Range looked a little perplexed. "Jumpers, do what Lieutenant Whitehead said. Go back and lock them up now and let me have the key to that connex. If we lose them, it'll be my fault. I can't blame you."

Jumpers went back to do as he was directed. Range looked at Whitehead and asked, "What's that all about?"

"Could you find another lock for a connex and put the carbines in there by themselves?"

"Sure that's easy. Why?"

In a minute." Whitehead responded as Jumpers came back.

Range gave Jumpers the keys to the chain and lock

of the supply truck along with the paperwork. Whitehead and Range watched him go. Whitehead then motioned for Range to follow him back to the connex which Range opened.

"I think I found what whoever rearranged our room was looking for," Whitehead said as he picked up one of the carbines from the connex.

The two lieutenants then took the carbine apart, with Whitehead explaining that Jumpers must have switched the stocks.

"Norm, this is what Cook wanted me to hold. He didn't care about the carbine, just what's inside the stock."

Whitehead took a small sack out of the stock. Opening it, he showed Range the contents. In his hand shined several pieces of jade.

## CHAPTER 8

The next morning began with coffee in a bowl as usual. Whitehead had been drinking out of a bowl for nearly three weeks now. Sometimes he held it between his thumb and the side of his forefinger. Other times he held it in his two hands.

Norm sat across from Whitehead reading a letter from his wife. Putting the letter down, Range looked at Whitehead.

"Oh I forgot," he said smiling. "You're paymaster this month."

"What?" The bowl almost slipped out of Whitehead's hand. "What does that mean?"

"It means that tomorrow you sign out a pistol, then go with Sergeant Blutik to pay the troops. First here, at the company, then Da Lat. The next day, you're off to Nimh Hoa and Duc My to pay the troops there."

"Great. At least you gave me plenty of warning with that one, Norm."

Still smiling, Range said, "You ready? It's almost 0800 and I have to get to the supply room."

"Go ahead, Norm. I'm going to walk down to Goldfinch. It'll only take ten minutes. I need to think some more."

For another ten minutes, Whitehead sat and pondered. He knew that tomorrow was October 1, payday. But he couldn't figure out what day of the week it was. He searched his mind but just couldn't remember. Three days later was his birthday, yet he couldn't figure out on what day of the week it would occur.

The walk to Goldfinch did him good. Walking the other way was a group of Vietnamese air cadets. The kid in charge saluted him and giggled. Whitehead saluted and couldn't resist it, so he giggled back.

Walking across the LZ of the 8th Field Hospital cut

off a lot of time.   At the LZ he saw evidence of hard fighting to the North.   Bloody bandages, left behind after the ambulance and chopper, were laying near a large pool of stuff that had to be blood.   He began to jog.

Arriving at Goldfinch, he was in a cold sweat and would have puked if Franklin and Boggs weren't there.

"Well, lieutenant, who's chasing you now?" It was Boggs, and he appeared in better spirits.

"No one new.   I ran out of people to piss off yesterday."

Boggs fumbled, "Lieutenant, about that.   I was out of line.   Franklin told me what happened.   I also ran into Blutik.   He was really pissed.   I figured you weren't really out of line if you could piss off Blutik.   That mean bastard must've had something terrible in mind for Wilson.   Maybe you were right in getting him out of the way."

"I guess.   I wish I could be that sure now."

Franklin, who had been listening, excused himself to get to the details that Boggs had given him.   It allowed Boggs to ask about Duc My.   "Anything new about Burgess?"

"Not a thing Boggs.   I guess it's all over.   No choice but to accept it."

Boggs nodded.

Whitehead continued, "Anything I should know about the site or what happened up North?"

"No, sir.   Everything's under control.   I may have to talk to you about Collins though.   He says he wants to get married, but let me talk to him first.   Maybe when you get back from Da Lat he will have changed his mind."

"How did you know I was going to Da Lat?"

"You're pay officer this month.   Everyone knows it."   "How come I didn't know until an hour ago?"

"Should've ask me, sir. I would've told you."   Boggs smiled, saluted, and left.

\*

Whitehead had the Goldfinch number that Cook had left for him. He went over to the communications hut and picked up the phone, giving the operator the number. The number belonged to a guardhouse in Nha Trang. The sergeant who answered said he hadn't heard of Cook, then hung up on Whitehead. So much for Cook.

Norm called around 1100 hours and told Whitehead the jeep was in the motor pool for its regular checkup. The two made plans to go downtown after dinner that night. Whitehead decided to spend the afternoon at Goldfinch.

The day went slow. The Goldfinch site ran pretty well with no one around to supervise it. Whitehead wrote some letters home and watched the Vietnamese trainers take off.

Once again he walked out and looked at the containers of agent orange. For the next hour, he watched a series of choppers bring in wounded to the 8th Field Hospital. Then, he had a lunch of soda and candy--great for the teeth.

Norm came around 1700 hours with the three quarter truck. A little larger than a pick up truck, the three-quarter had been used for many years and was always scheduled to be replaced by the Army with a cheaper truck. Norm said he liked driving it and offered to let Whitehead drive it a while. Whitehead declined, saying he was learning too much too soon.

The drive downtown was quiet. They skirted "100 Pee Alley" where you could buy anything you wanted for 100 piasters. After finding a parking space near Duc Lap Street, and fighting off the street urchins again, the two lieutenants walked along the shops and the black market stands on the sidewalk.

Whitehead stopped and looked in a tailor's window. It had poncho rain coats. The GI would bring in a poncho, then the tailor would take the GI's measurement and cut the poncho into a pattern he sewed together.

Another item was a silk jacket with a map of Vietnam. Over the map, a slogan read: "When I die, I'll go to heaven, because I spent my hell in Vietnam."

Range and Whitehead walked about an hour and tired themselves out. The bars didn't look inviting. The whores still didn't look very good. Whitehead figured three weeks in Vietnam wasn't long enough to transform the whores into beauties. He'd wait a while longer.

Walking back to the three quarter, Norm pointed out the Red Cross shop on the corner. It was closed at that hour, but during the day, they sold ice cream. It was terrible. They used canned milk to make the ice cream. Norm thought it was tasting better each time he had it.

An explosion rocked the area knocking both men to the ground. There was dust all over and the sound of crying filled the air. Getting to their feet, they headed back to the truck just around the corner.

The corner was there, the people were there, but their truck wasn't. The only things remaining were the frame of twisted metal and bits of burning canvas and tires. Walking over to the wreckage, Whitehead found the steering wheel and chain with the padlock Norm had used to lock it. Several MPs and Vietnamese policemen arrived seconds after the two lieutenants.

To one of the MPs, Norm nearly yelled, "That was my truck. What am I going to do?"

The MP looked at Norm, and said, "Take it easy lieutenant. We'll write up a report and you'll submit it to your unit. It's no big deal. It's enemy action. Too bad you didn't get cut. We could've recommended you for a Purple Heart. Give me your name and unit. Then I'll get the two of you a ride home."

"Mine's in New Jersey," Whitehead said with a straight face.

The MP looked at Whitehead and said, "Sir, if you were an enlisted man, I'd arrest you for interfering in an investigation. Bad jokes are bad jokes, no matter where you are in this God forsaken country. Can I do my job?"

Whitehead backed off. He whispered to Norm. "That shithead can't take a joke."

"Dave, do you realize we could have been in that truck?"

Norm said the magic words. No, Whitehead hadn't thought that they could have been in the truck. He hadn't thought at all.

"Uh, no. I hadn't thought about it. I'm sorry you said it." Silently, his mind was moving fast and the questions were rapid. Was it just any truck that was blown up? Was this a message to them? Was it a timed device that went off too soon? Never had these problems teaching school, he thought. Spitballs on the ceiling, yeah, a little back talk from a wise kid, sure, but no one ever blew up his car.

Riding in the MP's jeep, Whitehead thought of tomorrow. Maybe he'd just sleep in, use a sick day.

*

Back at the villa, Dancer and Custard were both sitting in the main room. It was bland and had cracks in the wall. The furniture was early Salvation Army; the nylon had rips and the chrome was rusted. But the two officers seemed quite comfortable as they sat there and talked about events of the day. Norm and Whitehead changed that.

One recounting of the explosion led to another before Custard made his comments that both lieutenants were stupid and dumb and he wanted a complete report by Norm. He looked at Whitehead and suggested that he better not screw up the payroll. He stamped off to his room. Dancer performed his ritual shaking of the head and walked off to his room.

*

The next morning was the first of October. Someone told Whitehead at breakfast that it was a Thursday. Later, he found it was really Wednesday. It didn't really matter to Whitehead. He had over three hundred days left.

Norm was sitting across from him having breakfast, trying to write the report that Custard wanted. Once he had it outlined, he was going to drive Whitehead to the paymaster's office in the jeep that was waiting in the motor pool.

"OK, Dave, I think I have it all. I'm glad you were here. At least our stories match."

At the table, Norm briefed Whitehead about the pay system. The officer sat at a table. Then the GI would come to the table, salute, give his name, and put his payroll signature on the pay form. If he wrote the signature in any form other than his previous signature, he didn't get his money.

"Some guy will leave out his middle initial, Dave. You're not suppose to pay him till next month."

"Hey, what am I? A prick? I couldn't do that."

"Dave, you'll have no choice. Blutik's there, he'll do it. He's also there to collect his debts. He loans money to the troops at an even ten bucks a month. He charges outsiders interest of about 20% a month."

Paying the bill and saying hello to a few others in the club, Norm and Whitehead began their walk to the motor pool. Reaching the motor pool, Whitehead grabbed Norm's arm.

"Do you think we should check out the jeep before we start it? Maybe it's wired. You know, I've been thinking that it was quite a coincidence that 'our' truck was blown up."

"You can bet your ass I'm checking that jeep! Tomorrow, I'm having the motor pool begin welding locks on all the gas tanks. We were supposed to do it months ago. The VC wrap tape around the grenade, pull the pin, and put the grenade through the large opening on our gas tank. The gasoline eventually eats away the tape, the lever flies off and blows the vehicle to kingdom come."

"You think that's what happened?"

"God, I hope so. Better that then someone out to get us."

After looking the jeep over carefully, the two lieutenants drove over to the paymaster's office. The office was in the new area that was being constructed for what had to be a large influx of troops.

Cement pads and wooden structures were being built for newly arriving units. No word on whether a signal unit was coming in to help the 228, but it was possible. New equipment would mean a shot in the arm for morale. The 228 was tired.

The paymaster had the money waiting. After counting it, Whitehead thanked him and found Norm outside going over his notes for Custard.

Back at the company, the pay table was set up and Whitehead sat behind it. After the first soldier saluted him, he made it a point to tell the kid to sign the form correctly.

Blutik was getting pissed off and finally said, "Lieutenant, stop babying these kids. They know how to sign for their pay."

Whitehead said nothing to Blutik. He kept his warning up and there were no faults. Getting up, he thanked Blutik and left for the supply tent. Whitehead signed for the 45 Cal. and slipped it in the leather case which was attached to a web belt. Norm then drove Whitehead to Long Van. From there, a plane ride to Da Lat and more troops to pay.

## CHAPTER 9

The flight to Da Lat was pretty nice, for about twenty minutes. Then the plane climbed higher and disappeared into a cloud.

The village of Da Lat was out of the way in the highlands, a secluded spot used by both the South and North Vietnamese. Its farms provided produce for the wealthy of South Vietnam. Several restaurants there had worldwide reputations and were frequented by South Vietnamese officials, including the Vice Premier, Nguyen Cao Key. In fact, GIs couldn't enter the town because a GI supposedly insulted Madam Key in one of the restaurants.

The landing was rough and Whitehead was glad to get off the plane. Walking to the terminal, he began looking forward to the visit. He was just beginning to really enjoy being away from Custard and Nha Trang when he heard someone calling his name.

"Whitehead. Whitehead, over here."

He knew the voice. It upset his stomach. He wanted to throw up on the owner of the voice. It was Cook. Out loud and not caring who heard him, he said, "Oh, shit. Oh, double shit."

Turning, Whitehead saw that he was right. It was Cook. He was wearing a white pullover shirt tucked into a pair of chino slacks. On his feet he had work boots. He was sitting in a land rover. Whitehead noticed the lock on the gas tank.

"Need a ride, Lieutenant?"

Walking over to the land rover, Whitehead said, "You know, Cook, you sound just like the big bad wolf in those Little Red Riding Hood stories. And I think it's in character."

Looking Cook over, Whitehead added, "You seem to be out of uniform. As a matter of fact, out of two uniforms that I know about. Who are you today?"

"Never mind. We need to talk. Get in. I'll drive you to the radio site and you can pay your troops."

"How did you know I was in Da Lat?" But Whitehead stopped Cook's answer before it even started, "Never mind, I know, everyone knows I was going to Da Lat."

*

After Whitehead finished paying the troops, the two men drove down to have lunch at a café. At Cook's request, of course. Cook drove for about ten minutes saying nothing. He let Whitehead look at the village of Da Lat. Cleaner than most towns he had seen, it was still not attractive in light of Whitehead's recent arrival from the States. It would look better months from now.

Once inside the cafe, Cook ordered. Salad, soup, wine, and bread. Cook was the perfect host.

Whitehead began the conversation, "OK, what's the topic? Carbines? Burgess? Harris? Or what?"

"Let's try 'what'." Cook was smiling.

Whitehead didn't smile. "Hey, I'm really confused. You said you wanted to talk. Instead, you buy me lunch. You are buying, aren't you?"

"First, I apologize. I'm screwing around and you're looking for some answers."

"Are you going to give me some?"

"Some. Right now, I don't think you need to know all of them. And you really don't want to know. Take my word for it."

The food came and it was delicious. The salad was crisp, the soup was onion, and the bread was fresh. The wine, a light fresh table white Chablis, was dry and mild. Cook certainly had good taste in cafes.

"First of all, I'm not Army or Air Force. I just am. You must have figured I'm in some branch of intelligence, and that's all you should know. I gave you the carbine for safe keeping. I'm going to need it in a couple of days. I want to be able to call you in Nha Trang and set up a meeting to get it. Can we do that?"

"Is this the carbine that someone broke into my room to steal?" Whitehead asked.

"Yeah, I guess someone saw us exchange it. You did a good job keeping it safe."

Whitehead figured he'd play stupid. He asked, "What's so important about the carbine?"

"Well, it's a keepsake from a buddy who died carrying it through Laos. He gave it to me when he was dying and told me to keep it as a remembrance of him."

"Boy, Cook, you're just one bundle of sentiment. You're bringing me to tears."

"No, seriously, that's all it is."

Whitehead was enjoying the wine too much to really get too excited about Cook. Maybe it's better like this, he thought. Just give the carbine to Cook and get it over with.

So he finally said, "OK, call me and we'll set up the meet. Got any idea when I should expect you?"

"Maybe as early as tomorrow," Cook responded. "You'll be in Nha Trang later today. I'll drive you back to the airport and you can get the next flight out. I'll probably leave tomorrow morning, close to noontime. I have some other business to take care of and then I'll call you."

Whitehead thought about bringing up the subject of Burgess and Harris again, but before he could, Cook was on his feet throwing piasters on the table. Whitehead gulped down the last of his wine and got up, knowing the conversation was over.

\*

Whitehead caught the "Nha Trang express" and fell asleep on board. He woke when the plane hit the runway.

The back door opened and he got out.    Thank God it was Nha Trang.    He probably would've gotten out even if it wasn't.    The wine did a great job on him.    He was literally wiped out.

Walking to the nearest phone, he gave Norm's exchange to the Goldfinch operator and waited for Norm to come on the line.    Hearing his voice, he said, "How's your ass, Lieutenant Range?"

"Who is this?" asked Range sounding a bit confused.

"I'll give you three guesses.    The clock is running. You have only 30 seconds to come up with the correct answer."

"Dave?"

"Correct, on the first guess.    You win three days in Da Lat, the finest resort in a shithole of a country.    Can you come get me before I fall down?"

"Are you at the airfield?    Or are you someplace you don't know?"

"I'm at Long Van, but my heart's in Da Lat."

Norm was about ten minutes getting to Long Van and another ten minutes parking the jeep.    He found Whitehead snoozing in the terminal.

Shaking him, he said, "Dave, it's bye-bye time. Mother is here to take you home."

"Mother never looked so good," Whitehead said, getting up and putting his hand on Norm's shoulder.

"You must have had a busy day."

"I met Cook.    We had lunch in the nicest cafe. The wine was fantastic."

"I'll bet," said Range as he helped Whitehead to the jeep.

\*

After turning in the 45, Jumpers drove Whitehead down to Goldfinch.    The wind from the jeep ride cleared his head.   Once there, Franklin updated the lieutenant.   No word from Southland after three days and Boggs was out with the three-quarter.   Blutik had called down and said the old man was looking for him.

"First of all, I'm not here.   You haven't seen me. Not yet anyway.   If the telephone rings and it's for me, write the name of the person down and show it to me, then I'll tell you what to say.   OK?"

"I got it, sir."   Franklin would do anything now after the Wilson affair.   Well, almost anything.

Just around five o'clock, the phone did ring. Franklin answered and wrote the name, COOK, on the pad.

Whitehead nodded that he would take it.   Taking the receiver, he spoke into it. "Whitehead here."

"Dave, it's Cook.   I'm back in Nha Trang.   Can we meet later for the exchange?"

"Sure.   When and where?"

"You know where the big white Buddha is?"

"Yeah."

"Meet me there at midnight with the package."

"Midnight?"   I'm asleep at midnight, Whitehead said to himself.   "Can't we make it earlier?"

"We can't be seen.   Just come and I'll find you. Trust me."   Then he hung up.

"Oh, you son of a bitch, you son of a fucking bitch!" Whitehead slammed the phone down and kicked the chair. Franklin just stared at him.

He smiled and said, "That was a friend.   He wanted to say something nasty to someone.   He asked me if I knew something rotten to say to someone.   That's what I told him."   The stare continued.   "Franklin, go check the generators or something."

After Franklin left, Whitehead called Norm.

"Norm, Cook's in Nha Trang.   He wants the carbine.   Would you mind bringing it with you on your way over?"      "Sure, I'll be right there."

87

In the back of his jeep, Norm brought the carbine. It was wrapped in a blanket. Whitehead didn't want to touch it, but he couldn't leave it in the jeep. Grabbing the blanket, he jogged over to the MRK 54 rig. "Collins!"

Hearing his name, Collins came out on the ramp between the huts.

"Hi, lieutenant. What's up?"

"Collins, I want you to hold onto this carbine for about an hour. Don't let it out of your sight. OK?"

"Yes, sir. I'll be here for the next eight hours. I'll hide it in the back behind the radio gear."

"Thanks, Collins. I owe you one."

All through dinner, Whitehead was trying to figure out how he was going to meet Cook at midnight. He could borrow Norm's jeep, but he couldn't find the Buddha by himself.

Finally, Norm asked the million dollar question, "When are you going to meet Cook?"

"He wants me to meet him at midnight."

Eating the last of his pie, Norm asked, "Where?"

Whitehead hesitated, "The big white buddha."

Norm almost choked. "You must be crazy! You can't even find it! How do you know what's happening up there at midnight?"

"I don't. I was hoping I could borrow the jeep and ...." Whitehead's voice trailed off.

"You son of a bitch. You want me to drive you there. Oh, no. You can take the jeep, but you're not taking me." Norm sat there shaking his head violently. "I don't care how many times you ask me, the answer is no. No sir!"

"OK, Norm, I was just inviting you. You can give me a map and start me in the right direction. I can handle this. Don't worry."

The rest of the dinner was in total silence. Norm was steaming mad. The jeep ride to Goldfinch was the same.

While Whitehead retrieved the carbine wrapped in the blanket, Norm went to the operations hut and wrote out directions to the Buddha.

When Whitehead got there, he said, "Here's the directions. You've got to be careful of some of these turns. Don't make any stops unless you have to."

"Norm, let's get you back to the villa. It's almost eight o'clock."

Night had just about reached Nha Trang as Norm and Whitehead drove to the villa. There was a full moon. That meant good light. But it was also cloudy, and every once in awhile, the moon was covered. Then it was pitch black.

Both of the lieutenants remained quiet. No one else was in the villa. By nine o'clock, Whitehead began getting ready to leave. He asked Norm for the keys, but Norm ignored the question.

Finally, Norm burst out, "Shit, you're not going to be on my conscience. I'd lay here and worry all night. I'll take you, but this is it. No more. Never again. Come on, let's go, but don't say a word to me."

CHAPTER 10

The jeep moved quickly through the streets of Nha Trang and out into the little village northwest of the city. Norm turned up the hilly drive and carefully used the moonlight to guide his path.

As they reached the top, the clouds covered the moon, plunging them into darkness. The moon was covered for the rest of the drive until the jeep approached the clearing.

With the Buddha now in sight, both Norm and Whitehead were silent. Norm began turning the jeep around.

"Leaving so soon?"

"No, but I want to be in a position to leave fast."

Whitehead smiled. "If I was by myself, I think I would leave."

"You just made me sorry for coming."

They sat in silence for a few moments.

"Norm, look. By the Buddha. Someone's over there."

"How come you didn't remember to bring a flash light?"

The clouds covered the moon again bringing a light rain with the darkness. The rain sounded like footsteps. Norm and Whitehead got out of the jeep. The shacks along the edge of the clearing were deserted. Slowly, they walked toward the Buddha. Whitehead had the blanket in his arms.

"Norm, why didn't we bring your carbine, loaded?"

"Now you have a good idea. I can't believe I came with you."

"But you did, and I'm glad you did."

"Fuck you."

Stopping at the corner of the base of the buddha, a voice called out.

"Whitehead."

"Yeah, it's me.   Cook?"

"Don't come any closer.   Stay right there.   Pass the carbine around the corner and I'll take it.   You're being watched."

Facing the wall, Whitehead leaned against the base and passed the blanket with the carbine around the corner without looking.   Norm stood behind him.

Whitehead looked at Norm, and said.   "Let's get the fuck out of here."

One step away, maybe two steps.      A gun shot. Then the moan.   They looked at each other, and without a word, they turned back and looked around the corner.   A body was laying on the ground. They moved toward it.

"Dave, be careful.   Is it Cook? "

"I can't tell. Let me see if I have a match."   He did and struck it, holding the flame close to the dead man's face. "Shit, it's not Cook."

Whitehead stood up, struck another match, and saw the blanket.   He picked up the blanket.   No carbine.

"Come on, we better get out of here.   Let Cook handle this mess."

They ran back to the jeep.   The ride to the villa seemed to last only seconds.

In the villa, Norm led the way to the room.   All the other doors were closed.   It was almost 2200 hours.   The others were still out or asleep.

Once inside the room, Norm reached into his footlocker and brought out a bottle of "Old Grandad."   He took a long drink and coughed.   While coughing, he handed the bottle to Whitehead.   They drank half the bottle sitting on their beds.

"Dave, did you know that guy?"

"Do you want an honest answer?"

"God dammit, yes."

"Norm, it was Major Lakeland. From Duc My."

"Oh, shit."
They killed the rest of the bottle and fell asleep.

228

CHAPTER 11

Whitehead's mind swirled with thoughts of the last few days.  The midnight meeting at the great white Buddha. Lakeland and Harris.  The jade.  And, of course, Cook.

That morning, Custard ordered the new lieutenant to find out who was sleeping with his Vietnamese secretary, Lan.  But more importantly, breakfast was probably the worst meal Whitehead had eaten since coming to Vietnam.

The arrival of Dancer at the table where Range and Whitehead were eating didn't make the morning any better. Dancer told the two lieutenants he was heading for Cam Ranh Bay to attend a briefing on the company's future. Whitehead had heard rumors about a possible transfer of the company to combat areas.  A development neither the 228th nor the young lieutenant were ready to face.

According to Dancer, Custard was supposed to attend the meeting, but an hour ago excused himself leaving Dancer with the task.  Whitehead and Range were to report to the captain at 0900 hours for some new assignments and jobs.  The morning was growing worse by the minute.

While Norm checked into the supply tent, Whitehead went directly to the orderly room.  Apparently, Custard took the latest issue of Stars and Stripes into the latrine with him.  The only person around was Lan sitting quietly waiting to do her typing.

Whitehead looked at her and asked, "Lan, who is your lover?   Tell me and I'll see that you two are married." The only response from Lan was a giggle.

Before he could continue, Norm came in.   "Trying to make time with the help?   Did she tell you who did it?"

"Yes, she did.   She said it was you."

"Funny guy, aren't you?   Where's the old man?"

"Good morning, gentlemen!"   It was Custard.   He had come up right behind Range and nearly shouted in his ear.   "Give me a minute, then come in."

After waiting a few moments, they filed into the office. Custard motioned for them to take the two chairs against the wall. Custard had decided to stand and walk, giving a kind of oration. With the two officers against the wall, he wouldn't fall over them.

Looking out the window, he began, "Men, we are at the beginning of a momentous time for the 228. Lieutenant Dancer is in Cam Ranh Bay right now getting the details. We will soon be leaving Nha Trang and assuming a new mission."

So much for rumors, thought Whitehead.

"That mission," Custard continued, "will be in a direct combat support role. Not a few teams here or there, but the whole company. We are going to An Khe and will be attached to the First Calvary, Air Mobile. We are going to war."

"Oh, shit!" Whitehead couldn't help it.

"What did you say, Whitehead?" Custard said staring at him. So was Norm.

"Excuse me sir," he stopped and tried to think fast. It came. "Sir, I said 'oh shit' because we are now ill equipped for a combat mission. Our trucks are old, the radio gear is worn, and we're badly under-strength."

"Well put, Whitehead," Custard stared with total eye-to-eye contact. "You're right. But all that's changing. First, we are getting new trucks and jeeps. Then some new equipment. And, of course, we are getting officers and men. How does that sound, Lieutenant Whitehead? Lieutenant Range?"

Together, they said, "Fine, sir."

"But first," stopped Custard, for effect and breath, "we have two missions. One is to prepare the area for the incoming 459th Signal Battalion. They've left Fort Huachuca and will be here in three weeks. Range, that's your job."

"How do I go about that, Captain?" Range asked.

"Dancer will give you all the details. To you, Whitehead, goes the task of installing Nha Trang LD, the LD stands for long distance. That's the pair of trailers parked at the rear of Goldfinch."

Range got away with a dumb question, Whitehead figured he'd ask it too, "How do I do that, Captain?"

"Shit, Whitehead, do I have to tell you everything? You're a first lieutenant. You're suppose to know something." Looking directly in his face, he shouted, "Find out how to do it! Just get that switchboard installed as soon as possible! Dismissed."

The lieutenants stood, saluted, and walked out of the office, leaving Custard to stare out the window by himself. They both went to the supply tent without a word between them. The rumors were true. They were going to war.

*

Norm dropped off Whitehead at Goldfinch that afternoon. It seemed everyone at the switchboard site knew about the turn of events. The men inundated Whitehead with questions.

His thoughts turned to installing the switchboard as he left the operations hut and the questions, to sit on the Agent Orange tanks by the airfield. After a short time he saw Boggs pull in with his three-quarter. He got up and walked over, deciding to corral Boggs and bring him back to the new switchboard.

It must have been the "please." Boggs agreed without little hesitation.

After looking over the equipment in the trailers, Boggs made a few little suggestions such as cement pads under the rigs and having a tractor trailer driver place the rigs in place. The most important suggestion was that Whitehead should find a sergeant to lean on and use that sergeant to really do the work.

Their talk was interrupted by Sergeant Franklin.

"Sergeant Boggs, Sergeant Southland is back. Looks like they had trouble."

Boggs jumped down from the trailer. Whitehead followed.

Coming off the main road and into the Goldfinch site was a large Army tow truck with 4th Infantry markings. It was pulling one of the 228's old M211 deuce and a half trucks.

Southland got out of the tow truck and directed its driver to the rear of the site. He walked over to where Boggs and Whitehead were standing.

Saluting, Southland let out a great sigh, then said, "I hope you two are ready for a large tale of woe. There's nothing good to hear."

Whitehead spoke first, "Well, it can wait until you get yourself together." Looking around, he asked, "Where's Wilson?"

Southland hesitated, then said finally, "He got hit, sir. By a mortar. And we don't know if he'll survive."

"Oh, shit." Whitehead couldn't think of anything else to say. Then he didn't have to. He puked right there. And then he heard someone else doing the same. Turning, Sergeant Franklin was leaning over the containers of gasoline feeding the generators.

Whitehead had seen three bodies since coming over to 'Nam, but this was different. Wilson was just an innocent little guy in the wrong place doing the wrong thing just once too often. If he'd had left Wilson alone, he'd be alive right now.

"You said that Wilson may be dead, Sergeant. Don't you know?" Boggs asked, giving Whitehead a chance to regain his composure.

"Sarge, when we got to him, he was breathing but unconscious and covered with blood. A chopper flew in and took him to a hospital ship. We waited until this morning, but no news.   Then, we were ordered to leave."

After taking a deep breath, Whitehead told Southland to go in the hut and sit down.   Then he ordered Franklin to transport Southland's men up to the barracks.   He also told Franklin to find somebody to throw dirt over his breakfast.

\*

Inside the hut, Southland was smoking and leaning in a chair against the wall.   Boggs sat on the desk and said nothing.   Whitehead came in and squatted opposite Southland with his back against the wall.

"Give me a brief rundown of what happened. Sorry, I didn't control myself there.   It caught me by surprise."

"No problem sir, I puked this morning," Southland admitted.

While Boggs and Whitehead sat and listened, Southland related the events of the last six days with the 4th Infantry Division.   They arrived late on the day they left Goldfinch.   The infantry brigade's first sergeant ordered them to stay at the 4th's base camp as the reserve unit.

"We were there for two days and saw a couple heavy mortar attacks.   No hits, but we were all scared shitless."

Southland got up for some coffee.   He stayed standing, but leaned against the opposite wall for support.

Whitehead tried to help him a little and asked, "When did the mortar get Wilson?"

"Yesterday morning, sir.   We were just getting our shit together when they started.   About 0800.   Wilson had slept in the truck.   I saw him get out, walk about 20 feet and stretch.   Then the mortar hit."

Southland drank some coffee and then continued, "I've never seen so much confusion.   We were on the ground for 10 minutes while the mortars came in, maybe longer.   When I got up, I started counting noses.

"I was short one. Wilson. I found him about 20 feet away from where I'd seen him stretch. He never said a word. Didn't even move a muscle. I'm thinking the worst." He stopped.

"Boggs," said Whitehead, "take Southland somewhere and get him together. Southland, see the old man ASAP." Whitehead then looked at Southland and said, "I'm sorry. I fucked up. I guess it could've been worst, but I really don't see how." With that he left Boggs and Southland in the tent.

Outside, Whitehead began walking up to the orderly room. Half way there, Sergeant Franklin pulled up alongside with the three-quarter. "Sir, the captain wants to see you right away. Hop in and I'll take you."

Whitehead walked around to the passenger side and got in. Grinding the gear, Franklin floored it for the orderly room. The ride was awkwardly quiet for Whitehead. He felt he should apologize, but how do you tell a man you're sorry for sending his friend to die.

"I think things may work out," said Franklin, breaking the silence as they reached their destination. "Maybe he was only wounded."

Whitehead could only nod. Getting out he slammed the door. Looking back at Franklin, he said "I hope you're right about Wilson." Whitehead turned and headed into the orderly room, repeating his last statement as Franklin pulled away.

Ignoring Blutik seated behind the desk in the front room, Whitehead walked up to Custard's door. He knocked and entered, giving only the barest of a salute.

"You wanted to see me sir?"

Custard nodded and then related what he had heard. Whitehead added a few things and stated that Southland was putting a report together and would have it ready tomorrow.

"I hope you learned a lesson from this," Custard said matter of factly. "Wilson was not the man to send on this mission. He was a zero before and now he's a real zero. Get back to work."

Something inside caused Whitehead to remain silent at hearing that last statement. Any remark would probably be wasted on a man like Custard. It would also create more problems between himself and the captain. Instead, he simply saluted and left.

*

Walking over to the supply tent, he found Norm filling out some requisition forms for the company's new trucks.

Seeing Whitehead walk in, Range stopped and then picked up a piece of paper.

"Here. A note from Cook. The first sergeant brought it over earlier when he couldn't find you. Told me to get it to you at lunch."

Whitehead took the paper without looking at it.

"Call Cook and see what he wants," Norm told him. "It may get your mind off Wilson."

Holding the paper, Whitehead wondered if anything would get his mind off Wilson right now. He got Goldfinch and gave them the number. It rang twice then a voice answered, "Hello."

"Cook?"

"Yeah. Dave?"

"Yeah. What do you want?"

"The carbine."

"You got it. And I got more than I wanted in the process. You do things to people I don't like."

Cook was silent.

"What do you really want?" Whitehead asked. He was beginning to feel sorry for calling.

"I'm serious. You gave me the wrong carbine."

"Hey, shithead, check the serial number."

"The serial number's right, but the stock isn't. You took the stock off. Get it. I'll call you in a few days. I want that stock." With that he hung up.

Whitehead sat with the receiver in his hand. Norm must have picked up the rifle using the serial number to identify it. They still had the jade.

## CHAPTER 12

Whitehead needed a change of scenery.  The beach was the first place he thought of.  After lunch, Range and Whitehead drove out to the shore.  Both were quiet as they sat watching the waves.

About thirty minutes passed by without a word from either man.  Whitehead sat in the jeep thinking about the situation with Cook.  He decided to leave the jade alone for the time being.  It was safe.  At least safer than he was. He also felt it was better not to tell Norm about the mixup unless he had to.

Norm started the jeep and drove back to the supply tent.  Back at Norm's desk, Whitehead reviewed what he thought he needed for the installation of Nha Trang LD. Cement, wood, cables, and tools were all ordered.  Jumpers and some men would get most of the stuff tomorrow.

"I forgot to tell you," Norm said.  "I know someone who may be able to help you with Lan.  His name is Phuc."

"What can he do, besides make me laugh because of his name?"

"Well, since he's the camp's interpreter, you may want him to ask Lan your questions in Vietnamese.  Then, you can laugh because of his name."

"O.K., I'll look for him later.  Thanks."  Putting the paperwork in order, Whitehead left the supply tent.

Whitehead found Boggs, and the two headed over to Long Van Air Base where Nha Trang LD would be installed. Whitehead had to meet with Major Lang, a Signal officer who was building the communications center for Nha Trang under a civilian contract.  The switchboard would tie into that and work off the large microwave antennas.

It took about ten minutes to reach the rear of Long Van Air Base.  On the way over, Whitehead asked Boggs about Major Lang.

"Major Lang?  Nice fellow.  He manages the

contract for the Oriental-American Engineering Company. They construct buildings, build runways and do just about anything that makes money.

"Don't like his company, though. They're all civilians of the worst kind. When they're not working, everything they do is done without much class. Many of them are just slobs. Not a nice group of people at all."

Boggs pulled the truck into a small road just past a large microwave screen nearly a hundred feet long and about fifty feet wide. Boggs motioned toward it and said, "I think that's the antenna you're going to tie into for long distant commo. You'll run some lines out to this one and the other one out there near the end of the runway."

Parking the three quarter, Boggs and Whitehead explored the area prior to entering the large corrugated tin building that was the communications nerve center for the Nha Trang area. Compared to this effort, the 228 was just playing games with its little switchboard and radio relays.

Satisfied with the lay of the land, Boggs and Whitehead entered the building. No one came near them. After walking around, they were stopped. A large burly civilian, having one of the largest stomachs Whitehead had ever seen, approached them and put a hand up.

"Now just where the fuck do you two soldier boys think you're going? Do you know this is restricted?"

"I'm Lieutenant Whitehead and this is Sergeant Boggs, we're from - "

"Who gives a shit. How about you two turn around and get the fuck out of here!" The fat stomach began moving toward them.

"Hold it Bradley, they're here to see me." The voice came from behind Whitehead and Boggs. "Hello, I'm Major Lang." Looking back at the stomach with legs, Lang said, "Thanks, Mr. Bradley, I'll take these men with me. They're here to install the long distance switchboard for the Army."

Bradley nodded and left.

Lang, Boggs and Whitehead watched him go. It was Lang who spoke first. "Well, I appreciate you two coming over here. I just got here from Fort Monmouth about a month ago. Bradley keeps forgetting that I'm around. Let's go outside and see if I can help you find someplace for the switchboard."

With Lang leading the way, they walked about a thousand yards. They stopped behind one of the large antennas. Whitehead began to plan the location. He started to pace out the footage of the two trailers. Taking out a notepad, he then drew a diagram and shared it with Lang, who agreed with Whitehead's sketch.

About ten minutes later, and a few more questions and suggestions, Lang apologized saying he had to leave for a meeting with his friend, Bradley. Lang added, "Bradley's a slob, but he keeps his men working and they meet their deadlines. As a result, I don't really bother him. Check with me, and I'll make sure he stays away from you. Lieutenant, good luck with the installation. We'll be talking."

Lang left Whitehead and Boggs to deal with some details about how much cement and how the trailer should be turned and stationed. The two lieutenants finished up and headed back to Goldfinch.

*

At Goldfinch, Whitehead had a visitor. An Army major with crossed pistols on his collar was standing by the communications hut. "Are you Whitehead?"

"Yes sir. What can I do for you?"

"Can we talk quietly somewhere? How about out by those silver tanks?"

"Lead the way, sir."

Out at the tanks, the major lit a cigarette, then looked

at the tanks, and said, "Are they gas?"

"No sir, I understand they're Agent Orange canisters."

"Oh, I guess we're safe then. Cigarette?"

"No sir, I smoke cigars."

"Don't have any of them." The major looked pained that he didn't. He then proceeded, "I have to ask you some questions about an incident at the large buddha outside of Nha Trang a couple of nights ago. It's a little strange. I'm an investigator, but I've been told to stay off this one. So this is a personal inquiry and you can tell me to kiss off if you want."

"A guy was shot up there. I think he was murdered. Know anything about it?"

Whitehead decided to stick to the story he and Norm agreed to and answered, "No, sir, should I?"

"Well, I was in charge of the investigation for about 2 hours before I was pulled. Just before I was pulled, I was ready to call you. I found a piece of paper in the dead man's pocket with your name and the word 'Goldfinch' on it.

"You were easy to find, but I got zapped. I'm trying to figure out why."

"Major," responded Whitehead, "I'm at a loss. What was the guy's name?"

"No name. No identification on him."

"Sorry, Major, can't help you. Wish I could give you a hand." Getting bold, he went another step. "Want me to look at the body? Maybe I can give you a name."

"Too late. The body was picked up and the paperwork taken with it. For us, the body and the case doesn't exist."

"Sounds spooky," said Whitehead.

The major got quiet and appeared to be deep in thought. Finally, he said, "My name's Major Cohn, with the MPs. If you think of anything, call me at Goldfinch 433. Thanks."

The two walked back to the major's jeep. The MP officer got in and accepted a salute from Whitehead and drove off. Whitehead went back to the operations hut and called Norm.

"Norm, an MP major was here asking about Lakeland. He was pissed because the case was taken away from him to hush it up. If he calls, just tell him you know nothing about it. He didn't ask where I was or anything. Maybe it's all over."

"I hope so." With that Norm hung up the phone.

\*

Whitehead stayed at Goldfinch for some time, then headed back to the company orderly room. Walking through some rows of tents, two young Vietnamese bumped into him. Backing off, they quickly apologized and one then said, "You are Lieutenant Whitehead?"

Caught by surprise, Whitehead at first didn't understand the words that were tangled up with a heavy accent.

The young man spoke again, "I am Phuc."

Bells began to ring for Whitehead. "Oh, you're the interpreter," he put out his hand to shake.

At first, Phuc only looked at the hand. Then he jumped to shake it.

"I was just thinking about coming to see you," Whitehead said looking at the young man. "Do you know our typist, Lan?"

"Yes, I do. I was just speaking with her. Lieutenant Range told me what your problem was. I went ahead and asked her about her lover. She refuses to answer the question."

"If you like, I will ask her friends about her lover. They may be a better source of information."

"Thanks, Phuc." Whitehead had difficulty saying

the name.   He almost called him fuck.   "Well, I think you may be right.   Any help you can provide me will be greatly appreciated."

He offered the hand again and Phuc shook it warmly. Phuc then excused himself and introduced the second young man as his friend, Truc.   Truc and Whitehead exchanged hellos.

Finally, Whitehead said good-bye to them and was about the leave when Phuc spoke again, "We have a mutual friend."

Whitehead stopped and said, "Don't tell me you're from New Jersey."

"New Jersey?"   Phuc looked puzzled.   "No, I don't know New Jersey.   I know Cook."

Whitehead stared blankly as the two boys then excused themselves and left, ducking into a tent about twenty feet down the walkway.   Whitehead began to follow them.   Looking in the tent, he found it empty.   Phuc and Truc had vanished.

## CHAPTER 13

Whitehead, like every American in 'Nam, lusted after having a jeep of his own. Now that he had Nha Trang LD as an assignment, he was on the verge of making the move. But he had a few other issues to deal with.

One was Phuc. Whitehead had thought that the Cook situation was winding down. Now Phuc appears and claims friendship with Cook. Cook certainly gets around and meets all the right people.

Also Whitehead needed a sergeant to take the lead in installing Nha Trang LD. Leaving Norm that morning after breakfast, Whitehead headed to talk to the first sergeant.

Entering the orderly room, he saw Sergeant Blutik working on his morning report. He didn't look up so Whitehead said, "Good morning, first sergeant." He was trying to say all the right things.

"Good morning, lieutenant, what can I do for you?"

"I need a sergeant. To be exact, I need a sergeant for Nha Trang LD, first to install it and then to run it."

Blutik said nothing. He continued to work on his report. Writing a few last numbers, he closed the folder, put it on the side and leaned back in his chair.

"Well, you came to the right man. You must be learning. Tell you what I'll do. I think we're getting some NCOs from Group in the next few days. Maybe they'll have telephone backgrounds for the job. All of the current crew is radio; they hate switchboards."

"In the meantime, I need someone to pour some cement and get the site ready."

"I know, I know, hold your horses. I'm not finished yet. Maybe you didn't learn so fast after all."

"Sorry, sergeant, I'm just anxious to get this thing started."

"OK, lieutenant, I'll have Sergeant Rameirez help you with that. He should be able to get the site organized and ready to put the trailers over there. I'll send him down to Goldfinch later this morning. He was up at Da Lat before he went home on leave. He just got back yesterday. How's that, lieutenant?"

"Fine, sergeant. I appreciate it. One other thing, I think we need some transportation. Who assigns vehicles?"

"The motor officer. Lieutenant Range. You know where to find him?"

"Yeah, sergeant, I guess I can find him. Again, thanks for your help."

"OK, lieutenant." With that, Blutik put his head back into his morning report and Whitehead left the building.

In the parking area near Group, he was walking with his head down thinking about the LD when he heard his name. He looked up and it was Colonel Duel.

"Lieutenant, you walk around like that and you'll get your ass run over." Duel was sitting in his jeep.

Whitehead pulled himself together and saluted, then said, "Sorry, sir, I was in deep thought."

"I hope it was about Nha Trang LD. I want that installed and installed quick. We depended on those Air Force bastards too long. Get it over there, hook it up, and get it working. Kick some ass if you have to, but do it."

"Yes, sir." Whitehead began to tell the colonel about how he needed a sergeant and some specialists in switchboard, but Duel was already saluting and telling his driver to pull away. He left Whitehead with his hand to the peak of his cap saluting the wind.

Captain Custard had just left the latrine with the Stars and Stripes when Duel pulled up beside Whitehead. Walking to the orderly room, he watched Whitehead and Duel converse. To him, the talk looked intimate. Out loud, he said, "Shit, I knew it!" He then looked around, but no one had heard him. Slapping the newspaper against his thigh, he said it again, "Shit!"

Oblivious of Custard, the two lieutenants got into Norm's jeep. The supply officer started it and began pulling away. "Norm, I need transportation for Nha Trang LD."

At that, Norm drove to the motor pool. At the rear of the garage area, he stopped in front of a jeep that was missing its cover.

"I promised Van Rankin that he could have this jeep when it came back from maintenance. It was wrecked during a beach party three months ago. The mess sergeant got drunk and rolled it over on the beach.

"I understand it's difficult to steer," he said looking at Whitehead. "I'm afraid to let a sergeant take it, so I think I'll ask the old man to let me assign it to you. Then you can keep an eye on it. I'll also get you a couple of deuce and a halfs to carry cement and sand. They're a little less attractive to thieves and also harder to lose."

Whitehead looked the jeep over and even sat in it. The steering was very tight, but it was a jeep.

"Van Rankin will love this, but I don't really care. I covered for him three times when he was drunk on duty. I didn't want him to have the jeep anyway."

"Thanks, Norm, I appreciate it. It'll help with the switchboard. Not only that, you won't have to taxi me around anymore. It'll give us a little more flexibility, too. Now, we can just trade off on driving."

"I have to get going. Van Rankin will weld the lock on the gas tank and then it's yours."

Back in Norm's jeep on the way to Goldfinch, Whitehead asked, "Phuc is a friend of Cook."

From the look on Norm's face, it was obvious that he didn't know. "How did you find that out?"

"He told me. I met him between tents near the orderly room yesterday. It slipped my mind last night. I was too wrapped up in Nha Trang LD. Never entered my mind this morning."

"Wonders never cease," said Norm. "You know, he was smiling when I asked him to check with you about Lan. I thought his teeth would fall out. He must have been looking for an excuse to reach you. And I gave it to him."

*

Whitehead headed for the operations hut after Norm dropped him off.

Franklin was in the doorway of the hut. He saluted and said, "Good morning lieutenant. Want to read a letter?"

"If it's from your wife, telling you that she wants a divorce, I can't help you." Going in, sitting down, and throwing his cap on the table, he looked back at Franklin, "Sorry, bad joke."

"No problem, lieutenant, I'm not married. The letter's from Wilson."

Whitehead jumped up and hit his head. "Does that mean he made it?"

"Yes, sir, he made it. There's a message for you in the letter."

Sitting down and rubbing his head, Whitehead said, "I couldn't handle a hate letter today. Maybe you should only tell me what it says if it's good."

"Sir, it's good. He's happy to be home. Here, I'll read the part about you."

Franklin unfolded the letter, found the section, and read, "Tell Lieutenant Whitehead that I appreciate his efforts on my behalf. I was afraid Custard was going to crucify me. The assignment got me out of the way. It was just bad luck.

"The doctors on the ship operated and saved my leg, patched up my chest, and ordered me home. I'll be discharged as soon as I get out of the hospital.

"My old employer thinks I'm a hero and told me I

have a job if I want it.    He also told me that I may get a
town celebration when I get home.    I'll be able to wear my
Purple Heart one time before I put my uniform away.    Tell
Lieutenant Whitehead to be careful.    I'll pray that he and all
of you will get home safe."

Whitehead was quiet for a few moments then said,
"Thanks, Franklin.    Thanks for sharing that with me.    I
feel better.    God, I feel better."

Whitehead got up, picked his cap up and told
Franklin he was going out and sit on the agent orange.    He
needed to think.

Out on the canisters of Agent Orange, Whitehead
forced himself to put the Wilson incident behind him.    It
would be easier now that Wilson was okay.    He had to
think through his next steps.

About a half hour later, Rameirez approached the
tanks and reported to Whitehead.    After the exchange of
introductions, the two headed for the trailers to examine the
switchboard.

For the next two hours, Whitehead and Rameirez
worked over the requirements for the switchboard.    They
identified material and manpower needs and wrote up lists
they would bring to Norm and the first sergeant later in the
day.

Around 1600 hours, the two hitched a ride up to the
orderly room to see the first sergeant.    Looking over the
manpower needs, Blutik was able to spare six men for three
days.    It seemed the 228 would be busy in the coming
weeks preparing for the arrival of the new battalion.    The
men were ordered to build platform tents in the new camp
area.

Next was a stop at the supply room to go over the
forms for the materials they needed.    As long as Whitehead
could supply the men to transport the materials, Norm could
get them without a problem.

The next three days were going to be hectic for

Whitehead. Whitehead told Rameirez to get some personal time then be prepared to work as long as it takes to get the job done. Within seconds of Whitehead's suggestion, Rameirez was gone.

"What are we going to do for dinner, Norm?"

"There's a show in the officer's club down the street tonight. Maybe we could go to MACV for dinner and come back here and catch the show. Sometimes they're pretty good. Tonight, it's a stripper."

\*

The ride to the club was uneventful and ended with a parking space that was convenient to the club. They got out of the jeep and were in the club with ten minutes to spare. Ordering a couple of drinks, they found a table with three officers from an artillery unit.

Whitehead looked around and was amazed at the number of civilians. A few days ago, he would have thought they were journalists. Now he suspected they were civilian contract employees.

His feeling was reaffirmed when he heard loud laughing and some real dirty talk near the left front of the stage. The words weren't all that obscene, but the sound and tone of the voices were. Whitehead knew who it was, too. Bradley.

Nudging Norm, Whitehead pointed him out relating the other day's meeting with Lang.

"Looks like a nice guy. You do have such nice friends, Dave."

Turning his attention to the side, Whitehead watched the sport-shirted middle age club manager looking over notes about the act. He waved his hands and the lights went down.

He climbed on the stage and shouted, "Gentlemen! Gentlemen, let me have your attention. We have a special treat for you tonight.    All the way from Australia, we have a lovely dark-haired beauty who has more bounce to the ounce than you've ever seen."    He stopped and turned to the side and said, "Is she ready?"

Getting a signal from a doorway, he then turned back to the audience, "Here she is, Hurricane Gloria.    Let's have a big welcome for Glooooorriiia!"

The lights went out and a spotlight came on.    The music, naturally 'The Stripper,' played over the PA system. First, a leg appeared and finally the girl.    While she had a plain face, her body was no more than twenty years old.

She was everything that the club manager said she was.    Her dance was good.    Pretty artistic.    At least, for a while.

Down to just a small top piece and a G-string, her dance got a little more erotic.    Each bump and each grind set off cries from the officers and civilians that would embarrass their dependents at home.    War is hell, but someone has to fight it.

She teased with the top a little but continued her dance.    More drinks and more bumps got the audience to a torrid level.

The cat calls went beyond the suggestive to the downright obscene.    Leading the audience was Bradley who from his seat down front was also demonstrating what he wanted her to do to him.

The lights went out again. The stage was in total darkness.    And then once again the spotlight came on, with Gloria standing tall in her brief outfit.

"Gentlemen," she shouted over the screaming crowd, "now I want to share with someone my newest dance steps. If one of you would care to come up and join me, I will show him some things he's never seen before."

Bolting up to the stage was Bradley.    "Honey, there ain't nothing you can show me that I haven't seen before, but I'm game."

She looked at him with obvious disgust. She would have preferred someone not so wild or drunk, but Bradley was there. She was stuck with him. She began her act again.

"First, let's add a little mystery to the dance."

She went to the side and got a blindfold. Her dance had been smooth, but now she was a little rocky with her performance. This was obviously a little new for her. "What's your name?"

"My name's Eddie." Bradley was screaming and drooling. "But you can call me anything."

"OK, Anything, put this blindfold on."

Whitehead laughed at her little joke. He started to feel that this show was going to end up a little wild. Bradley was not the kind of guy to be cute. He was putting the blindfold on, but turned to the audience and winked.

She signaled for the music. Thinking Bradley was really blindfolded, she started to do some movements up and down his body, staying about a foot away from him.

Bradley, without removing his blindfold, grabbed her and pulled off her top. He was biting her on both breasts and making loud slurping sounds. He was also able to get her bottoms down and got his hand on her buttocks, enabling him to do some humping motions. Most of the audience was roaring and yelling.

Someone finally went up on stage to stop Bradley. Gloria was screaming wildly. But Bradley's cohorts were not to be outdone. They jumped to his rescue. Pretty soon the whole stage was in a riot, with Gloria in the middle.

Norm suggested it was time to leave.

In the jeep and heading for home, Norm said, "Remind me never to ask you and your friend Bradley to a party. He's not just wild; he's crazy."

\*

After a quick breakfast the next morning, they met Rameirez and the men at the supply room. Rameirez informed Whitehead that three of the men went with Jumpers for the material while the remaining three would go with him to get the site ready.

Norm told Whitehead that there were two deuce and a half trucks as well as the jeep waiting for them at the motor pool. With the small group in tow, they ran into Custard while walking to get the vehicles.

"Well, I hope you three are working on Nha Trang LD?" Custard asked looking at Whitehead.

"Yes sir." Whitehead filled him in on the details, laying out all the plans and schedules in a few minutes.

Then Custard spoke, "OK, it sounds like things are progressing." Looking at Range and Rameirez, he said, "Let me see Lieutenant Whitehead alone for a minute."

Range saluted, and said to Whitehead that they would wait for him in the jeep.

Once alone, Custard said to Whitehead, "What do you and Duel have going? You're assigned to this company out of the blue, then I see the two of you talking in the parking lot."

It caught Whitehead totally off guard. He had completely forgotten his encounter with Duel yesterday.

"Sir, he stopped me and asked me how Nha Trang LD was going. The conversation lasted only a minute or two."

Custard leaned into Whitehead's face and whispered, "If I learn of any secret reports going to Group about our work, you're done." With that, he walked off.

\*

Whitehead drove slow so he wouldn't lose the truck, but mostly so he could get used to the jeep. It literally drove like one of the trucks following him. The steering was stiff and very difficult, but the motor sounded good and it held the road nicely. Even better, the gears shifted very easily. He was feeling comfortable already.

Too soon he was at the site. He parked so he could leave easily, then showed Rameirez the site, walking around with him while the others unloaded the few tools they brought with them.

Whitehead left the men there. He told Rameirez he wanted the sergeant to use the morning to make forms and then pour cement this afternoon if he could.

Whitehead planned to spend the next hour getting use to his jeep then stay at Goldfinch with the switchboard that afternoon going through the manuals.

Pulling out and grinding some gears in the process, he decided to drive out to the fringe of Nha Trang and see how the jeep performed. He turned onto Farm Road, a sandy road that ran along the rear of Long Van Air Base. To the right were farm and rice fields which apparently gave the road its name.

The day went as planned. At dinner, Whitehead told Norm that he was going to stop at Nha Trang LD and check on its progress. Norm begged off wanting to write a letter to his wife.

Arriving there, Whitehead found the six GIs but no Rameirez. The soldier left in charge by Rameirez reported that the cement would be laid first thing tomorrow. Whitehead ordered the men to the barracks, wished them all good night, then got back into the jeep.

Pulling out onto the airfield road, he thought of what he would say to Rameirez the next morning. It was a full ten minutes before he noticed an ARVN army truck in his rear view mirror.

He made several turns, all of which the truck made. He was not only sure now, he was positive.

Once he hit Beach Road, he sped up to almost 45 mph. So did the truck. The truck followed as Whitehead hooked a sharp left.

The truck was staying closer now, much closer.

He looked ahead and was trying to figure out his next turn, when his head snapped to the rear. Another jolt as the truck began playing 'tag' with the jeep.

The truck sped up positioning itself for another hit on the jeep. The roar of its motor was enough to scare anyone. It was doing an excellent job on Whitehead.

Desperate, Whitehead slammed on the brakes turning the steering wheel sharply to the right. Skidding badly, the jeep kicked up a lot of dust and debris.

The truck barreled past him; the driver struggling with the wheel, trying to match Whitehead's turn.

Swerving as its driver lost control, the truck hit a pole dead center.

Getting out, Whitehead walked around the front of the truck. He found the driver on the hood where he had come through the windshield. Blood had already dripped down the sides.

Checking for signs of life, Whitehead lifted the head of the dead driver. It was Truc.

## CHAPTER 14

Life is full of symbols. In 'Nam, one of the most important for support troops was a pair of jungle fatigues. They had pockets, dried quickly, and were loose fitting. Support troops needed them so they looked as if they were part of the war.

At breakfast on the morning of the Nha Trang LD installation, Whitehead sat across from Norm. Last night's excitement had died down a little. His story about finding the truck on the side of the road satisfied the MPs so he felt a little more relaxed. He sat watching Norm eat his breakfast with a gleam in his eye.

"Alright, what's up?" Whitehead asked.

Norm stifled a laugh, then said, "You know, most guys think that supply officer is a shit job. And they're right. It sucks!" Norm started to smile. Not just any smile, but the largest smile Whitehead had ever seen. "But I acquired something that'll blow the socks off everyone. I'll have everyone kissing my ass for weeks."

"Norm, have you had this desire for everyone to kiss your ass long? I think you can get out of the army if this is a sexual hang-up with the ass kissing."

"OK, Dave, be funny. Come on, finish your coffee and follow me."

Whitehead did as he was told and followed Norm. Near the supply tent, Norm looked around like a private detective in a cheap movie. Whitehead did the same.

Norm went inside. The supply officer led Whitehead to the back of the tent, unlocked a connex, reached in and pulled out a set of jungle fatigues.

Looking at the fatigues, Whitehead asked, "Jungle fatigues? How many?"

Norm nodded his head saying, "Two hundred and fifty pairs."

"Are they hot?"

"Hell, no, but supply picks who they give them to. We've been on a list because of the outlying sites of Nimh Hoa and Duc My. They're perfectly legal." Norm paused then asked, "Dave, what do we do with them?"

"What? You're the supply officer. Do what you want."

"Dave, I'm torn between trading for a big goody or giving them to the troops."

"Shit, Norm, then give'em to the troops." Whitehead looked at the fatigues again. "Norm, you ought to set up a system of who gets what first. Give all the key people fatigues, but let the troops feel that they got their first. Got enough to give each GI two pairs?"

"Yeah, no problem. I can even get more."

"Norm, what did you do for that guy over there in supply? I hope you didn't compromise yourself sexually."

"Ha! I did it all with C-rations."

Whitehead walked out front as Norm put the fatigues back into the connex and locked it again. He waited until Norm came out to join him to ask, "How about jungle boots?" "Jesus Christ, Dave, I just got all those fatigues. You mean everyone I give the fatigues to will want jungle boots too?"

"Gee, Norm, I was only asking." Whitehead began to smile. Picking up his cap, Whitehead walked out of the supply tent, saying, "Norm, I'll call you later. Tonight is the big night. Nha Trang LD is being set up."

Waving good-by, Whitehead went to his jeep. Near Group headquarters, he saw Phuc leaving the tent. He couldn't avoid him. In fact, Phuc, with his head down, almost walked into Whitehead.

"Oh, excuse me!" Then Phuc realized it was Whitehead he bumped into.

"Good morning, Mr. Phuc. Have you heard anything about Lan yet?"

Phuc said nothing. There was hate in his eyes.

Without saying a word, he passed Whitehead and walked away.

Driving to Goldfinch, Whitehead looked behind almost as much as he watched the road ahead. But there was no sight of anything or anyone.

*

At Goldfinch, Whitehead found Rameirez waiting for him. They reviewed the whole plan for getting the switchboard to its new site and in position. It would begin after 1700 hours.

They had to borrow a tractor to pull the trailer. A transportation unit would let Van Rankin use one if it was used after regular work hours. A wrecker was also borrowed under the same conditions.

At 1400 hours, all the parties would leave Goldfinch. Van Rankin was to pick up the trailer with another driver for the wrecker. Whitehead would leave with Rameirez and the men for the new switchboard's site.

Midway through the morning, a visitor came looking for Whitehead. It was Major Cohn.

"Well, lieutenant, we meet again," said Cohn. "We seem to be destined to have these regular conversations."

"Good morning, Major. Something new about the incident at the Buddha?"

"No, but I was reading the incident blotter for last night and, lo and behold, I find your name associated with another death. Not a pretty death either. That was you, wasn't it?"

"You mean the Vietnamese in the truck last night."

"Yes, lieutenant, that's exactly what I mean. You seem to have an affinity to be in the wrong place at the wrong time."

"Sir, I was driving by and found this guy on the hood of the truck. What should I have done? Keep driving?"

"Very commendable,Whitehead. Very commendable. Did you know the Vietnamese national that was killed?"

Looking Cohn straight in the eye, Whitehead told the major that he didn't.

Major Cohn paused, then looking at Whitehead asked, "Do you know a national named Phuc?"

"He's the interpreter at Group, isn't he? I just met him. Why?"

"Truc was Mr. Phuc's lover." Cohn paused then said, "I asked him why Truc was driving a truck in that area. Do you know what he said?"

Whitehead shrugged his shoulders.

"He said to ask you. Then he walked away."

Both Cohn and Whitehead stood in silence. Cohn broke the peace, claiming to have an appointment.

"I'll be checking with you again. Can I give you some advice?" Without waiting for Whitehead's answer, he said, "Watch out for Mr. Phuc."

*

Whitehead spent the day dealing with the installation of Nha Trang LD. He was back and forth between the new site and Goldfinch several times. All things seemed to be going well.

With the help of a wrecker, Van Rankin put the trailers in place that evening. By nightfall, most of the job was complete. The headlights of the trucks were turned on to help in adjusting the struts and blocking the wheels at the base of the antennas.

As the men finished, Whitehead looked around the site. Something in the distance caught his eye. There was a person standing in the glow of the headlights. Over the many yards which separated them, Whitehead knew who it was. He could feel the hatred. Phuc.

The Vietnamese boy appeared only for an instant as the trucks began to move. Phuc disappeared into the darkness as quickly as he came.

Whitehead stood motionless for a few seconds before heading to the jeep. Looking around one last time, he made sure everything was squared away. The men were waiting only for Whitehead.

He got to his jeep and started it. Nothing exploded.

The trucks followed him most of the way, blowing their horns as they left him near the villa. Minutes later, Whitehead was in the villa and his bed trying not to wake Norm.

*

The next morning, he told Norm how well all the night's activities went. He even mentioned Phuc. Norm listened but said little. Jungle fatigues again, thought Whitehead.

Together they walked to the supply tent and found Jumpers with a message that Captain Custard wanted both of them in his office at 0900 hours.

On the way to Custard's office, Norm said, "What do you think this is all about?"

"Simple. He probably heard you had jungle fatigues."

Whitehead said nothing as they continued walking to the orderly room. Entering the building, the two men walked up to Custard's door, knocked and walked in.

Custard was reading Stars and Stripes at his desk. He saw Norm and Whitehead and told them to sit by the windows.

"Gentlemen, the 459th gets here in four days. I hope you are ready. Dancer will meet them in Cam Ranh Bay and lead the convoy to the edge of Nha Trang. I'll meet them there and lead them the rest of the way."

Looking at Norm, Custard said, "Range, I was out to the new camp. You need to do a lot more work out there."

"Yes, sir, I'll be out there all day for the next three days."

"Good!" Then he looked toward Whitehead. "What about Nha Trang LD?"

"Well, it looks like we may be operational in a few days. Rameirez isn't really a switchboard NCO, but he's got a few GIs who seem to know how to wire up the board. I'll be working with them for the next few days."

"OK," said Custard. "Anything else?"

"Yes sir!" It was Norm. "Sir, I just acquired 250 pairs of jungle fatigues."

Whitehead couldn't believe his ears. Norm was just too nervous to deal with the fatigues.

"Great, Range. Excellent." Custard seemed to be dazed at the news. "I'll let you know tomorrow what to do with them. Good morning, gentlemen. Get to work."

Outside, the two lieutenants said nothing until they got to the supply tent.

"Dave, last night I brought some fatigues back to the villa. I've actually got 275 pairs. Let the old man figure out what to do with the rest. I don't want the responsibility."

"OK, Norm, you know what you're doing." With that Whitehead left for Nha Trang LD and to see if Rameirez had started the wiring job.

On the way to the site, Whitehead was expecting to search for Rameirez. But when Whitehead arrived, Rameirez found him. He walked directly over to Whitehead and said, "Sir, I need to see my whore in town. I think she's screwing someone else."

"Sergeant Rameirez," Whitehead responded in a low voice to contain his anger. After taking a deep breath, he said, "I know you're concerned, but this little project is pretty important to the old man. If he knew I let you go whoring, he'd have my balls.   I'm afraid you'll just have to wait until noon."

Rameirez was pissed, kicking the dirt then stamping away to check the cable lines.

Inside, the two specialists from Group were working on the frame which matched the wires coming from the antenna to the switchboard.   Everything seemed to be going okay at Nha Trang LD so Whitehead decided to drive over and check the wire team doing the satellite job with the Air Force.

Riding out to Farm Road, he found Sergeant Willis and the team in a ditch.   Had he been driving by, he would have thought they were hard at work.   But he stopped and walked over to the ditch to find the four of them drinking beer and telling jokes.

Willis looked up and said, "Oh, shit.   I didn't see you come up, lieutenant."   Not knowing what to say, he asked Whitehead if he wanted a beer.

"No, Sergeant Willis, I don't want a beer.   Get your men out of here and find something to do that is less obvious than drinking beer on a main road!"

"But, sir, we're all done!"

"I know that.   Just look busy here, or hide out somewhere else.   Colonel Duel could have stopped and court-martialed your asses along with mine.   Now, if you'll excuse the language, get the fuck out of here."

He heard a "yes sir" as he got in his jeep and pulled away.  He arrived back at Nha Trang LD to find more problems.   Rameirez had left, telling the switchboard people that he had business in town.   They were also having problems with the wiring.   Whitehead got back in the jeep, told the men to do the best they could, and drove away.

In the jeep, he realized that he didn't know where Rameirez or his whore could be.   Goldfinch seemed the best place to start.

He got there in 15 minutes and found Franklin talking with Boggs and Southland. Pulling up, he walked over to the threesome. They all saluted and said "good morning."

"Maybe for you. Have any of you seen Rameirez?"

One way or the other they said they hadn't seen him.

Putting a hand on his forehead, Whitehead said, "I know where he is. What I don't know is how to get there. Where does he live with his whore?"

"Down town on Duc Lap Street," said Boggs.

"Thanks!" He turned and headed for his jeep.

Boggs called out, "The lieutenant isn't thinking of going there himself and getting the man?"

Whitehead turned and said, "Yes, the lieutenant is thinking of doing the very same."

"Be careful," warned Southland. "Rameirez is a tough character when he's pissed off."

Whitehead walked back to the group. Franklin, who had remained quiet, then said, "Maybe a few of us ought to go with you."

"Thank you, Sergeant Franklin. Perhaps Sergeants Boggs and Southland agree."

Boggs now looked pissed and said to Franklin, "When are you going to learn to keep your mouth shut?"

Boggs and Southland looked at each other. Finally Boggs spoke. "Southland and me will go with you. Franklin, you stay here. You might get hurt." Turning to Whitehead, he said, "Lieutenant, we'll take you to Rameirez, but it's our show. You listen to us and be very careful."

In 20 minutes, they were locking up the jeep about a block away from where Norm and Whitehead had their three-quarter blown away. Boggs led Southland and Whitehead to a building where a faded sign proclaimed "TRUNG."

Boggs said, "Here we are."

He led the way up a flight of stairs. In a long hall,

an old Vietnamese sat on a stool.    Boggs looked at him and asked for Sergeant Rameirez.    The old man responded, "Room 5."

Leaving the old man, the three walked quietly to the door with a "5" on it. Whispering, Southland asked, "How do we get in there?"

"Kick it down," said Boggs.    "The lieutenant has the authority."

"I do?" inquired Whitehead.

"You're his platoon leader," countered Boggs.

"Okay, if you say so.    Let's get on with it."

With Whitehead and Southland on each side of the door, Boggs stood in the middle and raised his leg.    When Whitehead nodded, he kicked away.

The door was rotten and broke away like balsa wood. With the door gone, Whitehead and Southland moved inside.

Rameirez and a Vietnamese girl were on the bed, naked.    The girl's head was buried in Rameirez' crotch.

The noise of the door being kicked in awoke Rameirez from a marihuana high.    Kicking the whore off the bed, he reached for the table nearby.

Boggs pushed Whitehead and Southland as Rameirez picked up the revolver from the table.    Boggs then tried to kick the revolver out of Rameirez' hand.    The large foot missed the hand, but did get Rameirez' jaw.

The pistol went off.    Rameirez' teeth hit the floor as the bullet went through the ceiling and possibly a whore upstairs, maybe a customer.

Meanwhile, Whitehead had nearly made it under the bed.    Southland was on the floor beside him.    Boggs stood in the middle of the room with nowhere to go.

The whore was quick.    Picking up Rameirez' gun, she fired off three quick rounds.    The wall never stood a chance.    She would have emptied the pistol, but it jammed.

Quickly, Boggs moved toward the whore.    Taking the jammed gun from the girl, he then punched her squarely in the nose.    Blood gushed out of the girl's nose as she ran around the room, then down the hall, shouting Vietnamese and American obscenities.

Looking down at Whitehead and Southland, he said, "You two brave boys can get up now.    Your willingness to help in time of need was greatly appreciated."

Pointing to Rameirez, Boggs said, "Would each of you kindly take an arm?    I think we should probably take him with us.    I'll gather his clothes.    Ain't the army grand?"

## CHAPTER 15

Using Whitehead's jeep, Franklin took Rameirez to the 8th Field Hospital when the group got back to Goldfinch. The report would read Rameirez fell off one of the rigs.

Boggs and Southland, both covered in blood from Rameirez' whore, went to their barracks to change their clothes. Whitehead, alone, walked over to the Agent Orange tanks to wait for Franklin to bring his jeep back from the 8th. The airfield was busy with the Vietnamese Air Force planes taking off to fly some missions in some area of the country.

Whitehead wasn't alone long. A jeep pulled off the main road and entered Goldfinch. Instead of stopping at the operations hut, it came right out to where Whitehead was sitting. By the time Whitehead realized who it was, Major Cohn had pulled up alongside the tanks.

"Don't get up, Whitehead. I'm only here for what is fast becoming a regular daily visit." Getting out of the jeep, he asked, "Were you just in Nha Trang City?"

Standing up, Whitehead was now in a more respectful position. "Yes, sir, Sergeants Boggs and Southland joined me in getting some ice cream at the Red Cross."

"Just by chance, you and your ice cream crew weren't involved in a disturbance at a place called `TRUNG', were you?"

"No, sir. We saw some scuffling, but we certainly weren't involved in it."

"No, of course not. Not Lieutenant Whitehead. With finding dead Vietnamese on the hood of trucks, giving your name to men who then turn up dead, and getting ice cream, do you have any time to do your actual work?"

"Yes sir, I'm installing a long distance switchboard near Long Van Air Base."

"Thank you for your time. Again. Now, you'll

have to excuse me, lieutenant, I have to investigate a shooting and an assault." Looking down and then out to the airfield, he continued, "I'm sure if you knew anything about it, you would have reported it. You may go back to watching airplanes."

With those words, he got back in his jeep, made a u-turn and sped out of Goldfinch.

Passing Cohn on his way out was another jeep coming into Goldfinch. Knowing Norm would be out in the new camp area, he discounted the supply officer's vehicle. Whitehead realized that it was his jeep with Franklin at the wheel.

Stopping next to Whitehead, Franklin got out and announced Rameirez would stay overnight and be released for duty tomorrow morning.

Whitehead got in the driver's seat and, after dropping off Franklin at the operations hut, drove over to Nha Trang LD to spend the afternoon supervising the specialists.

At 1700 hours, Whitehead drove to the supply tent to meet Norm for dinner. He stopped by the orderly room and found a message for him to call Cook as soon as possible.

With the first sergeant gone for the day, he sat at Blutik's desk and made the call. Cook answered.

"Meet me at Chez Francois for dinner."

"Why?"

"We need to talk."

"Don't we always. Alright, where is this Francois?"

"It's in Cau Da, just south of Nha Trang on Beach Road. Francois' is an excellent chef, a real holdover from the French colonial days. It's nothing fancy, but the food is great."

Whitehead sighed, then asked, "When?"

"An hour." As usual, Cook hung up without another word.

Whitehead sat at the desk holding the open phone line.

"Shit," Whitehead said aloud to himself. He got up and walked to the supply tent to find Norm.

According to Jumpers, Norm was tied up at the new camp site. Whitehead left a message for him with Jumpers about his meeting with Cook that night. He hoped he would be back so that he could tell Norm about the food. Then, left to gas up his jeep for the trip to Cau Da.

*

With a full tank of gas and head full of thoughts, Whitehead drove along Beach Road. He passed a lot of shacks that were similar to the ones on the way to Nimh Hoa.

In about 20 minutes, he entered a small village with stucco structures lining the road much like an old western town in the states. He saw one store front with a small sign that said "Francois."

Pulling up in front, he looked to the back of the building and saw the South China Sea. There was a small platform running out about 25 yards into the water. Obviously, the fishing boats docked there bringing their daily catch to the opening between Francois' and the next building so that the fishermen could sell it on the street. Francois probably got all his food right here.

Whitehead had about a half hour wait for Cook. In about an hour, it would be dark. Sitting around wasn't something he liked doing lately, so he decided to explore the waterfront which ran no longer than five to six hundred feet.

Locking the jeep, he walked slowly to the edge. The cement walkway gave way to sand. Looking back to Francois, it seemed desolate, so he walked on. Finding an old fishing boat overturned, he sat down on it and looked out over the water.

"Enjoying yourself, Lieutenant Whitehead?" The words were singsong and spoken by a Vietnamese.

Without even thinking, Whitehead knew they were from Phuc's mouth.

"Hello, Mr. Phuc." Getting up, Whitehead didn't know what to say. "Nice night, isn't it?" Looking down at Phuc's hand, Whitehead saw the pistol. The town seemed to disappear in the waning light.

Standing in front of the American, Phuc brought the pistol to bear on Whitehead.

"You made it very easy for me, Lieutenant. I thought you would stay near large numbers of people. But you're here. Alone. In the dark. You even walked to my boat here. The gods must be with me."

Phuc's face hardened. His eyes narrowed as he spoke. "You killed Truc."

"I had no idea he was the one driving that truck. He was trailing me. I turned a corner to get away from him. He tried to follow, but the truck couldn't handle the turn." Whitehead thought the pun would be funny someday, but not at this moment. "When I got to the cab of the truck he was already dead."

Phuc shook his head. "No, you killed him. Because of you, he is dead."

"You told him to follow me, didn't you? Why? Was it Cook?"

"Enough talk." Phuc looked down at the boat. "Turn the boat over and push it into the water."

Righting the old boat, Whitehead then pushed it toward the water. Phuc pointed the gun at him, watching him carefully.

"Lieutenant Whitehead, get in the boat, please." Waving the gun, Phuc followed Whitehead into the large rowboat. Sitting in the bow of the boat, he ordered the lieutenant to row out to sea.

The water was relatively calm which made the rowing less of a chore. Darkness made it difficult for Whitehead to figure out where they were going. Phuc seemed to have no trouble.

Whitehead rowed for about twenty minutes before Phuc ordered him to stop. Turning around, Whitehead saw a larger boat. By the smell and the sea birds flying around it, Whitehead figured it was a fishing vessel of some sort. No one appeared on deck to help tether the approaching row boat. They were all alone.

"Guess no one's home, Phuc. Maybe we better go back to shore and try another day."

"Only I will see shore again. Put the oars down and climb up to the fishing boat." Waiving the gun as he spoke, Phuc warned, "Do as you are told or you will die here and now."

Once on board, Whitehead thought to attack Phuc as he climbed onto the boat. The Vietnamese was so quick that it was too late to do anything. Lifting himself aboard, Phuc was standing in front of Whitehead before the thought was finished.

Phuc spoke, "Walk ahead and turn to your right."

As they approached the cabin door, Phuc took a flashlight from his rear pocket, shooting the beam down the stairs. He motioned for Whitehead to follow the beam.

Once downstairs, Phuc lit several lanterns, always careful to keep Whitehead in full sight.

"Sit down, lieutenant, but I am afraid you do not have the time to get comfortable."

Phuc then lit a cigarette, performing the task confidently and without any hurry.

"Phuc, listen to me. I don't know what you think I did, but I don't want to die. I'm prepared to do anything to live, including begging for my life."

"I haven't heard a word about jade, lieutenant."

"You really are a friend of Cook's. Just say the word and the jade's yours."

"If you had said that before, Truc would be alive." The gun hand began to waiver a little. Phuc approached

Whitehead.    Looking into the lieutenant's face, Phuc said, "You stupid fool.    You should have brought the jade to the Buddha.    It would have been over."

The boy stood up, still staring at him.    "Now Truc is dead, as you will be."

Phuc cocked the pistol and pointed at the lieutenant's head.    Beads of perspiration were on both men's foreheads. The two men stared eye to eye for what seemed like an eternity to Whitehead.    The world around them seemed to freeze as no sound could be heard except for their breathing and Phuc's finger tightening on the trigger.

The silence seemed to amplify the noise on the deck overhead.    Phuc stepped back, looking up at the ceiling. Whitehead stood up and turned to the door.    Then, all went black.

*

Slowly, consciousness returned.    His head hurt, hurt a lot.    All he could smell was the stench of fish oil.    Sitting on the floor, he opened his eyes.

"Oh shit, what a way to wake up."

Standing over him was Cook.

"Have a nice sleep?    You ought to be more careful in picking your company.    I ask you to dinner, but when you get there you take off with someone else.    Phuc is a nasty person, or at least he was."    Cook began to smile.

"Should I ask where he is now?" said Whitehead.

"Oh, the bottom of the harbor.    First, he bounced a pistol off your head, then came on deck.    I was waiting for him.    I shot him, tied a chain around his body and then pushed him overboard."

"You look pretty broken up over Phuc's passing."

"Phuc's greed did him in.    It's that simple.    If he didn't want the jade, he wouldn't have lost his lover, Truc. Isn't love terribly destructive?    When you put love and greed together, death can't be far away."

"You're getting philosophical in your old age, Cook. You ought to write a book and make your views widely known."

Ignoring the comment, Cook went on. "Even you, Whitehead. You've got some greed in you."

"What?" Whitehead looked at Cook, confused by the statement.

"The jade. I don't see you going to the authorities with the jade."

"At the beginning I thought you were the authorities. Are you?"

"Sometimes. I do what I my job requires. There's a very thin line between good and bad in this place." Helping Whitehead to his feet, Cook said, "Come on, get up and help me row back to shore."

Once on deck, Cook led Whitehead to the side of the ship. In the water was a second row boat. Apparently Cook had rowed out in pursuit of them.

Climbing into the boat, Whitehead asked, "How did you know where to find me?"

"I was in Francois when you pulled up. Then I watched Phuc follow you walking toward the beach. After I finished my drink, I walked over there, saw the two of you, and listened to your discussion."

"I'm glad you hadn't started dinner before you decided to tag along."

"Shut up and keep rowing or we'll be out here all night."

"Well, Cook, you could spell me a while."

Cook ignored Whitehead's last suggestion. They remained quiet for the rest of the boat ride. It was nearly midnight, when they reached shore.

Standing on the dock in front of Francois, Cook offered Whitehead a drink at the Frenchman's bar. Declining, Whitehead turned and headed for his jeep.

Halfway there, he stopped and walked back to Cook.

"When and where do you want your jade?"

"Hold onto it for a little while longer. I'll let you know soon."

Cook turned and went into Francois'. Whitehead got in his jeep and realized that he had a half hour drive back to Nha Trang. He started thinking about getting a gun. Norm had connexes full of them. He would feel more comfortable with one after tonight.

For the next half hour, Whitehead drove his jeep hard, stopping for nothing and looking straight ahead. The thought of breaking down out here without a weapon was a very unpleasant one this late at night. If he met "Charley" on the road, he'd never see his jungle fatigues. Great time for jokes, he said to himself.

The ride seemed hours long. By the time he got to the villa's gate, he was totally exhausted and had almost forgotten the headache Phuc gave him.

Inside the villa, he found Norm asleep. Whitehead tried not to wake him as he made his way to the bed. Norm never moved a muscle.

On Whitehead's bed were two sets of jungle fatigues. He picked them up, held them to his chest and laid down on the bed. Sleep came quickly to Whitehead that night.

## CHAPTER 16

The monsoons made their first appearance in early October. Rains suddenly burst on the scene, only to be followed by the heat of a bright sun. Frequently, the sun disappeared from the sky. The rain would fall continuously only to have the sun once again beat down upon the men.

For Nha Trang, the monsoons brought rough waters. Waves were two to four feet higher than normal. The calm South China Sea which had caressed the beautiful beach turned angry as GIs abandoned the beach for inside fun and games.

The big winner was the Club Nautique, a French-operated hotel and restaurant on Beach Road. Late afternoons and evenings were loud and rough affairs for those who could afford the prices. Most frequently, those who could afford it were civilian contract employees. Even in Vietnam, a soldier's pay didn't go far in night clubs.

For most GIs, entertainment came with evenings in the beer halls run by the individual units. Drinking was followed by passing out in the barracks, perhaps with a fight on the way.

Officers tended for more refined pleasure, usually a whore house. For Whitehead, the Nha Trang whorehouses still seemed less than inviting.

After the events at Trung's and then the adventure in Nha Trang harbor, Whitehead was more interested in a quiet evening. So when Norm suggested dinner and a movie at the Special Forces compound, Whitehead quickly agreed.

Pulling into the Special Forces parking lot, the two men saw that a lot of people had the same idea. In the officers club, they ate fast and got into the movie theatre before the popcorn was made. Once in their seats, Whitehead volunteered to get both of them popcorn from the lobby before the movie started. He got up from his seat and walked out the back of the theatre.

In the lobby, GIs of all ranks and branches were lined up for popcorn. When it came to popcorn, rank had no privilege.

Getting two boxes, Whitehead returned to his seat next to Norm. When the screen credits came on, Whitehead began booing.

"What's the matter, Dave?"

"I saw this movie on the plane from New York to San Francisco."

"And I don't like Gregory Peck too much. Let's go to the O club and get a drink."

Back at the officers' club, a five-girl band from Korea was playing American songs while the club patrons enjoyed a happy hour. Buying two drinks each, they found a table and settled in to enjoy the music.

For the next hour, assisted by two more drinks each, the two lieutenants watched the band. While the band played, no one seemed to care about the war or not being home. Only when the girls sang, "I left my heart in San Francisco" did the crowd seem sad or upset. Downing their drinks, Norm returned to the bar to get refills. He came back a little wobbly with another round.

Sitting down and nearly missing the chair, he leaned over the table and said, "Dave, your friend Cook is at the bar and he wants to talk to you."

"Fuck!"

"You going over?"

"Hell, no. Let him stand there for all I care. He seems to find me when he wants to. I don't need to go to him."

Finishing their drinks, they stood up and started to leave. Cook walked over to them as both men appeared lost while they looked for the exit.

"Follow me fellows and I'll show you where you left your jeep." Outside, the rain had stopped. Cook brought them to Norm's jeep and asked if they wanted a ride back to their villa.

"No, we're alright," said Whitehead, as he slipped getting into the jeep.

Coming around to Whitehead in the passenger's seat, Cook asked, "Tomorrow, why don't you two join me for a little get-together with some of my friends?"

"Can't do," said Norm, "but Dave is free."

"Good, Dave, I'll pick you up at noon.    Dress casual, but nicely.    Good night."    He turned and walk off into the night.

"Why did you tell him I'd go?" asked Whitehead.

"I don't know.    You look like you need a party. Sorry."    The apology went unheard as Whitehead passed out.

Norm put the jeep in gear and drove home with Whitehead snoring in cadence.

*

The snoring continued uninterrupted until a little before 0900 hours on Sunday morning.    Whitehead's body was ruined from the drinking of the night before.    He couldn't even begin to identify the fellow officer who was telling him that he had a telephone call.

Staggering to the phone, he took the receiver and muttered his name.    From the receiver came Cook's voice.

"Dave, are you awake?    How's your head?    Did you forget my invitation?"

It was Whitehead's turn.    "No, bad, and no.    Did I take care of all your questions?"

"Yeah, I'll be there at noontime."    Again he hung up without an answer.

By noon he was just about all together.    He walked out on the porch and looked at his beige slacks and blue button down broadcloth short sleeve shirt.    On his feet were brown oxfords.    He didn't look down at them in fear he would puke.

Looking for his jeep, his stomach took a turn for the worse. His jeep was gone. A jeep was there but this one had a roof. As he turned to re-enter the villa to phone the MPs, he noticed the number on the front bumper. The jeep was his. Someone had added a roof overnight.

On the seat was a note. It read: "We hope it's the right color."

Cook's land rover pulled up as Whitehead read the note. A short burst of the horn told him that Cook did not want to wait. Looking again at the jeep, Whitehead put the note in his pocket and got in the rover.

Cook drove down Beach Road toward the town of Cau Da again. About five minutes out of Nha Trang, he made a left turn onto a private drive. The jeep approached a large French provincial mansion. Immaculately kept, the structure showed no sign of being anywhere near a war. It was also well protected.

Cook was waved in by several Vietnamese police. Each one held an automatic rifle pointed at the oncoming vehicle as it passed by the guard post. This didn't seem to affect Cook as he began lecturing on the history of the mansion.

"This place used to belong to Madame Nhu. She summered here for several years. Then Premier Ky used it for meetings. Now it belongs to a friend of mine. You'll meet him inside.

"By the way, if anyone asks my name here is Mr. Ralph."

"And I'm ...?"

"David Whitehead. Why?" Cook stopped the land over and looked over to Whitehead and said, "Relax. And enjoy yourself."

Getting out of the vehicle, they walked together to the entrance. The double doors were made of glass and wrought iron. An aide in formal dress opened the doors and bowed inviting the two men inside.

"I feel underdressed." said Whitehead.

"Relax.   There is a war going on, you know."

"Not here."

*

Once inside, a brocaded hall led into a room as large as a football field.   In the far corner, a three-piece string ensemble filled the high-ceiling room with the sounds of Bach and Vivaldi.   Tables of food and drink lined the walls.   To the right, Whitehead saw shrimp and oysters. An elegant server filled with a champagne punch sat on the next table.

Most of the party-goers were men.   A few women dressed in traditional Vietnamese clothing were quietly accompanying their spouses.   At least two of the women wore Western clothes; one seemed to have round eyes. Whitehead had read in an old Time magazine that it was popular now for oriental women to have operations on their eyes to make them look more western.

Cook leaned over and said, "I'm going to visit with some friends.   I'll be back in a little while.   Enjoy yourself."   As he walked away, he warned, "Stay away from the women.   Vietnamese husbands hate to have their wives approached by westerners."

Whitehead nodded.   He had already decided to eat and drink.   As Cook wandered into the crowd, Whitehead headed for the food.

At the shrimp table, Whitehead selected several large shrimp. Looking for a place to sit, he headed toward a set of French doors which opened onto a veranda.   A floral garden consumed most of the acreage beyond.   The sun seemed to make the garden more radiant than it really was.

He put the plate of shrimp on the balustrade and ducked back in for champagne.   When he returned, another man was standing on the veranda.    Looking at the garden with his back to Whitehead was the well built, slightly gray-haired figure of Major Cohn.

"Christ, they let all kinds in here," said Whitehead.

"What the fuck are you doing here?"    Cohn was pissed and showed it.

"Take it easy, Major Cohn, you're among friends."

"I'm not Major Cohn."

"Oh?"    A smile began to appear on Whitehead's face.    "And just who are you now?"

"I'm Mr. Robert Conner, a civilian contractor."

"Well, hello, Mr. Conner.    I'm Bill Westmoreland, general of the army.    Here, have some shrimp.    They're delicious."    Whitehead offered Cohn the plate.

"Very funny.    I'll see you at your signal site tomorrow afternoon at 1500 hours.    Remember, you don't know me."    With that he drifted away and started to mingle.

For the next hour, Whitehead watched the party-goers from the veranda while eating the plate of shrimp. Every few minutes he would see Cook, engrossed in conversation, pass by the double doors.    Each time he walked by, Cook was speaking with a different person. "Mr. Ralph" is a busy man, thought Whitehead.

Whitehead had just finished his plate of shrimp and glass of champagne when Cook appeared on the veranda. Accompanying him was a heavy set Vietnamese man well into his sixties.

"Dave, I want you to meet Nguyen Van Phan, a plantation owner in nearby Buon Ma Thuot."

"Welcome, Lieutenant Whitehead," Van Phan said as he shook the lieutenant's hand.    "I hope you are enjoying the day."

"Yes, I am, thank you.    The shrimp's delicious.    I didn't think parties like this went on in this country.    At least, not now anyway."

"We try to have these get togethers at least once a

month.   Now, if you will excuse me, I must go back inside and meet some of my other guests.   I'm sure my friends and I will see you again.   Have a good day."

With that Cook and Van Phan went back inside. For Whitehead it was more shrimp and champagne.

It was then Whitehead realized that Van Phan knew he was a lieutenant.   "Mr. Ralph" is indeed a very busy man, he said to himself.

By mid afternoon, Cook rejoined Whitehead outside and announced, "Dave, it's time to go."

Looking back into the party once more, Whitehead scanned the room for Cohn.   Apparently the major had already left.   Whitehead couldn't find him among the guests.

In the land rover, Cook asked, "Enjoy yourself?"

"Oh yes.   Lovely time.   And you?"

"Too busy working.   Most of those people impact on the work I do."

"And what work would that be Lieutenant Cook. Or are you still Mr. Ralph?"

"Some other time, smartass."

Turning right and heading toward Nha Trang, the land rover approached a red pickup truck.   At the wheel was a familiar face. Bradley.

Both Bradley and Cook recognized each other, blowing their horns and waving.

"I see you know Bradley," said Whitehead.

"You know Ed, too?"

"I only know him from his performance at the officers' club.   He's a terrific dancer."

"I heard about that," said Cook smiling.   "As a matter of fact I posted bond for him.   He's a regular 'good ole boy.'"

Cook was silent all the way to Whitehead's villa. Once there, Cook simply waved and said, "I'll be in touch."

Whitehead watched him pull away as a steady rain

began to fall.    I'm sure you will, he said to himself as he walked inside.

## CHAPTER 17

The next morning, Whitehead recounted the events of the day for Norm over breakfast. The two hadn't spoken with one another since the night Cook invited Whitehead to the party. Yesterday, Norm went to a nurses' party and didn't get in until after midnight. Whitehead had been sleeping when Range came home.

Whitehead talked about the mansion, the orchestra, the shrimp, as well as Cook and Cohn. Norm seemed impressed at the opportunity to rub elbows with the rich. As for Cook and Cohn, he said he rubbed elbows with those two too much.

They left the Officers' Club and headed over to the company area. Near the parking area, Dancer intercepted them.

"Whitehead, get your jeep out of the Group area. Someone stole Colonel Duel's jeep top and I think it's now on your jeep."

"Oh, shit!" Whitehead wasted no time. He was in the jeep and on his way to Goldfinch. Pulling in, he yelled for Franklin. The young sergeant came out of the hut.

"Where did you get the jeep top?" asked Whitehead.

Franklin hesitated then said, "I can't tell sir."

"Alright. Franklin, did you know that someone stole the top off of Colonel Duel's jeep?" Whitehead paused for a reaction. "Did you know that Colonel Duel's top is now on my jeep?"

"Oh shit, that top was supposed to have come from Cam Ranh Bay. We paid ten cases of beer for it. The guys here took up a collection."

"The guys? Bought the top? For me? What brought that on?"

"Nothing sir, they just wanted to do something for you. Sorry we fucked up."

"It's Okay, Franklin." Whitehead, feeling like an

ass, apologized.    "I was out of line.    I should've known you guys wouldn't have done that on purpose."

"Should I take the roof off?"

"Hell, no, I'm going to keep it.    I'm not giving up a gift from you guys just because it's the group's commanding officer's.    Let him get another!"

Lopez, the switchboard operator, poked his head out of the switchboard and told Whitehead he had a call on the operations line.

Picking up the receiver, Whitehead was greeted by the sound of a very happy Norm.

"Hi, Norm.    What's new?"

"Please, Dave, call me First Lieutenant Range.    It sounds much better don't you think?"

"Congratulations, Norm.    When did that happen?"

"Just now.    Custard pinned my bar on a few minutes ago.    Dancer also got promoted to Captain.    And I even have good news for you.

"Remember your little assignment to find out who knocked up our typist, Lan?"

"Oh God, it was you, wasn't it?"

"No, damn it.    You know, I really should let you stew a little, smartass."

"Alright, alright.    I'm sorry.    Are you going to tell me?"

"Yeah, I guess so.    Lan had her period.    She's not pregnant."

"Yes.    It's celebration time!    More beer tonight."

Norm went on to tell him that Dancer and he had to host a promotion party at MACV tonight.    All the signal officers in the area will be there.

"Dave, one of us has to stay sober tonight.    I elect you to do that."

"How could I refuse such a request?    See you at the villa."    With that, Whitehead hung up the receiver.

\*

Both lieutenants met at the villa, changed into civilian clothes, and drove in Norm's jeep to the MACV compound. At dinner, Norm took several rounds of congratulations and jokes with promises to see him at 1900 hours upstairs on the roof bar.

Norm and Whitehead moved upstairs. Afterward they ate and started the evening with a couple of beers. Groups of officers started to arrive and Norm had to greet them. Whitehead drifted off to the edge of the veranda and looked out over Nha Trang.

In the near dark, city lights were coming on. Some were electric; many were probably candles. The clouds were rolling in, but the party would be over before the rains came in.

Whitehead started to think about Nha Trang LD. Working, but not quite right, the switchboard seemed to be like the weather. Sometimes it was bad. Other times it was even worse.

Whitehead finished the beer and held the empty bottle in his hand as he looked out at the city. The music from the party inside seemed to grow louder.

"Time for another beer," he said out loud.

He turned to go back inside and walked into Major Cohn.

"How much did you drink tonight, Whitehead?" Cohn was smiling and in civilian clothes.

"Hello, Major Cohn, what brings you to a Signal Corps party?"

"You do. We need to talk. Privately. Get a beer and come back to the railing here."

Whitehead did as he was told. Returning, he asked, "What can I do for you, Major?"

"Call me Bob. I'm not really a Major. I'm a civilian."

Taking a drink from his beer, Whitehead asked, "Am I the only person here who's really in the Army?"

Still smiling, Cohn stopped talking and looked out over Nha Trang.

"Nice city."

"Fuck the city. What do you want?"

"I want Cook!" Cohn nearly shouted, then looked around to see if anyone heard him.

Cohn looked at Whitehead and then leaned back against the wall of the veranda. He began talking but watched the crowd so he could stop if anyone came close.

"Cook was CIA, but he's gone bad. He wants some big money quick, and he's on the verge of getting it. Through you."

"What?"

"You're holding his jade. I think he's using it to parlay a big profit in the exchange of heroin and other drugs from the Golden Triangle for a large supply of weapons for the VC."

Whitehead listened and then said, "Where do I fit in?"

"It took me awhile to figure that out," said Cohn. "I had you checked out. You're a junior high school teacher with two degrees from Rutgers."

"Would you like to sign my yearbook? I hope you didn't go to spook school just to read my biography."

"No," Cohn laughed. He became serious again saying, "You're just a pawn to Cook. A means to an end."

"So, I'm a pawn. Cook is CIA. And you? Are you CIA?" asked Whitehead.

Cohn's answer, if he gave one, was drowned out by the yelling from the men inside. In the middle of the room, the two new officers were being dowsed with beer in honor of their promotions. Both Whitehead and Cohn paused their conversation during the initiation.

Cohn leaned close to Whitehead, and said, "Dave, I

need your help."

Whitehead said nothing. He watched the fooling around some more and then looked at Cohn. He remained quiet for a while, then finished his beer. He turned to the railing looking again at Nha Trang.

"What do you want me to do?" His tone signaled that he was giving in.

"When Cook gets in touch, play along. We're watching you twenty four hours a day. Just do what he asks."

"And if he wants the jade?"

"Give it to him. Just let us know first if you can."

"Sounds too easy," said Whitehead.

"It is. But don't take any chances with your life," Cohn warned. "You're not trained. We may miss the meet. If we do, just give him the jade and get away." Cohn paused and then added, "Cook is a very dangerous person. He killed Burgess, Harris, Lakeland, and Phuc -"

"And maybe me next," said Whitehead.

"I knew those degrees weren't wasted on you."

Cohn turned quiet again. He joined Whitehead in looking over Nha Trang. Finally, he said he had to leave.

"Be careful, Dave. Move slow and obvious. We'll try and stay with you like we were your shadow. Take care."

Whitehead was alone on the veranda again. As a Boy Scout, he remembered going to the dedication of the Basilone Bridge, a structure named after a Congressional Medal of Honor winner from New Jersey. Whitehead thought of being killed in Vietnam by an American CIA agent. They'll never name a bridge after me for that, he thought.

Whitehead faced the party. At the bar, Dancer was singing with three or four officers. For the first time, he seemed to be having a great time. Tired of watching them, he turned and again looked out over the city.

Someone walked up next to Whitehead. Looking to his right he found Dancer.

"Enjoying yourself, Dave?"

"Actually, I am. It's kind of pleasant to find a nice quiet spot to forget where you are."

Dancer just listened and drank his beer. He seemed to want to talk but couldn't seem to get it out of his mouth. Finally, he said, "Enjoy the view, it's free. When you're done, go have some beer. It's free too. Take care."

Dancer walked back to the bar, stopping just before reaching it. Whitehead stood there watching the new captain. Looking back Dancer raised his glass to Whitehead in kind of a silent toast and walked on.

"What the fuck was that all about," Whitehead asked himself. "Must be time to go home, especially when you begin having a serious conversation with yourself."

In his silent contemplation and brief talk with Dancer, Whitehead had lost Norm. When he did find him, Norm was in bad shape. Sitting with four other officers, Norm was drunk and soaked in beer from top to bottom.

Getting an arm over his shoulder, Whitehead lifted Norm up. "Party's over for us. We're heading home. Lieutenant Range has to meet our new battalion tomorrow." They banged against the wall going down stairs, almost falling and then slipping on the last three steps. Whitehead wrestled with Norm to get him into the jeep. Then Whitehead realized the key to the jeep's chain was in Norm's pant pocket. After some more wrestling with the drunken just-promoted first lieutenant, he found the key and started the jeep. The ride home followed.

After another bout to get Norm into the villa, Whitehead put Norm on his bed, laying a blanket on him.

"Sleep tight, buddy."

Picking up another blanket, Whitehead fell back on his bed and drifted off to the United States.

\*

The next morning found them both with terrible headaches.   Drinking coffee from a bowl proved disastrous for Whitehead.   After two sips, it slipped and went all over the floor.   At that moment, he gave up on the coffee all together.

They walked slowly up to the supply area.   Norm went in to take aspirin.   Whitehead headed to the company operations room.

Walking in the orderly room unannounced, Whitehead found Sergeant Grace and Lan in very close contact.

"Excuse me, sir" Sergeant Grace said, jumping away from Lan. Grace was obviously surprised and a little worried.

Lan, of course, giggled.

"I guess I solved my little mystery," said Whitehead without a smile.

"Sir, you can't tell the old man.   Custard would have my stripes and my ass.   I'll do anything to avoid it. Anything."

"I'll think of something, Grace."   Shaking his head, Whitehead said, "Just use extreme care here in the orderly room.   It could have been anyone walking in the way I did."

"Okay, sir," Grace said.

"You better get back to work, Sergeant Grace." Whitehead then looked at Lan, "And you get back to not doing work."

Whitehead followed Grace back to the operations room.   Grace was trying to look like he was working hard. Whitehead was waiting for Dancer, but couldn't help joking with the Sergeant.

Whitehead watched him, then finally said, "Grace, I forgot everything I saw when I came in.   I don't want any

150

favors.   You don't owe me anything.   Just be careful."

Grace listened and simply nodded his head.

Maybe he would have said something, but Dancer walked in.

"Well, I see you survived last night, Dave.   Norm didn't.   I think he may have to go home and sleep, or vomit."

"Where's the old man?" asked Whitehead.

"Captain Custard's just outside the city limits.   He went to meet the convoy coming up.   They should be here by 1300 hours."

Whitehead listened.   Dancer sat at his desk.

"Is Nha Trang LD and Goldfinch in good shape?"

"We painted everything a bright orange yesterday."

"Dave, I think we're going to be in a world of trouble.   A friend of mine at Group said he talked with the new battalion commander.   He heard that the 228 was the worst outfit in 'Nam."

"Christ, if I were him, I'd send us all back to the States and wouldn't let us back in until we shaped up." Whitehead smiled, then continued, "In fact, I think I will recommend that course of action."

Smiling, Dancer said "Just go visit Goldfinch and the LD, then get back here by 1300 hours."

"Aye, aye, Cap'n," Whitehead responded in a pirate voice.

"I could have you flogged for that."

*

At 1330 hours, the 459th arrived in all its splendor. All that was missing was an accompaniment by the works of Sousa.

The NCOs of the 228 had been milling about since 1300 hours.   At the approach of the convoy, the men stood in loose formation.   The officers, who had been waiting in the orderly room, walked outside when they received the signal that the jeeps were approaching.

Custard's jeep, newly washed and polished, led the convoy. The new battalion commander, wearing a helmet, flak jacket, a side arm and a brand new M-16, rode in his own jeep following the Captain.

"Don't you say a fucking word." Whitehead overhead Boggs' comment to Southland. Southland was smiling as he watched the commander's sandbagged jeep pass by. The 459th had obviously come to fight a war. They were armed and looked ready to enter combat immediately.

Four more of these battalion "battle wagons" followed. All were laden with sandbags. The tops had been removed and the windshields folded down. Mounds of sandbags had been placed on the hoods, the front fenders, and on the floors. Southland's smile seemed to grow bigger as each vehicle came into view.

The battalion commander rushed in to see Colonel Duel. The other officers along with Captain Custard talked with the adjutant. The NCOs of the 459th stood at attention ready to assist their officers.

Dancer told the officers and NCOs of the 228 to go back to their jobs or sites and do their regular job. Hearing that, Whitehead got a lift to Goldfinch and then drove his jeep to the Air Force officer's club.

Around 1600 hours Whitehead stopped back at the company area. The 459th jeeps were still in the parking area. The officers and the NCOs sat waiting to be brought somewhere. The new arrivals did little to hide their feelings of superiority as they looked at the 228 and its men.

Staying in his jeep, a smile began to break Whitehead's mouth. A few drops of rain fell onto the ground. Then the rain fell like water from a faucet, drenching the men of the 459th.

He started laughing as he drove back to the villa.

Welcome to Vietnam, he said to himself.

## CHAPTER 18

The 459th had finally arrived. The 228 looked like a beaten enemy next to the fine new signal outfit. The 500-plus contingent of American soldiers, armed with new M-16s and equipped with new radio, microwave, and switchboard rigs, was a stunning sight to see.

Even the men assigned to the unit looked grand. They wore jungle fatigues and jungle boots. On their fatigues, the insignia consisted only of black and brown colors. The 459th in all aspects outshined the run-down 228.

And they knew everything. They frowned at the sight of Goldfinch and Nha Trang LD and made no effort to hide their contempt. Speaking to each other out loud about how things would change seemed to be the new unit's favorite past-time.

Tempers soon flared. Van Rankin tried to punch out the battalion motor sergeant who made comments about the shoddy condition of the motor pool. Blutik barely spoke to the battalion sergeant major.

Not surprisingly, Custard misread the criticism and agreed with it, thinking he was carving out a post for himself on the battalion staff. In private he derided the 228 and expressed contempt for his own officers and NCOs.

Whitehead felt the sting of the new arrivals as well. The second day after the convoy pulled into the company area, he and Norm were summoned to the battalion orderly room.

Pulling their jeep up to the tent serving as the battalion's orderly room, they watched the hustle of the new troops. Many were sandbagging the wooden-platformed tents which the 228 had built for the battalion.

The two lieutenants walked into the orderly room, reported to the adjutant, and were ushered into the commander's office.

Whitehead stopped in front of the commander's desk, brought his hand up in a salute and announced, "Lieutenants Whitehead and Range reporting as directed." Without waiting for a return salute, he brought his hand down and stood at attention with Range.

They seemed to have stood there for a few minutes until the senior officer finished his reading. He then looked up and told the lieutenants to get two chairs and sit down.

He began reciting a list of questions about their jobs in the company. He reacted with a series of frowns and sighs obviously disappointed in their work.

Turning to Whitehead, he asked, "How many men do you supervise?"

"I would guess somewhere in the neighborhood of 70 or 80 men," he then added, "sir."

"You don't know the exact number? What kind of platoon leader are you?"

"Sir, the men in company perform all jobs, including the construction of this camp. The first sergeant assigns the work details and then we run the facilities with the manpower that's left over. It's not the best way to carry out our assignment; it's the only way. We have too much to do with too few and too little."

"Sounds like an excuse, lieutenant."

The colonel stood up and walked about the rear of the tent.

"You young men have a great opportunity here in Southeast Asia. When I was your age, I was lost in peacetime Germany. You two should be striving to perform at your best.

"I'll be looking you two over during the next two weeks. I only want excellent officers in my outfit."

The colonel sat down again. Looking up from his paperwork, he said, "That's all, gentlemen."

Range and Whitehead then stood up, saluted, and left.

Outside, Range started to speak, but Whitehead motioned to say nothing. Norm turned around and saw the sergeant-major standing in listening distance.

Once in the jeep, Whitehead spoke, "Nice people! Do you think they're on our side?"

"Dave, I think we're in a world of shit!"

Whitehead nodded as the jeep headed back to the company area.

*

At Goldfinch, Norm turned to his supply duties. Whitehead picked up his jeep.

Ready to pull away, Franklin called him. He pointed to the telephone receiver in his hand, meaning that Whitehead had a call.

Shutting off the motor, Whitehead walked back to the operations hut.

Taking the phone, he said, "Whitehead here."

It was Cohn.

"Dave, Cook's back in Nha Trang. He flew in this morning. I think he's going to be doing business. Watch for him. Keep an eye out for a guy named Bradley, too!"

"When do I run my signal sites?"

"Next war." Cohn then added, "Just help us with this and then you're on your own."

"'Us?' Who's 'us'?" asked Whitehead, but Cohn had already hung up.

Whitehead slammed the receiver down and headed outside.

Back in his jeep, Whitehead decided to catch lunch and then take a ride. Nha Trang LD wasn't going to get any better. The outlying sites were set. The wire team needed no supervision. And the two telephone installers were ready to go home. So, here he was with nothing to do.

Leaving the traffic of the Army area and then the Air

Force base, he drove slowly out to the farm area. The air was warm and, for the first time since he got the top, he missed the air in his face.

Going faster, he sped along the road watching the Vietnamese working in their fields. Life as usual for them, he joked to himself. Must have a war every year.

He found himself at Goldfinch. Parking his jeep, Whitehead headed out to the Agent Orange.

The airfield was busy. It seemed as if the whole South Vietnamese Air Force was taking off on a mission somewhere to the north. The planes stood out against the gray sky as they grew smaller until they disappeared from view.

Whitehead needed time to think out his next moves. Cook was back. Cohn knew it. He was also watching Whitehead as intently as he watched Cook. He thought instantly of the jade. And Norm.

He had left Norm in the dark about the mixup with the carbines up at the Buddha. Norm did his part, helping Whitehead all he could.

Now, with Cook back wanting his jade for whatever reasons he had, Whitehead would need help. Norm had gotten involved. If anything went wrong between Cook and myself, Whitehead thought, Norm would probably be next. There was no other choice for either man.

With the planes gone, the airfield was quiet again. No one was around. With the 459th in place, the 228 didn't seem to be necessary. It seemed the usual routines were gone. Especially the afternoon breaks out at the tanks.

Whitehead heard the footsteps from behind. He whirled around expecting to find Cohn behind him. It was Franklin.

"This came in a few minutes ago, sir. LD told me you weren't there. I thought here would be the next place to look."

Franklin handed him the message.

"Call Cook, 722."

"Shit." Whitehead said as he crushed the message and stuffed it in his pocket.

\*

A half hour later, Whitehead called Cook from the operations hut. The discussion lasted no longer than a minute. Cook answered the phone and told Whitehead to meet him at Francois' at 1700 hours. Francois, Whitehead thought to himself, the one restaurant I'll remember for the rest of my life without even trying the food there.

Still holding the phone, Whitehead closed his eyes and began to curse. He cursed Cook, he cursed Cohn, but he cursed himself mostly. When he stopped cursing, he put the phone back into its cradle.

The phone rang as Whitehead stood up. It was Norm. "Dave, there's some big meeting in the old man's office tomorrow morning. We're all ordered to be there."

"Great. This day keeps getting better." Both men went silent for a moment. Then Whitehead spoke up, "Norm, Cook's back. I just talked to him."

"What? What does he want? I thought all this spy crap was over."

"He wants to meet. Tonight. At Francois'." Whitehead paused, then added, "I need your help."

"You didn't answer my question. This isn't over, is it?"

"It's a long story. I'll tell it to you on the way over."

"I'll pick you up at 5 o'clock."

"Make it four, Norm. The meeting's at five."

"Okay, I'll be there."

Norm pulled into Goldfinch at exactly 1600 hours. Whitehead waited for Range outside the switchboard tent. Boggs and Southland were with him.

Getting into Norm's jeep, Whitehead asked them if

they had ever been to Francois'. They hadn't, but planned to go in the next few weeks.

Both men looked at Whitehead. The lieutenant had been pacing and looking at his watch for the last ten minutes waiting for Norm. They were actions neither man was used to seeing in Whitehead. Boggs was the first to speak.

"Is everything okay, lieutenant? You don't seem quite right today. A bit edgy."

"Yeah. Everything's fine. We're just going to dinner. Take care of my jeep until I get back." With that, Range and Whitehead left Goldfinch heading to Francois' and Cook.

The two men rode in silence for few minutes. Turning onto Beach Road, Whitehead opened up.

"Norm, in case anything unusual happens, get in touch with a Major Cohn, Goldfinch 773."

"What could happen at dinner?"

"I don't know Norm. I've got a feeling that things are going to go wrong. I don't trust Cook."

"We still have the jade, don't we?"

Whitehead hesitated.

"It's okay," Norm said. "I realized that when you said Cook was back, we must've given him the wrong stock. I remembered that because of the other day when you did it yourself.

"You told me to get the carbine and I grabbed the wrong one. Don't say you're sorry for my mistake."

"I didn't want you involved again, Norm."

"But I was before. And now, because of me, I'm still involved. Let's just get it over with." Range paused, then continued, "Maybe with me there, he'll be different. Maybe he'll back off."

"Norm, he just wants the jade. He doesn't care about who he has to go through to get it. Cohn said give it to him. Maybe we should've gotten it before we left." Whitehead got quiet, then said, "Fuck him, let him wait."

"Yeah, fuck him!"     Norm said it without any conviction.

*

They reached Francois about fifteen minutes early. Norm parked the jeep in front of Francois parallel to the porch.    Getting out of the jeep, Whitehead looked around. It was becoming almost natural to be suspicious of every situation.

The town seemed empty.    So did Francois'.    With curtains drawn, the old French restaurant looked closed. Whitehead walked onto the porch and up to the double doors leading into the place.    Opening the door, they went in.

The restaurant was empty save for one table in the back.    Cook sat in the back drinking wine.    He waved them to the table.    If he was surprised to see Norm with Whitehead, he didn't show it.

"Dave, good to see you.    Looks like you made it here this time without trouble."    They shook hands, then Cook looked at Range.    "You must be Lieutenant Range."

"Yeah, I couldn't resist dinner at Francois."

"Pleasure to meet you," Cook said, shaking hands with Norm.    "Sit down fellows.    Francois is just about ready with dinner."

The two lieutenants pulled out chairs and sat down. Cook poured some wine in their glasses.    For several minutes he entertained Norm and Whitehead with talk of the colonial days of Francois.    During the discussion, Francois brought bread and some small bits of fried fish to the table. He listened to Cook and nodded his head in agreement.

Finishing the history lesson, Cook said, "Francois is going to bring us some more wine.    But first, could I ask a favor?"    Looking at Whitehead, he continued, "I need a minute of your time, Dave.    I have something to give you. Could you come with me?"

160

"Where?" Whitehead asked.

"It's in my rover. Out back."

Not knowing what to say, Whitehead said, "I'm a little hungry, Cook. Couldn't we eat first and then visit out back?"

"It'll only take a minute, and Lieutenant Range can try out the wine for us."

Whitehead stared at Norm, wishing he could say something to avoid Cook's request.

Finally, he said, "Okay, but I want to leave before it gets dark on the road back to Nha Trang."

"No problem. Francois is just about ready."

They both rose. Cook led Whitehead to a doorway. He stopped and held back a curtain. He ushered Whitehead through the kitchen, scaring the hell out of a couple of rats picking at garbage on the floor.

"Now, what's this thing you want to give me?" Turning, Whitehead came face to face with the barrel of a pistol.

"I'm sorry about this, but we have to visit Mr. Van Phan again. He's waiting for us."

Grabbing Whitehead's arm, Cook led him through the outer door and into the alley out back. The land rover waited with its motor running and a Vietnamese at the wheel.

"Please get in the land rover." It sounded like a request, but with the gun pointing at him, Whitehead knew better.

Getting in the vehicle, Whitehead recognized the driver as the young man who answered the door at Van Phan's party. Whitehead sat in front, Cook got into the back seat.

Once the doors were shut, the land rover was off heading back to the elaborate French villa. The ride was silent and quick. Whitehead watched as the scenery passed by in the waning sunlight. He worried about what was happening to Norm.   He was even more worried about what would happen to him once the trio arrived at the mansion.

Whitehead broke the silence as the jeep pulled into the drive.

"What about Norm?"

"Lieutenant Range?   Oh, Francois should be, um, entertaining your friend while we're gone."

Approaching the villa, all appeared to be quiet.   No guards roamed the grounds.   Only a few of the rooms were lighted.

The driver got out of the rover and looked around before walking toward the porch and the double doors. Cook and Whitehead remained in the vehicle.   Finished surveying the area, the Vietnamese waved them onto the porch.

The driver opened the front door of the villa and stepped back.   Cook seemed to hesitate, then pushed Whitehead through the door.

With Whitehead in the middle of the foyer, Cook entered hugging the right wall, looking all about and keeping his pistol in a ready position.   The driver then entered and mirrored his boss along the left wall.

"I must be bait," said Whitehead.

"Shut up, till we find out if we're alone," said Cook.

Whitehead then shouted out, "Is anybody home?"

Cook ran to the side of the stairs and looked upward. When no one responded to the question, Cook announced the house was secured.

Cook then walked over to Whitehead and drove a fist into his stomach.

"You say another fucking smart ass thing..."   Cook didn't finish the threat.   He didn't have to.   Whitehead remained silent, happy to wheeze for breath instead of being worse off.

Cook told the driver to bring Whitehead with him to the large reception room where the party had been held.

The Vietnamese was nearly six-foot tall and muscular. Whitehead noticed it only then because the driver practically carried him to the room.

In the room, the man left Whitehead on the floor, then walked quickly to the French doors and looked outside. He was carrying an automatic weapon.

Whitehead also saw that Cook still had his pistol drawn. Something was wrong and Cook didn't bother to hide that fact. Winded, Whitehead crawled and fell over to a cement love seat and sprawled across it, looking up at the ceiling.

He laid there for a few minutes until his strength returned. Shifting his hands to the section of the bench by his hips, he prepared to raise himself up.

The room erupted with the sound of gunfire and human screams. Bullets tore into the walls. Whitehead couldn't tell where the attack was coming from or what had happened to Cook or the driver. As the initial volley rained through the room, Whitehead stayed on the couch perfectly still, the bullets passing over his body.

Shielding himself with his arms and hands, Whitehead rolled off the love seat and onto the floor. The gunfire was deafening. Then, as abruptly as it started, it stopped.

Only the sound of human agony filled the room. Then that was gone too.

Whitehead felt something wet on his fingers. There was blood on his left hand. He was hit. Then he passed out.

*

When he awoke, Whitehead found Norm shaking him and wiping blood from his face.

"Am I hurt bad?"

"Sorry, Dave, but you're dead. We did all we could,

but you pulled through anyway," Norm responded, smiling.

His vision slowly returned to normal. Besides Norm's voice, he heard one other. This one was giving commands to other soldiers in the room. It, too, was familiar. Cohn.

Sitting up, Whitehead could see the bullet holes in the walls. On the floor in the corner of the room was the Vietnamese driver. He was dead. All over his body were bright red blotches and ugly gashes. Cook had disappeared.

"Where's Cook?" asked Whitehead.

Cohn came over and said, "We don't know. By the time we got here, everything was over. No shooters, no Cook. Just you and the dead guy." Cohn shook his head, "He seems to have slipped away. Or he was taken away by whoever shot up the place."

Looking at Whitehead, Cohn continued, "Did you see Cook leave?"

"I saw concrete or whatever this floor is made of." Taking a deep breath, he looked at Cohn and continued, "I'm in way over my head. Norm and I are going to get killed over here. We'd be better off with the First Cav."

"Wait a minute, Dave. This was a mistake. This wasn't supposed to happen," Cohn said in all seriousness.

Norm was standing still just listening to the exchange. He finally broke in and suggested going home.

"Okay, guys," said Cohn. "Let's head for Nha Trang. I'll sort it out for you tomorrow."

"Forget it, Cohn," Whitehead said in a low tone. "There's no tomorrow for us. We're done." With that, he began to walk out to the jeep with Norm following.

Cohn watched the two lieutenants leave, then shouted, "I'll call you tomorrow."

## CHAPTER 19

The next morning Norm and Whitehead sat in the officers club sipping coffee. Whitehead didn't eat anything since his stomach was uneasy. Norm had just finished his order of hotcakes. Eating seemed to calm him down.

"What do you think the old man's going to tell us at the meeting?"

Whitehead just shook his head, muttering something about going home.

"Dave, pull yourself together. Later on we'll get the jade, give it to Cohn and kiss him goodbye. Then we'll just be waiting for our time to be up like every other normal soldier here."

Whitehead just listened. He pushed his coffee to the side and sighed. Looking at Norm, he said, "Had enough to eat?"

"Yeah, let's go see what Custard wants."

They walked the usual block and a half through the tents and buildings to the company area. Norm waived to Jumpers and motioned that he was heading to the orderly room.

At the orderly room, Blutik sat at his desk and sarcastically welcomed the lieutenants.

"Good morning, sirs. How is your day shaping up?" Before an answer came, he started up again. "Mine began with that son of a bitch sergeant major jawing at me for an hour. He called me at 0600 and proceeded to bitch about how I run this company. What a royal pain in the ass!"

"Sorry to hear that, sergeant," said Whitehead. "It seems the 459th is making friends all over this place."

The appearance of Custard coming back from the latrine with the Stars and Stripes stopped the conversation.

"Gentlemen, in my office. We have a lot to talk about." Custard threw the newspaper onto his desk, then continued.    "Over the next two weeks we are going to be relieved of all our duties in Nha Trang.    Company B of the 459th will take over and handle all operations.    We'll sit tight for another two weeks and organize our equipment for travel."

Custard spoke slowly and calmly, giving the impression that the move was what he expected and, in fact, had planned.    As always, Custard ended his oration and looked out the window.

It was then Whitehead realized that Dancer was not present.    When Custard finished his talk, he asked about Dancer.

Custard looked annoyed and then said, "Captain Dancer is now with the 21st Signal Group.    He's been transferred."    Stopping a few minutes to move something on his desk, he then added, "Whitehead, you are the new operations officer in addition to your other duties."

"Am I keeping Nha Trang LD?"

"Absolutely.    It's your baby, Whitehead, from beginning to end.    Do you think it's going to improve?"

Whitehead had no real answer.    "I think so."    He could do nothing else but lie.

Custard dismissed them and the two men went about the day's business.    Range headed for the supply tent. Whitehead followed since he had left his jeep at the supply area.

Once in his jeep, Whitehead headed toward the long distance switchboard.    He wished Custard had taken this monstrosity away from him.    For six weeks now, the LD was a major complication in his time here.    It didn't seem to show any signs of getting better.

Turning into the switchboard site, Whitehead noticed a jeep from the 459th parked in front of the steps.    The day just keeps getting better, he thought to himself.

Chaining his jeep, Whitehead tried to read the letters on the bumper.    They were covered with mud.    He had planned to kick the mud off, when a pudgy lieutenant opened the van's door and called him.

"Whitehead, get your ass in here!"

Whitehead recognized the man from the 459th. His name was Sandurski, one of his former students in OCS.

"Well, well, if it isn't Lieutenant 'Chubbs.'"

"Never mind the bullshit, Whitehead. I'm here to take over this fucked-up mess." The words would have hurt more had they not come from Sandurski. They stung Whitehead nonetheless.

Smiling, Whitehead responded, "Could always use some help. Glad to have you around."

"No, no! You're done, Whitehead. Relieved! That's R-E-L-I-E-V-E-D."

"Very good, lieutenant. You may go to the fourth grade."

Whitehead strolled past Sandurski and said hello to the men. Sergeant Rameirez looked a little confused.

"What do I do sir?"

"Run the switchboard. Do as the Lieutenant tells you."

Whitehead proceeded to make his regular rounds and insured that things were under control. He then went to Sandurski.

"Well, looks as if things are under control. I'll be at Goldfinch if you want me." Hearing Sandurski shouting in the background, he left and drove away.

Once at Goldfinch, he called Custard. Feeling a little less anxiety now that Nha Trang LD was out of the way, Whitehead was surprised at Custard's reaction. The old man was pissed. In fact, he hung up on Whitehead.

Thirty minutes later, the phone rang. Whitehead, expecting Custard, was surprised upon hearing the voice of the battalion commander. The 459th's C.O. proceeded to apologize for Sandurski, and then added his own apology for the events at Nha Trang LD.

Whitehead responded admirably. "I'm here to do my job. Whatever job you give me is the job I do. I took no offense and I certainly have no feelings of ill will toward you or Lieutenant Sandurski." With that, the commander hung up.

The telephone call over, it was followed by another from Custard. "Did that sona' bitch call you and apologize?" Not waiting to hear Whitehead's response, he continued. "Who the fuck do they think they are. Do you know you outrank that asshole Sandurski? The CO chewed his ass out. He won't be able to sit down for weeks."

Custard went on and on. All this was really bad news for Whitehead. He really would have liked to get rid of the switchboard. The only nice thing was watching people falling all over themselves with sorrow and anger. Finally, Custard ended the conversation, leaving Whitehead holding a phone and a job he had little interest in.

"Shit! Fuck!"

"Nice words for a lieutenant, ain't they?" It was Boggs. He was standing at the door with Southland. The two entered the room and heard the end of one half of the conversation with Custard. "All that schooling and he can't think of any other words?"

"Sergeant Boggs, those words fit the occasion." Whitehead then sat in silence for a few moments staring at the phone.

Boggs began again, "You found your jeep alright?"

"Yeah, it was by the officer's club. Thanks."

After more quiet, Boggs began again. "We were going to follow you last night. You looked a little upset."

Whitehead hadn't planned it, but he proceeded to tell the two NCOs most of what occurred last night. They were a little surprised.

"Sounds like you might need a little help in the future. Keep us posted."

He thanked them and warned them that he may do

just that.    He also told them how he was relieved at Nha Trang LD and then put back in charge.

Boggs responded, "It's coming sooner or later anyway."

"I know, Boggs," said Whitehead.    "I only wish it would come sooner.    The anxiety is killing everyone. Their whole shitass attitude is making all of us feel worthless."

Southland was looking at Boggs and blurted out a suggestion.

"Hey, Lieutenant, why don't you get into some civilian clothes and come with us to a show at the NCO club. No one will know you're an officer."

"How do you mean that, Southland?"    Whitehead was kidding, but Southland didn't know until Boggs told him.

"Treat's on us."    It was Boggs talking now. Whitehead weighed his options.    Norm was tied up in supply business and would be sorting out equipment and hand receipts until late this evening.

"OK, when and where?"

"Great.    We'll pick you up at 1900 hours.    I mean 7 o'clock."

*

The afternoon passed slowly.    Goldfinch never seemed more comfortable.    In the aftermath of the shooting, Whitehead looked at the switchboard site as the one place in this part of the world where he could surround himself with people he knew were his friends.    It was a place the world of Cook and the war couldn't touch.

Stopping by supply, Whitehead talked with Norm for a few minutes.    They went to the officers club for dinner. He told Norm about Boggs' offer, asking Range if he wanted to forget about his work and go with them.    The busy supply officer declined begrudgingly, then finished dinner and went back to his work.

An hour later, Whitehead was standing on the porch of the villa looking for Boggs' three-quarter. When they arrived, he suggested they take his jeep. Boggs responded with a polite, "No, sir. A jeep will make us look odd."

He then squeezed in with Southland at one end and Boggs at the wheel. Southland already had a can of Budweiser open and offered one to Whitehead. The empty cans started piling up on the floor of the truck.

The Nha Trang NCO club was quickly filling up as the trio pulled into the parking lot.

"Hey, sarge," said Southland, "I think we have a show on tap. It's too busy to be just a drinking night."

Southland proved to be right. The place was literally packed to the rafters to see the stripper. Guys were standing on chairs along the edge of the room, waiting for the show to start.

Whitehead had a chance to look around while Boggs and Southland went for drinks. Down in front was a familiar face. Shouting and drinking was Bradley. At a front table, Bradley and his friends were well on their way to being totally drunk and disorderly.

Boggs came along side Whitehead with four drinks.

"Two of these are yours, lieutenant. Saves going back for seconds."

"Sergeant, I think we're in for an interesting evening. Our friend Bradley is down front."

"Oh, shit." Boggs was now looking over heads to find Bradley. He leaned over to Southland and spoke, "Tub of guts is down front. That oversized moron busted up MACV two weeks ago. Scared the hell out of a five piece band from Korea. He jumped on the stage and called them all slope heads and gooks."

"Wonder what it's going to be tonight?" asked Whitehead. He stood there with his two drinks and began looking for the quickest route to the exits.

The lights flashed on and off. The soldiers started shouting. Now the room light went out and the spotlight hit the stage. Music came up and a middle-aged stripper bounced on stage.

Bradley started right away as if on cue.

"Oh, Christ, she's a senior citizen!" Pushing his chair away, letting it drop to the floor, he shouted, "Hey, lady, keep your clothes on. Nobody wants to see what you got!"

Nearby, a uniformed staff sergeant told him to shut up. Bradley walked over to him and punched him in the face. Blood gushed and the fight began. The stripper ran off stage, replaced by a half dozen guys fighting.

Boggs tapped Whitehead's arm, "Time to go!"

Whitehead started to move toward the door, adding, "Just when the show was getting good!"

In the truck, the three decided to try another club. Ten minutes later, they were at a table in the Special Forces NCO open mess. A club by any other name, thought Whitehead.

This club, though, was a little more plush, with Vietnamese waitresses in tight, revealing outfits. "What would you like?" became an open invitation for off color humor.

The drinks were good, the music was easy to listen to, and Boggs and Southland were good company. Whitehead was enjoying himself.

Just after 2000 hours, the trio left, weaving to the three quarter. Southland wanted to ride in the back, laying down on the side bench. Boggs told him to sit in the cab.

Boggs got the truck started and soon had Southland sleeping on his shoulder. The cool breeze of the evening kept Whitehead awake. His eyes caught a pair of headlights ahead. The long car pulled out in front of the three quarter along Farm Road.

Whitehead knew right away it was Van Phan and his Mercedes. Whitehead looked over to Boggs, and said: "Sergeant, that car ahead. Follow it a little ways."

"Anything I should know, sir?"

"Yeah, that's Van Phan. He's the one who owns the house that the shooting took place in last night."

For ten minutes, Boggs shadowed the car. It drove slowly along Farm Road and then took a left toward the beach. The limo drove to a section of the airport which appeared to be part of the ARVN air force academy.

Boggs stopped the truck up the road. He and Whitehead got out. Southland lay in the cab without any sign of life. Leaving him, they followed the fence so that they could see the landing area. Nearing the gate, they heard airplane engines rev up. Looking in, the two men saw the Mercedes next to an Air America twin engine plane. A dark figure got out of the car and into the aircraft. Almost immediately, the plane took off disappearing into the night sky.

Back tracking to the truck, Boggs started it and, without turning on the headlights, backed down to an opening on the side of the road. He was going to turn around, when the lights of the limo appeared coming in their direction. Without thinking, he just kept backing up, hoping nothing was behind him.

"Thank God, you didn't have the lights on!"

"Was that your friend, Van Phan?" asked Boggs.

"I think so. Couldn't really tell, but I'm pretty sure it was him. Who else could it be?"

"Van Phan's got to be working for the CIA," Boggs offered.

"I think Van Phan works for Van Phan, Sergeant." Whitehead shook Southland. He was sound asleep. "I think we better get our friend to a bed."

Boggs agreed and headed the truck toward Whitehead's villa.

"You keep the days and nights interesting around here, Lieutenant."

"Thanks.   I wish I didn't.   This much excitement can kill a man."

"Yeah.   Let's hope it's not one of us."

## CHAPTER 20

The following morning brought with it disturbing news. The 459th had officially assumed the responsibilities of the Decibel Devils. The decision came down quick and merciless.

In a morning meeting with his officers, Captain Custard, in a subdued tone, made the announcement.

"It's all over, men," said Custard. "We are officially out of the war."

"Just what does that mean, sir?" Whitehead asked.

"It means, Lieutenant Whitehead, that as of this moment we do nothing. But we do have to get new equipment and be ready to go elsewhere when we are told." Custard dipped his head. He was obviously upset.

Apparently, the decision to relieve the 228 was not one which was presented nicely to Custard. Getting up, the Captain began pacing behind his desk. Not once did he look at his men.

"We all have some new duties," Custard continued. "Lieutenant Range will remain Supply Officer. Whitehead, you are now Motor Officer and any other officer we may need.

"Your first task is to get the trucks, signal equipment, and other gear together and prepare them for whatever," Custard said, waving his hands in air. "The motor pool here in this area will be the staging ground. However, the troops will be moving to the tent camp and joining the 459th. Range, that's your job."

Custard then sat down and began looking out the window. Range and Whitehead sat in silence waiting for more. More didn't come. Custard was defeated and looked every bit of it. Finally, Range and Whitehead just got up and left.

*

With the 228 inactive, everyone who wasn't part of the 459th had little if anything to do.   During that time, Whitehead noticed that almost every soldier in Vietnam had a camera.   Some brought them from the States.   Most bought them in the PXs in Nam.

The new cameras were 35mm made by Pentax, Minolta, and Petri.   They were great for shooting pictures of the countryside while driving in a jeep or truck.   Just point and shoot.

Cameras were surpassing the rifle as the soldier's most important piece of equipment.   GIs would leave their rifles in trucks, under bunks, in air terminals, and in latrines; they'd never leave their camera.

Whitehead had held off for a long time.   His basic reason was he knew little about 35mm cameras.   Norm had a single lens reflex Pentax that could do everything, if you could figure out the settings.   Norm took pictures of everything and sent them home.

A visit to 8th Field Hospital got Whitehead his camera.   He saw a Vietnamese putting six Minoltas on a shelf.   Fully automatic, they were only $35.   He bought one; he almost bought two.   Being armed, Whitehead could shoot VC and send them home.   The pictures, that is.

With a new toy, the mess with Cook and the arrival of the 459th seemed unimportant.   He had a challenge now. Get the goddamned camera to take a picture.

Whitehead took pictures of everything.   He found that the camera was indeed automatic.   An electric eye adjusted the lens setting and shutter speed.   He brought the film to be developed to a Vietnamese photo shop on Long Van air base.

After leaving the shop, he remembered that he had taken pictures of gun emplacements, signal equipment, and fighter aircraft.   He started to fantasize how MPs would come along and arrest him for letting the enemy see these important government installations.    But none did, nor would they.    No one gave a damn.    The Vietnamese were working at the sites already and could take their own pictures, and probably did.

The camera could only keep reality away from Whitehead for so long.    He mastered the camera and its myriad of settings.    There was nothing more to discover about it, so Whitehead decided to get involved in the company again.

When he got to Goldfinch, two officers and a dozen men from the battalion were already there.    A captain took Whitehead's salute and advised him that Bravo Company would be putting their equipment next to the radio relay gear and shift the radio traffic to the new equipment.    The 228's switchboard would have to stay until the 459th unpacked its board from its shipboard crates.

Whitehead asked about the equipment at Nimh Hoa and Duc My.    The captain didn't know anything about them.    He was only responsible for Nha Trang.

Once the captain left, Whitehead drove over to the motor pool.    As motor officer, this was now his responsibility.    He envied the captain from the battalion. He had only one responsibility.    Nha Trang.    Whitehead needed more fingers than he had to count his assignments.

He parked the jeep in front of the motor pool. Taking his camera, he walked about the area, looking but not inspecting.    In the rear, out of sight of everyone except a careful observer, he came to an old three quarter truck that had been cannibalized.

Whitehead took a couple of shots from different angles.    He fantasized about telling people it had been blown up by VC.    Maybe it was.    He began to wonder why it was hidden away.    He didn't have to wait long for an explanation.

"I'm glad you're taking pictures of the evidence." Whitehead turned around and found the motor sergeant.

"What do you mean, Van Rankin?"

"Shit, Lieutenant, someone ripped this truck apart for parts. And you know that's against Army regulations. You can't cannibalize."

"Christ, we've been tearing apart generators since I've been here."

"Right, sir, and as motor officer, your ass is goin' to be grass." Van Rankin was smiling and enjoying himself.

"Don't be so pleased with yourself. You better have every green book up-to-date and ready for inspection." Whitehead was heading now toward the motor office where the green maintenance books were stored. Looking back at Van Rankin, he said, "I want to see every piece of paperwork on each piece of equipment."

"Why, Lieutenant, you gonna take a picture of it?"

Whitehead stopped, walked over to Van Rankin, and said, "If I go down, you do too! Now get your ass in gear."

For the next two hours, the two poured over the paperwork, aligning each requisition with each piece of equipment. Whitehead soon realized that Van Rankin was right.

There were too many troubling problems. Poor paper handling and loose administration of the motor pool was going to haunt him. It was no excuse that he was just made the motor officer; the problems were there. And they were his.

Things were changing. Whitehead could feel it. He felt alone. Range was in supply catering to the 459th's needs. Boggs and Southland were in the field area with 459th personnel. No one connected with the 228 looked happy. There was a great deal of sorrow in what was happening and how it was happening.

And Whitehead was left to stand around and watch the action. Walking to his jeep, he looked back and wondered if Goldfinch would ever be the same. He thought he hated the site. He knew differently now.

## CHAPTER 21

"Christ! Where the fuck is he?" Whitehead shouted, slamming his hat into the wall. He had been waiting for Custard about ten minutes with Boggs and Southland in the orderly room. Neither man knew what the Captain wanted. All three had received a call to report to the CO's office, but none were told what the meeting was about.

"A little impatient today, aren't we, Lieutenant?" Custard said as he walked into the orderly room holding a copy of the Stars and Stripes.

Following him into the office, Whitehead and the two sergeants sat down and waited for Custard to begin the meeting. Custard stood at the window of his office, looking out as if waiting for a signal to begin the meeting. Turning abruptly, he moved to his desk, sat down, and began talking.

"Okay, men, we have a little mission. Captain Dancer called a little while ago. He wants us to look at Hon Tre Island, that big clump of rock sitting in the harbor." He turned towards Whitehead and continued, "He asked specifically for you, Whitehead."

"I added you two to the pie," he said nodding at Boggs and Southland. "I think the battalion and group may be thinking of us to go out there. I want to be ready."

"What are we looking for, Captain?" Whitehead was puzzled about the assignment.

"Christ, Lieutenant. You don't have to be looking for something. Just look. You're scheduled for lift off from the Artillery base camp on the other side of Long Van at 1300 hours. OK, get to it!"

No more questions and, as usual, no answers. Whitehead, Boggs, and Southland left. Outside, they followed Whitehead to his jeep and agreed to meet back at the orderly room at 1230 hours, then head over to the chopper. Boggs and Southland went to lunch together.

Whitehead decided to find Norm and check out his schedule.

Finding Norm in the Supply tent, Whitehead recounted the morning's events. Norm listened, then said, "Hon Tre Island. Very unusual place. I remember Dancer discussing it with someone on the phone one day. I heard that it was a stopping off place for VC during the day. At night, they'd get back on their little boats and go south to Vung Tau. It's their rest camp."

"Great. Can't wait to get there," said Whitehead. "Hold my camera?" He handed the 35mm to Norm, then said, "You can have it if I don't come back."

"I'll have it waiting for you when you get back. Besides," Norm continued, "I already have a better one. Let's get some lunch before you go."

*

Forty five minutes later, Whitehead was flying above the harbor looking down on the naval ships and junks dotting the seascape. The water was a deep green, reminding Whitehead of the jade still hidden in Cook's carbine.

Boggs and Southland were quiet, looking out the side door. Neither had said a word since getting on board the chopper. Even the pilot grew quiet as they neared the small island in the harbor.

Soon the water gave way to land, and Hon Tre was directly below. The island was mostly rock with a heavy growth of trees and bushes. A couple of scars started to emerge near the shore and traveled up a hill. Near the bottom of the scars were three company-sized tents where the engineers made their camp.

The chopper climbed and rose with the mountain at the center of the island. The elevation at its highest point was 300 feet. Near the top, the chopper hovered and allowed the three soldiers to look at a flat section. In a corner of the small plateau were a half dozen pup tents.

The red haired gunner, seeing his passengers' curiosity at the sight, shouted, "They're Koreans. It's an isolated radio relay team that shoots a signal to Nimh Hoa. We drop them C-rations from time to time." Looking at Whitehead, he smiled. "Great assignment. The Korean lieutenant there says he fucked up on a patrol. Hon Tre was his reward. What did you do, Lieutenant?"

Whitehead didn't respond. He made believe he was too busy looking over his potential new home to hear the wiseass remark. For another half hour, the chopper roamed all over the island, then they headed home.

*

Back at Goldfinch, a lot of animosity began to develop between the troops of the old and new units. Fights erupted over how the 228 let the switchboard deteriorate.

At the switchboard, a message waited for Whitehead. The lieutenant was to go to Nimh Hoa and Duc My to get the 228's equipment up there. He sent Boggs and Southland to the motor pool to get trucks and trailers ready for the drive.

Boggs was back in ten minutes.

"You better come with me," he said to Whitehead. "There's an officer from the 459th in your motor pool. He found that three-quarter ton truck that's torn apart."

Hopping in, Whitehead started to feel sick.

"I guess we've been fucking up by the numbers. No wonder we're losing the war. The 228's at fault."

*

At the motor pool, a tall lanky captain shouted directions about to line up all the generators. Getting out of the jeep, Whitehead approached the captain and saluted.

180

Ignoring the salute, the officer addressed Whitehead.

"You must be the most sorriest fucking motor officer in the whole world!"

"Thanks for the compliment, but I'm sure there are worse." Whitehead looked around, then said, "You obviously don't like what you see."

"You're goddamned right I don't! This is pathetic. I can't believe this unit. Wait till the colonel sees this. Lieutenant, you'll be hearing from us. Soon!"

Whitehead saluted again as the officer departed. He added, "And a jolly good fucking day to you too, Captain."

Turning, Whitehead found Van Rankin smiling. "Got your ass reamed pretty well, didn't you, Lieutenant?"

"Shut the fuck up, Van Rankin." Whitehead began to walk away, calling to Van Rankin as he walked out the door, "Did you get the trucks and trailers for Boggs? I don't want any breakdowns."

"They're all ready," Van Rankin answered, then added, "They're all ready, sir."

Leaving the motor pool Boggs drove Whitehead back to the switchboard and the lieutenant's jeep, then the sergeant went back to get the vehicles for the convoy ready. Whitehead decided to head for the Air Force officers' club. By this time of day, the place would be in full swing and, after the short confrontation at the motor pool, Whitehead needed a drink. Maybe several.

In five minutes, he was parking his jeep and rapping the chain around the wheel. With one foot on the ground, he turned finding Major Cohn standing with his hands on the back of his jeep.

"Should I salute?"

"Whatever turns you on, Lieutenant." Cohn was half smiling. "But since you obviously like to trail people at night maybe saluting is a little too tame."

"You must have heard about another of my little adventures. I didn't intend it to happen; it just happened."

Visibly upset, the major moved closer to Whitehead. They were standing in front of the Officers' Club. Cohn seemed ready to go head to head with Whitehead.

"This isn't the place to vent our problems, is it, Major?   Even I know that.   Let's drive to the beach."

Cohn nodded and walked to the other side of the jeep and jumped in.   Whitehead slid back behind the wheel, unwrapping the chain.   He looked over to Cohn, and said, "I'd offer you a drink, but I know how wild you get when you drink."

Cohn turned and answered, "Fuck you, asshole."

In ten minutes, they were at the beach.   Cohn proceeded to advise Whitehead in very clear words that he was to play the next week straight to the vest.

"Be careful, Whitehead, it's almost all over and you're still alive.   One mistake could change all that. Following guys like Van Phan around is dangerous.   It's a very easy way to end up dead."

It was a one way conversation.   Cohn was angry about something.

"You can't be that pissed about last night.   What's wrong?"

"I don't know what's wrong; that's what wrong.   I should have a better handle on what's going on, but these bastards seem one or two steps ahead of us."

"That flight last night came out of nowhere.   We thought we had that son of a bitch figured out.   Then for some god forsaken reason, he drives to the airfield and flies away.   I turn around and there you are, sitting in a jeep as if it were a drive-in movie."   He looked out at the ocean, "Take me back to the club."

The drive back through the afternoon traffic was painfully long.   Cohn just sat and brooded.   At the club, he warned Whitehead again, "Watch your ass.   Things are proceeding erratically.   I don't know if you're one hundred percent safe.   Even with me around."

With those words he left and walked around the corner. Whitehead sat in the jeep for a moment and looked at the club. He suddenly didn't feel like a drink. Even in a crowded bar, Whitehead would feel as exposed as a target on the rifle range. He checked his back for a bull's eye, then went back to his quarters.

*

At 0800 the next morning, Whitehead sat in Norm's jeep waiting for Boggs and the convoy. Waiting with him, Range sat behind the wheel. Norm had decided to come along to inventory the equipment. He also wanted to get away from the 459th.

"Hey, Dave, I wanted to tell you this yesterday, but when I got back to the villa last night you were already asleep." Norm was working late again in supply thanks to the new unit.

"What's up?" asked Whitehead. He didn't turn when Norm spoke. Whitehead kept looking down the road for the convoy.

"I've got less than six months to go. I'm a short-timer." Norm was almost giggling as he spoke. At that moment the convoy appeared around the bend in the road. "Here they come," Norm said. "That's Boggs and Southland in the lead jeep." Norm started the motor as the jeep and two trucks and trailers approached.

Range and Whitehead took the lead with Boggs and Southland behind the last deuce and a half in the convoy. Southland asked the two lieutenants to keep looking back in case of engine trouble.

The convoy moved slow and steady through the jungle on its way to Nimh Hoa. At normal speed, the trip was about a half hour. With the deuce and a halfs, the journey lasted twice that. The next hour was filled with thought, noise, dust, and the lush green countryside. Norm and Whitehead talked about home as usual while at the rear, Boggs and Southland were having an animated discussion. The men driving the vehicles in the middle drove silently and watched for any signs of trouble.

As the convoy approached the bridge alongside the old monastery, the convoy came to a dead halt. An artillery truck jammed itself against the bridge's sides, the vehicle being too wide to make it through cleanly. With their progress stopped and the scene ahead unchanging, Norm and Whitehead turned their attention to the ruined monastery overlooking the bridge.

"Hundreds of years," Norm said aloud. "We must be the hundredth army those walls have seen. I'm surprised one of those armies didn't just blow the shit out of those walls."

Whitehead added, "Maybe we will."

Norm was apparently intrigued by the monastery. "I think those walls will be around for centuries more."

"Well, thank you, Lowell Thomas," said Whitehead.

"Who's Lowell Thomas?"

"Shit, Norm. He's the guy who first wrote about Lawrence of Arabia."

"Christ, Dave, do you think he knows about the monastery?"

"Sorry, Norm, I think he's dead."

The traffic began moving again. Once over the bridge, they passed the artillery truck and its driver. An MP was lashing into the driver for causing the traffic jam.

Whitehead looked back making sure the trucks followed. Boggs and Southland were visible as the little convoy turned a corner in the road. The two men were bickering as usual. Probably more sandbags, Whitehead thought to himself smiling.

About five miles out of Nimh Hoa, Whitehead heard a horn blowing from behind. Boggs' jeep had stopped. The remaining members of the convoy stopped as well.

The three vehicles began backing up toward where the two sergeants' truck died. Boggs had the hood up while Southland rubbed his chin diagnosing the trouble.

"Gas pump," said Southland as the sergeant turned to face Whitehead, who was still in the jeep as it backed in front of the stalled vehicle. The lieutenant got out of the jeep and ran back to the troubled vehicle.

"Shiiiitttt!" Boggs threw his hat to the ground. "Southland, you don't know shit about trucks and motors. It's the god damn water pump. That's why it's getting hot."

Range came up behind Whitehead joining the motor analysis team. As Norm and Southland focused on the problem, Boggs drifted off and began talking to the other members of the convoy. Whitehead turned and watched as the men grabbed their weapons and stood in front and in back of the trucks.

Whitehead drifted toward his jeep and caught Boggs' arm as he walked by. "Expecting trouble?"

"Just being cautious."

Range and Southland were doing a vaudeville routine about how to fix the motor. Neither really knew what to do, but it made for a good show.

Boggs had climbed up into the back of the deuce and a half and exited the vehicle dragging a chain. He threw it in front of the disabled jeep. Southland and Range ended their debate on the engine problems to watch Boggs as the sergeant looked at the chain, then the jeep, and then back at the truck.

"If you Einsteins would kindly step out of the way," Boggs said as he grabbed one end of the chain. "I may be able to correct our problem."

Boggs looked under the jeep for a place to hook up the chain. Moving from under the jeep, he stopped quickly and seemed to be staring through the tires at the road behind the convoy. Whitehead stood up and looked back as well.

Down the road, three young Vietnamese in black

pajamas walked towards the small group. Whitehead couldn't see if the figures carried any weapons, but he didn't want to see them get close enough to make certain. "Oh, shit," said Whitehead. "Get the chain hooked up, Boggs. If you can't do in 20 seconds, you're going to be laying there all by yourself."

"It's hooked up already, sir. Southland, hook the other end on the deuce and a half."

Whitehead continued to watch the young men. He looked around the large trucks in front. No one coming that way. He then pushed Southland toward the driver's seat of the deuce and a half.

"Get it started. We're getting the fuck out of here. Norm, start your jeep and get going."

But Norm was already in the jeep waiting for the rest of the convoy.

"Move out," shouted Whitehead. "Thank God, we're out of here."

The windshield of the truck shattered. Boggs and Whitehead fell to the road covering their heads waiting for the next shot.

"Boggs?" Whitehead asked without lifting his head.

"Now's a good a time as any, sir."

With that, the two men jumped into the towed jeep and the convoy moved out. The next three miles to Nimh Hoa and the Korean site were covered quickly. No stops and, more importantly, no gunfire.

## CHAPTER 22

The stop at Nimh Hoa proceeded without incident. The men stationed there would have the equipment, and themselves, ready to depart when the convoy returned from Duc My.

Leaving the site minus the overheated jeep, the small group continued its journey to the Special Forces camp. With Norm staying behind to oversee the wrap up of Nimh Hoa, Whitehead rode in Range's jeep with Boggs and Southland.

Boggs took the wheel, with Whitehead alongside of him. Southland sat behind them holding his M14. Boggs had turned the back seat around so that their backs would be covered. The men in the remaining deuce and a half rode close behind the jeep with their M14s close at hand.

There were very few vehicles on the road. In the tree lines off to the side, movement seemed to follow the convoy. Whitehead's grip on his rifle tightened.

Reaching Duc My, Boggs and Whitehead exchanged worried looks as their jeep sped through the guardhouse unimpeded. There were no guards, the compound's gates left unprotected.

Once inside the gates, they passed by a unit of Vietnamese Rangers returning from combat. At least four of the walking men were wounded and bloodied. The rest looked ragged and useless. They marched in a group, disorderly and beaten.

Inside the main compound, things were a little more orderly. Southland jumped off the jeep and walked over to the radio hut. After a few moments, he reported back to Whitehead that the team was just about ready to move. Whitehead and Boggs left the jeep and joined Southland and the remainder of the convoy personnel in surveying the equipment at the Special Forces camp.

Not having a crane to lift the huts, the radio gear was

going to be transferred to the 459th personnel.   But the generators were another thing.   They were so bad, the 459th didn't want them and wouldn't accept them.   But they were in a trailer ready for hitching to the deuce and a half.

As the survey of Duc My's equipment continued, Boggs and Southland wandered off.   Left alone, Whitehead went back to the jeep and sat down.   One of the men brought a C-ration carton over to him for lunch.

Sitting in the jeep's front passenger seat, Whitehead began to enjoy the dry, tasteless cracker when he heard someone approach from behind.

"That may be your last cracker if you don't get your ass out of here in a half hour."

Whitehead tried to get out of the jeep, but felt a hand pull him back.   He twisted and turned face to face with Cook.

"Christ, you're like a bad penny."

But Cook finished the line.   "Yeah, I keep turning up in all the wrong places."

"What's happening here?"

Cook walked around to the driver's seat and said, "Keep eating.   You don't have time to eat much though. The VC are about thirty minutes away.   Get your shit and get out."   Cook stiffened, looked around, then continued, "Go east.   They're coming from the west."

"How do you know all this?" asked Whitehead, finishing up the last bit of cracker.

Ignoring the question, Cook looked at Whitehead. "Tonight, this place'll be in VC hands.   Believe me. There's not much time."

"Cook, what the hell are you doing here?"

"Never mind why I'm here.   Just be glad that I am, or you and your men may be guests of the North Vietnamese tonight.   And they don't appreciate sarcasm the way I do."

As he spoke, three young Vietnamese came alongside of Cook.   Whitehead recognized them.   They were the same three figures that had drifted out on the road outside of Nimh Hoa during their engine problems.　And they were probably the people who fired at them.　Before he could mention it, Boggs appeared.

"Well, if it isn't our friends from Nimh Hoa."

"Yeah," answered Whitehead.　"And they're friends of Cook here.　I'd like to introduce you to him, but I don't know his rank, or if he even has any."

Moving away from the jeep, Cook offered a final warning.

"Like I said, Dave, haul ass out of here."　Cook then walked away joining a group of Vietnamese Rangers.

"Nice friend you have there, Lieutenant," Boggs said.

"Boggs, that son of a bitch is no friend of mine.　But I think we'd better take his advice."

Boggs nodded and headed toward one of the tents. Whitehead watched as he exited the structure carrying about six or seven clips of ammo for their M14s.

"We may need these to help get us home," Boggs said as he loaded the rifle and took the safety off.

*

The caravan travelled for about five minutes without trouble.　The jungle passed by in a green blur as the convoy moved as quickly as possible back to Nimh Hoa.　The two vehicles maneuvered through the twists and turns of the dirt road, the deuce and a half keeping up with the smaller, quicker jeep.

"We've got some company, lieutenant."

Ahead of the jeep, some Vietnamese troops positioned themselves in the road, attempting to stop the two vehicles.　There were about a dozen men, each holding an assault rifle.

"I see them.　Are they on our side?" asked Whitehead.

"Can't tell from here," answered Boggs.    "Get ready."

The jeep closed in on the squad of men.

Finally, Boggs said, "Lieutenant, would you give those fools ahead some warning shots?    They may be ARVN, but they may also be VC.    And I really don't want to stop to ask."

Pulling the bolt back, Whitehead held his M14 outside and next to the windshield.    He pulled the trigger not realizing the rifle was on full automatic.    The weapon emptied its full clip.    The soldiers scattered jumping behind whatever cover was available as the jeep and truck sped through the aborted roadblock.

"Nice job, Lieutenant.    I'm glad you fired over their heads.    I think they were ARVN."

"Shit, I was aiming to shoot them."    Whitehead put the rifle in the seat behind him, then asked, "What if I had shot one of them?"

"Sir, they would have given you a new assignment. Life at Fort Leavenworth."

"Thank God I'm not that good of a shooter."

*

Neither man spoke again until they reached Nimh Hoa.    Whitehead was upset at what might have happened back at the attempted roadblock by the ARVN troops.    He didn't really want to shoot the enemy, let alone people that were on the same side.

At Nimh Hoa, the Koreans had fixed the truck. They had cannibalized one of the other trucks at the site to replace the water pump in Boggs' deuce and a half. Whitehead smiled as Norm related the story to him.

"Didn't think we were the only ones," he said to Range and Boggs.

"But you were the one who got caught, sir," Boggs

answered.

Back on the road, Whitehead was now with Lieutenant Range leading the convoy. With an eye on the road ahead, they again tried to keep the other vehicles in sight.

In thirty minutes they were back in Nha Trang. Pulling into the motor pool, Whitehead told Boggs and Southland to dismiss the drivers then do whatever they wanted for the remainder of the day.

Norm drove back to the Supply Room and returned Whitehead's camera. Most of the troops had already left for evening chow, so Norm and Whitehead proceeded to discuss dinner plans for themselves. Besides being exhausted from their adventure, Whitehead found that he was very hungry. Only when the action had stopped and they were home did the hunger pains start. Deciding on the MACV Officers' Club, they returned to the jeep and headed for town.

Half way to the club, they hit traffic.

"Damn."

Norm smiled as he looked at Whitehead then at the line of vehicles ahead. "Why don't you go see what happened? I'll stay with the jeep."

"Yeah, okay."

Taking his camera, Whitehead left the jeep. He walked ahead about two hundred feet and found the cause of the traffic.

Whitehead raised his camera and scanned the accident scene. Through the camera's lens he focused on the grizzly sight of an ARVN soldier caught under the rear wheel of a large Vietnamese truck. Not wanting to take a picture of the crushed head and body, he scanned to the right and took several pictures of the crowd that had gathered to watch the cleanup.

Scanning further to the right, he stopped. Whitehead scanned back to the left and held the camera focused on a familiar face.    He pushed the button again, and then again.

Lowering the camera, he saw only the back of a head as the face moved away from the scene.

He knew the face.    He kept repeating the name to himself as he walked back to the jeep.

Getting back in the jeep, he said the name aloud, "Burgess."

He turned to Norm and said, "He's not dead."

Norm looked at him.    "What?    Who's not dead?"

"Burgess.    He's alive.    And I have his picture."

## CHAPTER 23

Body counts became an important aspect of the Vietnam War. How many enemy soldiers killed was a measurement of battlefield success. Whitehead had been keeping a body count, a count that was progressively getting larger. Or, at least, until yesterday, it was getting larger. It was now one less.

The appearance of Burgess at the Vietnamese accident scene chilled Whitehead. He realized that the mess he'd been dragged into was a lot more complicated and strange than he thought possible.

Whitehead's main goal was to avoid getting on the list of dead and wounded. At the shock of seeing Burgess, there was also a hope that all these guys who were dying were really faking it and, like Burgess, would all show up alive.

*

Dinner seemed to take forever. Both men sat silently while they ate, unsure of their situation. Burgess' death was one of the few occurrences that was easy to grasp. Now that he was alive, it appeared that anything was possible -- even dying, and returning to life.

After dinner, Norm dropped off Whitehead at the Air Force Officer's Club. Whitehead didn't want to be alone, but Norm's Supply Room and the 459th's needs beckoned. Inside, the music was loud, the room smoky, and the crowd was lively. Walking over to the bar, Whitehead ordered a beer.

The young lieutenant had just found an open bar stool and began to sit when someone tapped him on the shoulder.

"Dave."

"Shit." Turning, he found Major Cohn standing

behind him. "Now what," said Whitehead. "Did I cross against the red?"

"We need to talk."

"Now? I just had a very strange day and I just sat down."

"Okay. I'll join you." Cohn sat down as a soldier got up from the bar stool next to Whitehead. Ordering two beers, Cohn smiled at Whitehead. "Here you go. Maybe you'll be nice to me . . . at least for a little while."

"Yeah, sure. So, what brought on this generosity?"

"Bradley." Cohn answered, then took a sip from his beer.

"You sure you want to talk about that stuff here? In public?"

"I thought you may feel more comfortable here."

"What's my large, obnoxious, disgusting friend doing now?"

Cohn smiled. "From what I hear he's starting to make some moves. I think he's trying to figure out how you could be added to the weekly body count list."

"Another admiring fan? Great. What's the story with him anyway?" Whitehead shifted in his seat to face Cohn.

"Bradley's a civilian contractor," Cohn answered. "He's used this war to make his life . . . more comfortable. And he's looking to gain much more now that a half million troops are coming into South Vietnam. Those kinds of numbers mean big bucks. His problem is that he doesn't know where to start."

Whitehead listened closely. Cohn faced the bar as he spoke, his eyes never meeting Whitehead's.

"About four months ago he came across some valuable merchandise. He had little use for it, but, as stupid as he looks, he knew there were elements in 'Nam that would pay a small fortune for it."

Cohn stopped and turned to Whitehead. "The merchandise is a thousand Russian and Czech made automatic rifles. He has fifty crates of weapons that were stolen off the docks in Saigon."

"We've been watching him, but he's always been able to move the rifles without us knowing about it. He's moved the lot twice since then. I guess now he's decided to unload them as quickly as possible."

"So where do I fit in?" asked Whitehead.

"You are proving to be a problem. He's probably a little pissed about a mindless lieutenant who seems to be screwing up his deal."

"And you think Cook is helping him."

"Maybe," responded Cohn. "I know Cook from Laos. I was his supervisor. I trained him. He was good, probably the best I've ever seen over here. But drugs and big bucks seem to have turned him from the CIA to SELF. He's out for himself now, but he still uses his CIA connections. That may be how Bradley knows when and how to move the guns without us knowing."

"You spy guys are one big happy family." Whitehead stood up and finished his beer. "Well, it's been really swell seeing you again and thank you for the beer, but I really must go. But don't feel like I'm trying to get away from you, I just don't feel that safe right now."

"No offense, Dave," Cohn said drinking his beer. "But you are in more danger than you could ever realize."

"And good night to you, Major. I feel much better now." Whitehead turned to leave, but stopped and whirled around, then said, "Well, the least you could do after telling me all these wonderful things is give me a ride home."

Cohn smiled. A short while later, Whitehead found himself in his bed unable to sleep. I just love these kinds of nights, he thought to himself.

*

Whitehead spent the early morning of the next day thinking about Cohn's information and his own predicament. Breakfast time found both Range and Whitehead restless and ready to eat.

As the two men reached their jeep and began to back out of the driveway, a red pick-up truck pulled in behind cutting them off. The door opened and Bradley seemed to roll out of the driver's seat. Several empty beer cans also rolled out as well.

Drunk, Bradley walked over to the passenger side where Whitehead sat. In his left hand Bradley held a can of beer while holding a .357 magnum in his right. Range and Whitehead sat perfectly still as the fat man began to speak.

"Good morning, gentlemen. Sorry to interrupt your drive, but I need a word with you." He looked directly at Whitehead, breathing his beer odor in Whitehead's face. The lieutenant wondered if Bradley could actually see him clearly, let alone fire the gun he carried. He decided it would be healthier to assume the slob could do both.

"I need the stuff that Cook left with you, and I want it right away."

Impatient sonofabitch, Whitehead thought. As Bradley towered over Whitehead, Norm stared straight ahead, then looked at the two men next to him. Bradley was bigger than Norm had first thought. Whitehead glanced over at Norm. Range responded by shrugging his shoulders.

"Bradley, I'll give you anything you want," said Whitehead. "Could you be a little more specific?"

Cocking the hammer back on the Magnum, Bradley said, "Cut the shit, Lieutenant." He leveled the barrel against Whitehead's temple. "You'd look funny with no head. I guess then you'd be just 'White', huh?" The magnum began to shake as Bradley laughed at his own joke. "I'm not sure I know what stuff you're talking about."

"I'll tell you what, Whitehead. You think about it today. You figure out what I'm talking about and remember what this big ass gun looks like. I'll be watching you and your friend over here." Bradley nodded to Range, then continued, "I want whatever Cook gave you. And I really don't care who I have to go through to get it."

Whitehead and Range remained quiet as Bradley uncocked his Magnum and returned to his truck. Opening another can of beer, he pulled away from the jeep laughing.

"He certainly makes his point," said Whitehead.

"If he made it any clearer, you'd be dead, Dave. Where do you meet these guys?"

"Pen pals."

"Real fucking funny, Dave."

"Shit, the son of a bitch works for the government. I don't know where they get these guys."

"What are you going to do?"

"Good question, Norm. I hope you know that I don't intend to get killed. We have to get rid of this jade."

"Sounds good to me."

*

The following morning's breakfast was at the Air Force Officers Club on Long Van. Whitehead had stopped trying to eat big breakfasts; they interfered with his 1030 coffee breaks at whatever club he was near. After breakfast, Whitehead would be behind his desk at the Motor Pool. As motor officer, he had little to do, but a lot to worry about. Besides Cook and Bradley, the 459th was after his ass.

Coming out of the club, Norm pointed to a couple of Air Force "super" sergeants. They had curved stripes below and loads of stripes above the little star in the middle. They were watching the sky.

With his cap back, the sergeant with a mustache pointed to a group of black dots dropping out an airplane. After a few seconds, the black dots became little white puffs.

"Shit, it looks like they're all going to make it," said the other sergeant, talking with a cigar in his mouth.

"No! No! There's one. Shit, c'mon and open up you little bastard."

Norm and Whitehead both stopped. As he looked up, Whitehead asked, "Who are the black dots?"

"They're South Vietnamese rangers in training. They jump most mornings. These guys are betting on whether the chutes open." Norm spoke with a very matter-of-fact kind of tone.

The two sergeants, seemingly oblivious to their audience standing a few feet away, held their ground watching as the black dots continued all the way to the horizon.

The sergeant chewing on the cigar shouted and slapped his buddy on his back. He had won. The ARVN ranger lost, but that was another story.

Norm pulled Whitehead away. "C'mon we have work to do."

"Yeah. I guess so."

Whitehead followed Norm, but kept turning around watching the mustache pay the cigar his money.

Walking toward the jeep he was nudged by Norm. "Dave, up ahead. Do you know that guy? He looks like he's waiting for us."

"Yeah, I know him. It's Cohn. Remember?"

"From Van Phan's mansion?"

"Yeah. I thought it might be another 'new friend' of ours, pulling a Magnum on us threatening to kill us for the jade."

"Don't fool yourself, he may well do that, too. I don't know whose side he's on either." He kept the pace and added, "Great fucking war we got ourselves into!"

Cohn began speaking as the two men approached the jeep. "Must be nice to have time for breakfast. I've been going since 0500 hours."

"You're in the wrong army, Major," said Whitehead. He paused, then looked at Norm and smiled, saying, "I'm not even sure it's our army. Is it?"

Ignoring the remark, Cohn continued. "You're going to take me for a little ride so I can brief you on the latest."

Norm took the wheel, Whitehead the front passenger seat, and Cohn sat in the back. The major leaned forward as Norm drove, giving him directions. After ten minutes, he pointed to a turnoff and told Norm to pull off to the side and kill the motor.

"We all comfortable?" asked Cohn. Whitehead and Norm nodded.

"Well, I have some bad news, and some bad-der news."

"Hey, Cohn," broke in Whitehead, "you got some bad English."

"Shut the fuck up and listen. Your friend Van Phan wants you dead."

"Jesus, Dave, the list keeps growing."

"Why me? What'd I do to him, except eat a lot of shrimp at that party of his?"

"Because he believes you killed his son," Cohn answered.

Whitehead couldn't believe Cohn. "I haven't killed anyone. And what about all the people trying to kill me?"

"Maybe they don't like sarcastic assholes like you," Norm said.

"Add one more to that list. Van Phan. He's convinced you dumped Phuc in the harbor. Did you?"

"Shit, no, it was Cook. Phuc tried to kill me because he thought I caused his lover's death. Remember Truc?"

"You mean Truc, the driver of the truck that tried to run you down?" Norm asked.

"First, the truck hit the pole, then Truc went through the windshield." He then added, "I guess Truc got fucked with the truck while working for Mr. Phuc."

"Can't leave it alone, can you, Whitehead? You have to make a joke of it." Cohn sat shaking his head as he spoke.

"Hey, I'm not joking. I'm just describing what took place." He said it with a straight face and no sign of laughter. "How did you find out Phuc was his son?"

"Van Phan told me," said Cohn. "Remember, one of my roles is as a friend to the circle of sympathizers who meet with Van Phan. We had a little meeting and he expressed his hate to one of his VC friends. He has a distinct dislike for you."

Norm listened to Cohn, then added, "The list is even bigger. Bradley stopped us this morning and expressed a similar dislike for Dave."

"You'd better tell me what happened." Cohn was again very serious.

Whitehead and Norm described the morning's encounter for him. When they finished, Cohn just sat there and thought. Cohn then told Norm to start the jeep and drop him off near the Officers' Club. At the club, Cohn got out and offered one final remark, "Watch your ass."

Watching Cohn turn the corner of the street, Norm said, "Why don't I feel better?"

## CHAPTER 24

The two lieutenants continued on to the motor pool. Whitehead wondered what else could happen to make this day one for the record books. Well, that didn't take too long, Whitehead said to himself as the motor pool came into sight.

Just inside the gate three jeeps sat as if waiting for Whitehead. One was the Group's CO, another was the battalion's CO. It really didn't matter who owned the third jeep since the shit was about to hit the fan.

"If I were you, Norm, I'd drop me off and leave."

"Good advice, but I think I'm in trouble, too. I'm the maintenance officer, remember?"

"Yeah, but they've got to find you to burn you. Take off. I'll let you know what they said."

Norm pulled away without any more encouragement.

As Whitehead soon found, they had a lot to say. Colonel Duel studied the cannibalized truck when Whitehead entered the motor pool while the battalion CO examined the cannibalized generators. Whitehead walked over to Duel and reported.

Duel turned, shook his head and walked past Whitehead over to the generators joining the battalion CO. After a few moments, he turned back to Whitehead and said, "Christ, Lieutenant, did you do this all by yourself, or did you get help from the VC?"

Continuing their inspection, the two senior officers walked a few more feet exchanging whispers and frowns. Whitehead walked in the opposite direction around the generators. Wishing he smoked, Whitehead felt that a cigarette would show a measure of relaxed concern. He knew trouble was at hand.

"Lieutenant," Duel called.

Walking back to Duel and the other officer,

Whitehead came to a form of attention.

"Yes, sir."

"You must have an explanation for all this gross neglect of government equipment," said Duel. "But I can tell you right now that anything you come up with will be unacceptable. No kind of explanation can explain away these generators, that truck, and the utter destruction that has gone on in this motorpool. In any case, I would like to hear at least something on your behalf. Soon."

Whitehead stood at attention as the two officers turn, get in their respective jeeps and pull away without looking back. Two down, Whitehead thought as the owner of the third jeep came up alongside him. It was the Maintenance Officer that had visited before.

"Shit, you'll be in Vietnam forever trying to explain away this mess," the major said. "Why don't you volunteer for a grunt unit, get yourself killed. Be sent home in a body bag. It's the only way you'll ever see the States again."

Whitehead looked him square in the eye, took a deep breath, and said, "Respectfully, sir, would you kindly go fuck yourself!"

The officer smiled and commented, "That would read nicely in your court martial papers. But, I understand, and I'll let it go by. You're in enough trouble."

The officer continued smiling as he walked back to his jeep. When he got to the gate, he waved like a little school girl saying goodbye to her mother. Then the major got into his jeep and left Whitehead and the Motor Pool.

Alone, Whitehead knew he did everything wrong, especially telling the major to go fuck himself. He went over to the office and found Van Rankin sitting amidst piles of green maintenance books, one for each generator they owned.

"Well, sergeant, I hope you like this country. It

looks like we'll be here a while."

Van Rankin looked up and said, "Not me, Lieutenant. I ain't letting any of these assholes take me down."

"Well, good luck, sergeant! Let me know if you have any ideas."

For the next hour or so, Whitehead moped around the motor pool. He was sorry he let Boggs and Southland have his jeep. He wanted to take off, go to the beach. He could have looked at the water which led to the States. Maybe he could start swimming.

Reality interrupted his daydream escape as Norm showed up at the gate. Norm seemed as down as he was.

Whitehead spoke first, "What makes you so down hearted?"

"I just had a visit from Group and Battalion," Norm said.

"What did Duel say to you?"

"Shit, Dave, Duel didn't show. It was just two majors who were pissed off about everything. No records. Wrong rifles. Too little of this type of equipment. Too much of that. Wanted to see hand receipts. Those assholes wore me out."

Whitehead got in the jeep and recounted his visit by Duel and the Battalion CO. Offering a weak smile, Norm agreed that Whitehead got the worst of it.

Norm then added, "We better grab lunch in the company area. I think I got a lot of work ahead of me."

Whitehead wasn't interested in lunch or Norm's work. "Take me anywhere you want."

*

At the mess hall, Whitehead hardly ate anything. He could barely determine what it was he was eating. He finally looked up from his plate, pushing it away to the center of the table.

His view came to rest on Captain Dancer standing at the entrance to the mess. Whitehead watched as the new arrival looked over the room, his eyes passing from table to table. In one hand, Dancer held his hat and in the other a cigarette. When their eyes met, Dancer began to move across the room aimed toward the two lieutenants. When he reached the table, he stood for a moment and then spoke.

"May I join you two?"

"I'm sure the maitre'd won't object." said Whitehead.

Sitting down, Dancer said, "Well, at least you didn't tell me to go fuck myself."

"That was my next comment."

"You do have a way with words, Whitehead. Norm," Dancer said, nodding in Norm's direction. He crushed his cigarette after one last drag and lit another. Then he continued, "You two guys are in a world of shit. So's the company for that matter. Group and battalion are trying to figure out how to burn the company."

Norm dropped his fork. "Jesus! Don't you guys know there's war going on? Those generators are waiting for parts; they've all been ordered. What's this bad case of the ass that everyone has?"

"Relax, Lieutenant, I know that. I'm on your side here." The captain took another drag of the cigarette before continuing. "They just haven't found out yet."

"So, what do we do? Wait for somebody to hit them over the head with that little tidbit? Christ!" Norm pushed his plate away, joining Whitehead's in the center of the table.

Dancer looked at the table, then said, "They're not that dumb, at least not all of them. I've got a few favors in Group. Maybe I can take some of the pressure off. Loosen up some of the parts."

"Any other news to brighten our day, Captain?" asked Whitehead.

"I've heard rumors that the 228 is going to be re-fitted. You'll get all new equipment. That may explain all this shit with the generators and other equipment. I think Group wanted to siphon off some of it for other units." Dancer took another drag. "They didn't realize how bad off the 228 was. So maybe the problem isn't as bad as it seems. Keep in mind, I'll be working for you."

Sitting between Norm and Whitehead, Dancer crushed the cigarette and lit up a third. Turning to look for the waiter, Norm accidently knocked Dancer's cap to the floor. Reaching down to get it, Dancer stretched over. His fatigue blouse moved revealing his waist. Whitehead stared at the black holster clipped to Dancer's belt. Returning to his up-right position, his blouse returned in place and covered the pistol.

"Well, I'm late," said Dancer. "I'll catch lunch later. Remember, I'm looking out for you. Keep me posted from your side."

The two lieutenants watched Captain Dancer leave the mess.

"I told you Jim was a good guy, Dave. Maybe he can loosen up those pricks at Group."

"I don't know, Norm. Outside of you, Boggs, and Southland, I'm not sure if I trust anyone around here."

"You're just getting paranoid. He's alright."

"He's armed. Not many guys at Group wear pistols under their jungle fatigues."

"That was probably a wallet you saw."

"Bullshit, Norm, I know a holster for a small caliber pistol from a wallet."

Norm took a deep breath. "Maybe he's traveling to isolated sites."

"What good would a pistol like that be against the

VC, Norm?   He's got other things in mind.   And I'm not sure I really want to trust him with our lives.   And why all this friendship, Norm?   And why did he come in and join us at the table?"

"Jeez, Dave, it's lunchtime!   He didn't know we were here.   Coincidence, that's all."

"Norm, he came in looking for us.   I watched him from the door; this was no chance meeting.   I think we better be on our guard with him around.   He may be as hazardous to our health as Cook."

*

The two men left the mess hall and headed out to Nha Trang Beach.   Norm paralleled the shoreline for a few minutes then turned onto the sand and parked the jeep facing the water.   Behind them on Beach Road, Club Natique loomed over the jeep.

Whitehead began to feel a little less anxiety over the situation when Norm tapped him on the shoulder.   He was pointing down the shoreline.   In the distance, Whitehead watched as a red pickup truck came into view kicking up a dust storm as it crossed the beach.   They knew it was Bradley long before either saw the man behind the wheel.   They sat silently as the pickup pulled alongside their jeep.

Looking at Whitehead, Bradley nodded, then said, "Come down for a little relaxation?   The beach does have a nice view, don't it?   I suppose you don't have the jade." Without waiting for an answer, Bradley continued, "No, I didn't think so.   Oh well, I'm giving you all the chances in the world, but you just can't seem to understand that I'm not fooling around."

Bradley reached over to the passenger side. Whitehead went pale as he watched Bradley pick up something from the seat beside him.   There was a muffled click.   Whitehead began breathing again as he watched the fat drunk take a drink from the beer can he had just opened.

Whitehead watched, and then finally said, "No, that's alright. We don't want a beer. It's a little early for us."

"Fuck you, Whitehead." Bradley finished the beer he had just opened, then reached down for another. "You're so fucking smart. I still have my gun and you piss me off to no end."

"Sorry, I didn't know you were so sensitive," said Whitehead.

"Well, you're in for a real treat. Like I said, nice view. You can see just about everything from here. Just about everything." Bradley turned and pointed toward Club Natique.

"See that jeep up there?" asked Bradley.

Whitehead looked back at the Club's parking area. It was a couple hundred yards away and seemed to be empty, except for the jeep.

Bradley continued, "A certain major sent that jeep to follow you guys. He's only been there just a few minutes." Bradley emptied the second can. "I think that's long enough, don't you?

"Now look. See that, the guy on the motorcycle. Up there, coming up behind the jeep."

Whitehead and Range watched as the cycle came up the road and pass by the jeep parked in the lot. They looked at each other, then back up at the club. The cycle and its rider were no longer in sight.

"Watch!" Bradley began to laugh as he said the word.

Up on the hill, Whitehead spotted the cycle rider approaching from behind the jeep again. He was walking up slowly, crouching down. The soldier behind the wheel of the jeep was oblivious to the approach.

Just then, Bradley spoke and the two lieutenants turned to look at him. "I'm going to leave you now.

After I leave, go over and look behind the jeep."

Bradley laughed and opened another can of beer. He started the pickup and spun its wheels in the sand. Whitehead looked back up the hill. The rider, his cycle, and the soldier were gone. All that either of them saw was the empty jeep.

"What the hell was that all about?" asked Norm.

"Do you wonder what's behind the jeep?" pondered Whitehead out loud.

"If we were smart, we'd just drive back to the company area," suggested Norm.

"Yeah, but after all this, why start now. Get us up there."

Norm started the jeep. They pulled slowly off the beach, crossed Beach Road, and pulled in front of the empty jeep. They began to walk towards the vehicle when Norm grabbed Whitehead's arm. Range pointed to a puddle at the back of the jeep.

"Oh shit," said Whitehead as he watched the pool of blood grow in size.

Under the back of the jeep was the soldier lying in his own blood. The wire still wrapped around his throat cutting almost halfway through the neck. Whitehead almost threw up.

From the back seat of the jeep, they heard muffled voices. Tucked in the canvas cover was a walkie-talkie. Picking it up, Whitehead listened to the voice coming over the open channel.

"Come in Wild Cat One. This is Wild Cat Base."

Seeming to wait a lifetime, Whitehead reached for the radio.

"Wild Cat base, this is Wild Cat One. Do you read me?" Whitehead shouted.

"I read you 5-bye Wild cat One," the voice replied.

Whitehead tried to sort out what to say. After a few moments, he spoke. "I don't know who you are, but you have a problem at the Club Natique. Your man has been murdered."

"Who is this?"

Whitehead put the radio down in the back of the empty jeep. If Bradley was trying to frighten Range and Whitehead, he succeeded. They walked around to the front, feeling sick and too frightened to do anything other than sit in their jeep.

About ten minutes later, Cohn pulled up in a jeep. He hopped out and ran to the back of the empty jeep. Cohn stood over the body of the soldier then turned away, his eyes closed, cursing himself under his breath. He picked up the walkie-talkie and shouted some orders into it. Once he stopped barking orders, he threw the device out onto Beach Road where a passing deuce and a half ran over it.

"How did you find out about this?" he asked Whitehead.

"Like two jerks we watched it happen. Bradley had us on the beach, and told us to watch your man and another person on a motorcycle. Bradley distracted us and when we turned back to the jeep, the cycle and the rider had disappeared. We didn't see the driver either. We found him like that when we got up here."

"I'm going to get that son of a bitch." That was all that Cohn said, but Whitehead knew that the man was thinking much more. Cohn looked out over the water. "How did they know?" Turning to the two lieutenants, Cohn said, "Get out of here. Watch your backs. Stay together."

Whitehead stared out in front of the jeep all the way back to the compound. All I could do was sit there and watch it happen, he thought to himself. Reaching the Supply Tent, Whitehead decided to get himself and Norm out of this mess.

"Norm, whoever asks for the jade first, gets it."

"You'll give Bradley the jade?"

"You bet your ass.    I'll give it to Santa Claus if he showed up and asked for it.    I'm done with the mystery and the killing.    That kid at Club Natique should be alive. I don't want any more deaths because of this shit."

It was 2030 hours when they went back to their quarters. Norm, exhausted, fell asleep quickly.    Whitehead lay in his bed unable to sleep.    He didn't want to shut his eyes.    When they were closed, all he could see was the empty jeep and the pool of blood.    He could also see Bradley laughing, standing over his own dead body, and the jade.

## CHAPTER 25

In the Westerns Whitehead watched in the theaters back home, the good guys wore white and the villains wore black. Always. In Vietnam, both sides dressed in whatever the hell they pleased.   If the person wasn't VC, you couldn't always tell the good from the bad until it was too late.

In the company tent Whitehead sat looking out the screened-in section of the back of his office, his back to the desk.   He turned when he heard footsteps.

In the entrance of his office, the battalion motor officer appeared.   The major stopped a few feet inside the doorway and stood.   No salute, no greetings, not even a hint of recognition in the man's face.

"What can I do for you today, Major?" said Whitehead rising to his feet in mock respect.

"Please, sit, Lieutenant."   The motor officer looked around and commented, "I guess you're settling in here. Maybe the tents are better than the buildings you were in."

"We'll switch back anytime you want to, " responded Whitehead.   "Those buildings are dry and cool."

"I guess you're right."   Seeming to run out of small talk, the motor officer began anew.   "I need to talk to you."

"Go ahead."

The motor officer was obviously very pained to be here, and even more pained to talk.   "I need to discuss a very touchy subject."

"The generators."   Whitehead stood up again. "OK, no need to talk.   You want my bars, a signed confession, and you're going to leave a loaded pistol."

The motor officer put his hands up.   "No, no!   It's not going to be that way.   I've got a deal."   As the major spoke, Whitehead looked at the tall, nearly bald soldier.

"The old man told me to see you and take all the generators off your hands. You can hand receipt them to the battalion."

"Why?" asked Whitehead. Then the answer came to him. "You want the parts."

"We want to help the company."

"Bullshit," said Whitehead. "Get out. You should be talking to Custard anyway."

"The battalion CO won't talk to Custard. He thinks he's a horse's ass."

Whitehead was thoroughly pissed. After days of worrying about a court martial, the same man who threatened to lock him up for life for the generators now stood there telling him that the battalion was going to do the same thing.

"Listen, Major. For me to do anything, your boss will have to call me and apologize for all that bullshit in the motor pool. Who do you bastards think you are?"

The motor officer picked up the phone and gave the battalion CO's telephone number.

Surprised, Whitehead asked, "What are you doing?"

The motor officer smiled and said, "The old man said he was willing to do just that to get you to act. You can talk to him right now."

Whitehead grabbed the phone and hung it up. Shocked, he walked around. "OK. You can have them. I don't need an apology. I could use a little help now and then, but being left alone will do. For now." Sitting down, Whitehead asked "When do you want the generators?"

"Now. We need them for Tuy Hoa. We really just need the parts. Everything is breaking down. We just underestimated the wear and tear."

"You underestimated a lot of things," smirked Whitehead.

*

Once the motor sergeant finished the paperwork for the battalion motor officer, Whitehead headed for Captain Custard's office.

At the outer office area of Custard's tent, Blutik sat behind his desk, humming while he worked on the morning report. As Whitehead approached, Blutik looked up and smiled.

"Well, well. Good day, Lieutenant. You just saved me some work. The old man wants to see you."

Whitehead looked past the first sergeant into Custard's office. The Captain was nowhere to be found.

"Where is he?" asked Whitehead.

"He's in the latrine with *The Stars and Stripes*."

"You mean the flag, or the newspaper?"

"Very funny, Lieutenant. You must leave those kids you teach with a stomach ache from laughing so much." Blutik was not laughing; he just kept on writing.

Custard's words followed his footsteps, "Oh, there you are, lieutenant. I got a job for you. I know you're looking for something to do." With that, Custard walked into the section of the tent designated as his office. Whitehead followed as his CO continued to talk.

"You're going to Hon Tre Island. Plan to spend about three days there. Look it over. Map it out. Take this set of directions and locate the site. We're not going to An Khe; we're going to Hon Tre." Custard sat back and looked at Whitehead, then asked, "Any questions?"

"How much time do you have? I have at least 150 questions."

"Keep it down to 3 or 4. I have only a few minutes," said Custard.

Tempted to ask him what he had to do, Whitehead satisfied himself with some obvious ones. "Where do I stay over there? Do I go by myself? Is it dangerous over there?"

"Shit, lieutenant. Take anyone you want. Bunk with the artillery unit, or the engineers, or even the Koreans. Or maybe you want to set up your own camp. Suit yourself. If I were you, I'd arm myself with any weapon you can find. M14s, grenade launcher, pistol, machine gun. VC are all over that island. We'd be better off in An Khe with the whole fucking 1st Cav to protect us."

The meeting ended as Custard picked up his newspaper and headed out the tent. Whitehead began to realize that his boss had the shits, and was becoming extremely well read.

\*

Whitehead's next stop was supply. Norm would be there to hear about this latest adventure Whitehead would be enduring. But Norm had his own problem.

As he approached the supply tent, Whitehead saw the battalion jeep. Then Whitehead heard the familiar voice of the battalion supply officer. Norm was being called names, names Whitehead hadn't even heard before, and threatened with every law in the Uniform Code of Military Justice.

After a few minutes of eavesdropping, Whitehead walked inside the supply tent.

"Excuse me, sir," Whitehead interrupted the battalion man's tirade, "but could I use the phone a moment?"

"You'd better use the phone before either one of you ends up in the guard house for screwing up by the numbers."

"Thank you," said Whitehead. He dialed the battalion motor officer. Getting him on the phone, he said. "You remember our little conversation this

214

morning?" Whitehead then turned away from Norm and the battalion supply officer. After a few moments, he faced the two men again. "Someone wants to talk to you."

Taking the phone, the supply officer said his name. Nodding his head, he said, "Are you sure?" Listening more, he said, "Alright, but you better have a good reason for me to take such action."

Hanging the phone up, he looked at Whitehead saying, "I don't know what's going on, but I do what I'm told. Listen, Range. Inventory all your shortage. Write hand receipts for my signature. Bring them to my office tomorrow, and I'll sign them." Then he left.

Norm looked at Whitehead, then said, "What the fuck is going on? You make one phone call, and Mr. Hyde turns into Dr. Jekyll. Did you find the battalion commander jerking off with a five-year old?"

"I'll tell you later, but you'd better take advantage of this. Write up everything you need. I would even add a few more items that are nice to have. By the way," Whitehead smiled, "I just got word I'm going to Hon Tre Island."

"What?"

"You heard me. I'm being sent to Hon Tre as an advance party. I need everything for three, maybe four days. Rifles, ammo, food, tent, and whatever."

"You'd better take the carbine. Not for the jade, but for personal use. The forty-five is useless; the M-14's too heavy. The carbine is perfect. Who's going with you?"

"You!"

"No way, buddy. I'm staying right here. You need someone with smarts anyway. Someone you can trust. I'd take Boggs and Southland."

Whitehead was going to argue with some smart answer, but he knew Norm was dead serious. So he kept quiet, and started to plan how he was going to break the word to Boggs and Southland.

*

The three of them were shitfaced drunk, or at least seemed to be. Whitehead, Boggs, and Southland were in the lieutenant's jeep heading south along Beach Road. As Whitehead drove, he was beginning to feel the effects of the five or six drinks he had actually consumed. He had bought at least eight of the twelve rounds of drinks, usually straight whiskey, that they had in the half dozen NCO clubs in Nha Trang. Whitehead frequently poured his drink on the floor, or dumped it in the latrine, which he went to quite often.

Pulling up in front of the NCO quarters, Southland staggered out of the jeep then leaned back in and said to Whitehead, "Lieutenant, you ever need us for anything, just ask."

Sensing the right moment he said, "Well, there is one thing you could help me with."

He then told them about Hon Tre, or at least, he told Boggs. Southland was totally wiped out. Boggs was clearly alert. With little question, Boggs agreed to go along with Whitehead while Southland moved behind the jeep and threw up.

Thanking Boggs, Whitehead helped carry Southland into the villa. Once inside, Boggs said, "You know, lieutenant, you could have saved a lot of time and liquor if you asked us earlier tonight about Hon Tre. Jumpers told us this afternoon. I threw half my drinks away tonight."

"I guess I'm learning, but not fast enough. You don't have to go," Whitehead said as he headed for the door.

"Hey, Lieutenant, we're packed already. It's easier to go than unpack." With that, Boggs reached down and picked up Southland from the floor of the villa and dragged the passed out NCO toward his room.

*

The next morning Whitehead walked across the company area, planning a stop to see the company commander then Norm.     As Whitehead neared the company tent, a jeep pulled up alongside him.     Seeing the driver was the battalion commander, Colonel Duel, Whitehead stopped and saluted.

"Well, Whitehead, have you seen Nha Trang LD lately?" the battalion CO asked returning the salute.

"Yes, sir," Whitehead responded.     "It looks good. I like the sandbags; they're good protection.     I think the reception on the phones is better also."

"Bullshit, you're lying.     You still think we're the biggest bunch of assholes you've ever met.     Well, you're young," Duel said smiling, "you'll meet bigger ones.     We found out that the switchboard had bad parts.     According to the manufacturer, they were installed wrong.     You never really had a chance of getting it right."

Whitehead stood there and listened.

"I know you're going to Hon Tre.     Watch yourself. And I heard you called for your supply officer.     We'll take care of it."     With that, he saluted and pulled away.

*

Whitehead met Boggs and Southland at the supply tent before heading over to the launching area at the beach. Besides their weapons and supplies for the trip, the three men were equipped with a jeep.     They also received a small trailer which they hitched to the jeep.     After a final check of their status, they headed over to the beach. Whitehead was driving; Boggs sat in the front seat. Southland laid in back moaning about a headache.

"How do we get to Hon Tre if we're not going by chopper?"   Whitehead asked.

"Mike Boat," Boggs replied.

"What's that?"

"Landing craft.   The army used them in World War II at Normandy.   Only they were bigger."

From the backseat, Southland continued to moan. Boggs turned and told Southland to shut up.   He looked at Whitehead and said, "What's bothering you, sir?"

"Well, I have a bit of a headache myself, but that's not my problem.   My problem is how do I back this trailer onto the Mike Boat?"

"No problem," said Boggs. "We're going to get out of the jeep and walk on the boat.   Southland is going to back the jeep and trailer onto the boat.   He can then stay with the jeep and sleep off his drunk."

"Sounds good to me, Boggs."

"Are you going to fill me in on what we're doing?"

"Sure, Sergeant, but unfortunately Custard gave me some very strange directions.   He said look around, find a site, and report back."

"Anything else, lieutenant?"

"That's all."

They both got quiet and waited for the Mike boat to load up.   There was a lot of engineering equipment and some artillery personnel to be loaded.

As the landing craft moved quickly across the waters of Nha Trang harbor, Whitehead listened to the conversations between the other men on board.   Most of the talk centered on Hon Tre.   None of it made Whitehead feel more comfortable about the trip.

The soldiers spoke about the rumors they heard from others returning from Hon Tre just days before this advance party.   Stories of snipers shooting at the engineers on the bulldozers as well as shooting at the soldiers on guard duty at night circulated about the Mike Boat throughout the short voyage across the harbor. Hon Tre was becoming very unattractive compared to Nha Trang. Just when the battalion seemed to stop being the enemy, Whitehead thought to himself, the real enemy appeared.

CHAPTER 26

With its beautiful mix of blues and greens, Nha Trang harbor was totally out of place with the war that was going on throughout the countryside. The calm waters of the harbor seemed to be worlds away from the busy, hectic beach from where the Mike Boat was launched, where the Vietnamese children were hawking pineapples and the GIs were yelling obscenities at each other.

For most of the boat ride, Whitehead carried the carbine at his side. The weapon was light and, with all the rumors the young lieutenant heard on the boat, it proved to be reassuring. Boggs and Southland both had their M14s which they left in the jeep. The jeep was also the place where Boggs and Whitehead left Southland, asleep in the back seat.

As he held the carbine, Whitehead thought about Cook. The man appeared seemingly out of nowhere. Could he appear on the island, Whitehead wondered. Cook seemed to have the ability to go anywhere he pleased at any time without anyone knowing about it. Whitehead held the weapon tighter as the thoughts rolled around in his head.

"There it is, Lieutenant," Boggs shouted over the sound of the Mike Boat's engines. "Hon Tre."

"I think it looked better from the air, sergeant."

When the boat maneuvered onto the beach and dropped its landing pad to the beach, Whitehead and Boggs walked off, then watched as Southland drove the jeep off the Mike boat. Southland drove off to the left of the landing site where the engineers had carved out a beachhead from the rock and dirt which comprised the island. Whitehead and Boggs walked behind the jeep and trailer as it moved the short distance to the camp area.

At the engineer's camp, a young black lieutenant named Walker greeted Whitehead. After a short discussion with the engineer, Whitehead returned to the jeep and told Boggs of the arrangements. The three would use the camp's spare tent as their headquarters. Anything else they required would be provided to them if possible.

They drove the jeep to the tent, unhooked the trailer, and unloaded. Boggs decided to see the engineer's first sergeant as a courtesy and get additional information about the island.

Whitehead agreed, leaving Southland to stay with the carbine and jeep. Southland decided to get some more sleep leaving Whitehead to himself. Walking back toward the landing area, Whitehead looked toward the top of Hon Tre Island, trying to get a feel for what was on this seemingly isolated land mass.

From the air, the island didn't seem like such a nice place. Now that he was actually on the ground, Whitehead realized how much better the island was from that distance. There was little shoreline or beach. No sandy areas ideal for swimming. Hon Tre was all rock and dirt, literally a mountain in the middle of the sea.

After walking a little more, he found a rock just right for sitting. The sun broke out and he shut his eyes.

"Lieutenant Whitehead," a voice called out. Whitehead knew who it was immediately.

"Cook," Whitehead said. Opening his eyes, Cook stood before him. "How'd you find me, Cook?"

"I'll tell you all my methods some day. Right now, I need the carbine. Where is it?"

Whitehead looked around, "Do you see it?"

"No, that's why I asked. You had it when you came off the Mike boat. I need it today. Now. Right now!"

"It's back with my NCOs," Whitehead said as he sat up a little straighter. "I really didn't expect to run into you so I didn't feel the need to carry it with me."

"I have a suggestion for you, Whitehead. In fact, I

have two.   Don't walk around the island unarmed.   The second is, go get my carbine."

"I can't do that right now.   My sergeants will get suspicious.   Meet me later.   I can tell them I lost the carbine."

"I don't like the delay.   But maybe you're right. Your sergeant friend is walking this way now.   Be here at 9 o'clock tonight."

"You mean 2100."   Whitehead smiled.

"Don't screw around.   You know what time I mean.   Be here.   Make up a good story for your NCO. Tell him I'm a civilian engineer."   With that, Cook took off, walking past Boggs who was heading for Whitehead.

Nearing Whitehead, Boggs looked back, but Cook had disappeared.   Boggs stopped and turned around, looking in all directions for the man who had just walked by him.

"Who the hell was that?" asked Boggs.

"He's a civilian engineer with the Army."

"Sneaky bastard.   Where did he go?"

"That's how he came upon me," said Whitehead. "I sat down here, closed my eyes, and he appeared.   Asked me what I was doing here."

Boggs continued to look at the area where Cook disappeared.   He turned to Whitehead and said, "You know he looks a lot like that guy that was at Duc My who had the three Vietnamese trailing him."

Whitehead ignored the comment and began walking back to the engineers' camp.   "C'mon, we'd better find Southland and get about our business."

*

Back at the tent, they found Southland fast asleep in his bunk.   Boggs moved quietly to the edge of the bed, looked at the sleeping man, then punched Southland in the shoulder.    Southland immediately jumped to his feet shouting in pain at the unexpected awakening.

The three men began to pack up their gear when Whitehead discovered a very interesting thing.    The carbine was gone.

"Boggs, have you seen that carbine I brought with me?"

"Where did you leave it?"

Whitehead pointed to his bunk then lifted up his sleeping gear.    Walking outside the tent, he looked in the jeep.    There were two M14s, but no carbine.

"Oh well, easy come, easy go," said Whitehead.    "I guess Cook couldn't wait."    Now that Cook had the carbine, he wondered to himself, would he still have to meet the man at 9 o'clock, or at 2100, or ever again.

Back in the tent, Southland was fully awake and being apologetic about the carbine.   He offered his M14 to Whitehead, who refused it saying the sergeant was a better shot and more likely to be effective with it anyway.

The three got into the jeep and began their drive up to the area they flew over with the chopper a few weeks ago.

The road was steep.   Boggs shifted into four wheel drive, keeping it only in second gear.   The jeep churned along, hitting ruts and going around boulders.

They passed a few groups of engineers, all well armed and working.   Up on a high rock scanning the area, a GI held an M16, a bunch of grenades clipped to his suspenders and cartridge belt.   Welcome to Vietnam.

Further up the road, Boggs stopped the jeep in a small clearing where another group of engineers stood around taking a break.    Still further up, Whitehead watched as a GI scanned the area with his M16 and grenades at the ready.    Boggs struck up a brief conversation with the NCO in charge.

"I see all you guys have those new M16s.   Lucky.

We still have our old M14s," said Boggs.

"You might be better off," said the engineer. "The dust is killing the M16s. We're constantly cleaning them to make sure they don't jam."

The conversation was cut short by the sound of an AK-47 erupting from the forest. Whitehead turned trying to find the sound of the gunfire, then turned his attention back toward the group of engineers. They moved fast, faster than Whitehead expected. Shovels were dropped and rifles picked up and aimed in unison. Everyone seemed to fire at once. Whitehead, Boggs, and Southland stared. It was like watching a movie unfold.

"Hold your fire!" shouted the engineer sergeant.

He had to shout three or four more times before everyone did stop. Whitehead turned back toward the road. Up ahead, the engineer who had been on patrol lay dead in the middle of the road.

"Move that jeep out of here!" the engineer NCO shouted at Boggs. "And be careful. One of our guards reported some additional movement about a half mile up the road. Could be villagers, or it could be VC."

"We'll be careful," said Boggs, and pulled away.

Boggs turned to Whitehead and said, "Lieutenant, take my M14. Check it and be ready for trouble."

Southland checked his clip, pulled the handle back and cocked the weapon. Whitehead did the same thing. Whitehead noticed that the clip was actually two taped together, allowing the user to reverse the clip when the first emptied.

"How about putting the safety on, guys," said Boggs. "You're more likely to shoot me than the VC."

Boggs wasted no time going up the hill. The three men sat silently as the jeep moved swiftly past another group of engineers. These men held rifles rather than shovels. Boggs didn't stop the jeep when the NCO with this group waved. Being shot at once today is enough, thought Whitehead.

*

About fifteen minutes later, they reached a flat area which housed the Korean's communication site. Three or four of them were up on a hill and looked to be digging a hole. Three others could be seen at high points watching the surrounding countryside.

Stopping the jeep, Boggs suggested they wait awhile and maybe contact the engineers concerning any more sightings. Whitehead got out and was immediately caught in a bear hug.

"Lieutenant. I so glad to see another officer." The words came from a young Korean, about 5'9" with a big grin. "I Lieutenant Koo, first lieutenant, Republic of Korean Army. I use to be captain, but now I here."

"Glad to meet you. Heard of any action by the VC?"

"No, they afraid of Koreans. I have dozen VC ears. You come see."

"That's ok," said Whitehead. "I have my own ears in Nha Trang. I'll bring them the next time." Southland began to laugh. Boggs punched him to stop.

Two rifle shots were heard in the background. The four Koreans looking in a hole jumped and ran to a nearby hut and got weapons. They then scurried up the hill on the opposite side.

"No worry," said the Korean lieutenant. "Engineers always shooting up tree and rocks. No VC. No VC."

"Why are your soldiers going to their bunkers?"

"Good practice. No VC."

By now Southland and Boggs were both standing nearby. Whitehead introduced them. Boggs said a few words in Korean that he had picked up while stationed there.   Southland stood in awe of Boggs.   "I didn't know you spoke Korean?"

"I don't," said Boggs.   "I know a few words.   I also know that those soldiers looking in the hole were making Kimchee."

Lieutenant Koo nodded his head.   "You right sergeant.   We eat Kimchee every night.   You call it cabbage."

More chit-chat of war.   As before, the chat became gunfire.   The Koreans on the hill were shooting, and shooting in earnest.   Lieutenant Koo followed his men to the ridge.

Whitehead, Boggs, and Southland were looking for cover, but were interrupted by screams from the hill.   All three knew the screams were joyous, for the Koreans were now on their feet holding their weapons high in the air.   It was clearly a celebration.

The crowd of Koreans was now coming down the hill.   Behind them, the Korean sergeant was following. He was dragging something, but it became clear that the something was actually someone.

Lieutenant Koo approached and smiled with great joy, "We got VC! We got VC!"

Southland moved out toward the approaching Korean Sergeant.   The Koreans were indeed happy, almost out of control with laughter and good spirits.

Whitehead was impressed with the morale, but soon changed his mind.   He watched one of the young Korean soldiers walk over to the VC and kick the body two or three times.   Another Korean soldier did the same.   It became infectious.

Whitehead moved toward the group, thinking maybe he should stop the brutal attack on the body.   But Lieutenant Koo stepped in front of him, and spoke almost perfect English, "Leave them be.   Perhaps you should go now."

By now it was nearly 3 o'clock.   Boggs, joining the two lieutenants, said, "Sir, I think we better get back down the hill.   We don't have much time before dark."

Looking at the Korean officer for some signs of humanity, Whitehead finally gave up, "He's right, Lieutenant Koo.   We'll come back tomorrow for a longer stay?"

Returning to the jeep, Whitehead continued to watch the Koreans laugh and joke around the dead VC. The kicking seemed to have stopped, but Whitehead was concerned about what would happen when they left.

Southland was driving now.   Boggs was in the back seat and Whitehead in front with the other M14.

Southland pulled out onto the road and headed to the bottom of the hill.   Going down was easier, noisier and faster.   Passing the work crews giving waves, the three man jeep crew arrived at the bottom a half hour later.

Pulling up at the tent, they got out, took a deep breath, and stretched out on the three cots inside. Sleeping or resting, no one spoke for a long time.

Boggs finally sat up.   He walked outside.   He went over to the jeep and began looking at its side. Hearing him move, Whitehead also sat up and followed him outside.

"What are you looking at?"   Whitehead asked.

"I may be wrong, but I think I'm looking at bullet holes."   Boggs was pointing to the side of the jeep where Whitehead saw five round holes on the passenger side.

"Do you think it was that dead VC?" asked Whitehead.

"First off, Lieutenant, that VC wasn't dead. Southland said he could hear the groaning when he got nearby."

"Just when I was feeling a little better, you have to ruin my settling conscience.   I left a human being up there to be tortured?"   Whitehead asked.

"You had no choice.   You were just an observer. It was their call." Boggs was speaking with great calm. "Do you think the engineers would have done much different if they caught the VC?"

"I hope so, sergeant.   I really hope so."

\*

Chow time on Hon Tre proved interesting. Whitehead, Boggs, and Southland had freshened up and were walking toward the mess tent.

"Let's get a table together so we can discuss tomorrow," said Whitehead.

Boggs grumbled, and said, "Sir, I might suggest you sit with the Engineer lieutenant.   We'll find seats with the NCOs."

"Sounds a little segregated to me, Boggs," Whitehead said in a low tone.

"Sir, you may be in the American army, but you're still in the army.   Rank has its privileges, and your privilege is to sit with other officers.   Ours is to sit with other sergeants."

"OK, whatever you say.   By the way, I'll buy dinner.   Put it on my tab."

Sure enough, the young engineer lieutenant had his own table with plenty of seats.   The others were all crowded.   The engineer, Walker, waved to Whitehead.

Before Whitehead entered, Boggs whispered to him, "Be sure to say 'as you were' after someone says attention."

Whitehead entered; someone shouted attention. Whitehead said, "As you were."   He joined the other lieutenant briefly, only to get up and get some food.   Not a very comfortable dinner for Whitehead.

Dinner over, he met Boggs and Southland.   The sergeants were going to take a walk and asked Whitehead if he wanted to come.   Whitehead declined and said he was going to lie down.

Left alone, he decided he was going to romp a little too. Lying down was just impossible. He headed back toward the landing and to the rock he sat on earlier. He was glad he didn't have to see Cook again.

No sooner had the thought entered his head, Cook's voice broke the spell.

"I thought I'd come earlier. Where's the carbine?" Cook looked around. "Dave, I don't see it. Go get it."

Whitehead jumped up lunging toward Cook.

"You son of a bitch. You took the carbine before. You snuck up to the tent and stole the carbine. I don't know what your game is, but leave me the hell out of it."

Inches away from Cook, with the words just out of his mouth, Whitehead felt a sharp pain on the left side of his head. First Cook was in front of him, now only darkness prevailed.

## CHAPTER 27

Coming to, Whitehead found himself tied up in the back of a dimly lit cave. The ground was hard and damp and in his mouth, he had some twigs, dirt, and some bugs as well. Whitehead could hear voices echoing and ringing in the cave, seeming to come from every direction. Lifting his head, Whitehead could see the cave was large, its walls lined with large wooden cases. Even in the dim light, Whitehead soon realized that the cases had markings of weapons, ammunition, and explosives.

He groaned, then felt a sharp pain in his side. Whitehead looked around and saw Bradley hovering over him. He groaned again, and Bradley kicked him once more. Shut up you stupid bastard, Whitehead said to himself, he kicks you when you moan. The kerosene lights gave the cave an eerie look; Bradley's face and breath made it downright ugly.

Bradley squatted down into Whitehead's face. "Well, Lieutenant Shithead arises! I hope you thanked Cook for stopping me. I really would have liked to kick the shit out of you."

"Bradley!" The voice came from the mouth of the cave. It was Cook.

Walking over to where Whitehead lay, he said, "It's about time you woke up. I thought Bradley may have hit you too hard."

"My stomach feels like a punching bag," said Whitehead wincing in pain. "I hope I didn't offend anyone by passing out."

"Always the wise-ass," hissed Bradley. "Another kick in the gut will shut his mouth."

"Leave him alone," said Cook. "I want him to be able to talk enough to tell me where the carbine is. No food or water for him either. It'll loosen his tongue a little."

Until Cook mentioned food and water, Whitehead was fine. Now he could think of nothing else.

Cook looked at Bradley who seemed to be focusing more on the beer he was drinking than what was going on around him.

"Do me a favor, Bradley," Cook said, "don't get drunk."

Bradley didn't say a word. He finished the beer then threw the empty can into the corner of the cave. The can bounced off one of the wooden boxes of explosives. Bradley then burped and passed wind.

Turning back to Whitehead, Cook said, "I watched the Mike boat land. Then I saw the construction vehicles pull slowly off the boat, followed by you and your jeep. Your sergeant was driving and your tall, lanky NCO followed the engineers."

"You had the carbine with you. And, for your sake, you'd better have the jade."

"What the hell is going on here?" asked Whitehead.

"It's simple, really. We're exchanging some . . . commodities." Cook smiled, then continued, "The jade goes to Bradley for the weapons; the arms would then go to Van Phan for drugs. The drugs would then go for cold, hard American cash."

"Sold by you, of course," said Whitehead.

"Of course. It's great, isn't it, Dave?" Cook began to laugh.

While Cook talked, a third figure appeared in the cave. He leaned against the wall looking at the cases of AK47s which Bradley had brought to the island several months ago. Whitehead knew who the third person was even before he could see his face. It was Burgess.

Cook turned to the new arrival.

"Great. One asshole is getting drunk and the other is getting high."

Burgess took the reefer from his mouth and said,

"Fuck you, Cook." He then sat on the cave floor with his back against the wall.

"My friend's eloquence overshadows his cleverness. His heartbeat was so low at Duc My no one could have detected it. Even you missed it."

"No one but Lakeland and Harris you mean," interrupted Whitehead.

Burgess began laughing. "Those two were in it from the start. They wanted the money, but they got restless and wanted it immediately. Now they got nothing but dead."

"However," Burgess continued, the hash making him talkative, "My friend Cook, now, he's something else. This son of a bitch appears, then vanishes. Amazing."

Struggling to his feet, Burgess began cursing, then kicked at the dirt. "I still smell those dead gooks!"

"The three Vietnamese who helped us carry the crates to the cave," Cook explained, "Burgess shot two of them; the other Bradley beat and left to die. Three months later, Burgess found the kid near the cave's entrance. He died trying to crawl out. Tough little guy."

"Looks to me as if your two friends could be your biggest problem, Cook," Whitehead said.

"You may be right, Dave," Cook said as he watched Bradley and Burgess begin arguing. "They attempted to kill Van Phan and me at the party."

"So they were the shooters?" said Whitehead. "You better watch your ass."

Cook added while walking away, "If I were you, I wouldn't worry about me. If I left, these two would kill you, and enjoy every minute of pain they would put you through."

\*

Bradley and Burgess bickered about one thing or

another for most of the night.    Burgess was high on something.    Bradley was drunk.

Whitehead was never so glad to have the dead man, Burgess, alive.    He was keeping Bradley occupied. They literally argued about everything, but mostly about beer and dope.    The bickering finally erupted into a full-fledged argument.    A few minutes later the two men separated.

Sometime during the night, Burgess took an AK47 and plenty of ammunition, then left the cave.    The next morning when Bradley went outside to relieve himself, Burgess shot at him.    When Cook appeared at the mouth of the cave, Burgess fired upon him as well.

"That son of a bitch is going to kill us and keep everything," screamed Bradley.

"Shut up you drunken fool," said Cook.    "Let me think!"    Cook acted quickly.    Grabbing a couple of AK47s from the crates lining the walls of the cave, Cook loaded both and threw one to Bradley.    Bradley never came close to catching it.    Picking it up, he looked at Cook as if to kill him.

Cook spoke, "We're going to the entrance.    On the count of three, you run to the left and I'll run to the right. He can't shoot both of us."

"No way I'm going out there," yelled Bradley.

Cook pointed the rifle at Bradley.    "If you don't go, I'll shoot you here."

"OK, OK.    You win. Let's try it."

"Don't try it.    Do it!    Run fast and keep changing direction."

Cook and Bradley headed for the entrance.

Crouching down, Cook counted.    At three, they both took off.    Automatic rifle fire ripped the cave's entrance.    There was a scream, then silence.

Cook then came back into the cave, sitting by the entrance.    Propping his rifle against the wall, he walked back to where Whitehead was laying.

"I'm glad you're awake. You can now see what's going on." Cook reached down and grabbed Whitehead's collar and proceeded to drag him to the opening of the cave.

"Now I can watch you while I clean up this mess with Burgess and Bradley."

*

Soon after, Whitehead heard the sound of a chopper. Now sitting up by the cave's entrance, he could see out the cave as a group of four very professional looking Vietnamese soldiers jumped out and proceeded to secure the area. A door-gunner also scanned the area with an M50 machine gun.

A stout Vietnamese was helped out onto the ground. White pants and shirt, white shoes, and a white straw hat was all that anyone could see. Whitehead knew who the man was without seeing his face. Van Phan.

All the old players were coming back into the action.

Whitehead watched as Cook walked swiftly from the cave, shook hands with Van Phan, and then made some small talk.

They turned in the direction of the cave. Bradley reappeared from the trees limping, his right pant leg bloodied. Bradley was dragging something behind him. The something was a man.

Bradley dragged the man to the door of the chopper. He then kicked the wounded man two or three times with his left foot. Bradley screamed in pain each time. He pulled his Magnum from his belt and fired two rounds in the man's stomach.

"I hope you enjoy the belly wound, Burgess." He then threw the man on the chopper and yelled to the pilot to dump him in the ocean.

The pilot looked to Van Phan, who nodded his head.

Within minutes, the chopper was airborne, heading toward the outward side of the island. It soon became a speck in the air though only a few hundred feet off the shoreline.

Still visible from Whitehead's position, the chopper hovered a few seconds. A black object fell from the chopper and headed for the ocean. Burgess was dead, again.

## CHAPTER 28

Still bound, Whitehead watched his captors outside the cave. Van Phan looked very disturbed. Whitehead lifted his head hearing the Asian's voice grow louder.

"I do not like the situation here. Mr. Cook. You said everything would be ready when I arrived. Yet, I am here, the weapons are here, but the jade isn't."

"Wait!" Cook grabbed Van Phan's arm. "The jade will be here. Then the guns are all yours. Bradley!"

From inside the cave, Whitehead looked on as Bradley limped into view.

"Bradley, help Van Phan's men load some of the arms on the chopper."

"Fuck you!" Bradley shouted. "This faggot all dressed in white doesn't touch a rifle without the jade in my hand."

Cook quickly said, "I apologize for my friend's poor taste in language. He's drunk." Stepping between Bradley and Van Phan, Cook continued, "I can get the jade in 20 minutes. Your men can begin to load some of the weapons on your bird. In an hour, the whole deal can be done. Then, you can bring a boat out for the rest of the arms cache."

"Get the jade, Mr. Cook. You have 20 minutes to get back here. Then you will have 30 minutes to get off the island. A boat is already on the way for the arms."

"Is the American Lieutenant in the Cave?" asked Van Phan.

"Yes," said Cook.

"I want him alive. He comes with me," Van Phan said. Whitehead could see the large smile on the man's face.

Turning back to the cave, Cook trotted back toward Whitehead. Reaching down, he dragged Whitehead to a standing position.

"I guess you want something?" said Whitehead with a grimace of pain.

"No fucking around, Whitehead. There's a guy outside who will shoot you, me, and a hundred other people to get what he wants. Right now," Cook said as he untied Whitehead's feet, "he wants these arms. And for him to get those arms, and remain alive, I have to get the jade for Bradley."

"I guess you want me to tell you where it is?" asked Whitehead.

"I don't know what it is with you. You joke when you should be scared shitless."

"I am scared shitless," admitted Whitehead without thinking.

"Now, we're going out the cave and down the hill to the engineers' camp to get the jade. Understand?"

"I think I do," said Whitehead. He didn't have the faintest idea where the jade was, but the engineers' camp was better than the cave.

Outside, Bradley glared at Whitehead. Looking at him, Bradley shouted, "Kill that son of a bitch if he tries anything funny. You hear me, Cook? If you aren't back in half an hour, I'm coming to look for you, Whitehead."

"Always a sweet guy," said Whitehead.

"Shut up and keep walking." Cook stuck a pistol in Whitehead's back. "Fun and games are over."

*

Whitehead needed time. Walking as slow as he could, Whitehead tried to burn up time to think. Nearing the bottom of the hill, the two men stopped to rest at a parked bulldozer.

"I need a break. Just a few seconds, okay?" Whitehead asked as he sat down on a large rock hoping an idea would come to him. Cook stood with his pistol pointed at the lieutenant. Looking at the bulldozer next to him, Whitehead thought it should be painted bright yellow, but it wasn't. It was olive-drab, like everything the Army owned.

"Let's get going, Whitehead," said Cook.

"Hey, what happened to 'Dave?' I thought we were friends."

Cook looked at him with deep scorn and cocked the pistol.

Whitehead held his hands up and said, "OK, OK. I get the message."

As they approached the engineer's camp, Whitehead saw his jeep parked in front of the tent.

"There. It's under the jeep," said Whitehead. It could be, he said to himself.

Falling to the ground, Whitehead moved under the jeep. He almost choked when he looked up and saw the carbine wired to the frame of the jeep.

"What's the problem, Whitehead?" said Cook.

"Nothing."

"Bullshit," said Cook, crawling under the jeep with Whitehead. Seeing the carbine, he yelled, "Get the son of a bitch and let's get the hell out of here."

Sliding out from under the jeep, Cook stood up and turned to find Boggs. The sergeant stood there aiming an M14 at Cook's chest.

"Hello, sergeant."

"Fuck you," said Boggs. "Move and I'll blow your chest away."

"Sergeant, I know you mean well, but if you get in the way, you'll be very sorry."

"Listen, shithead, I'm not sure what you and the lieutenant are fooling with, but I saw you and your fat-ass friend blind-side him, then go up the hill. If Lieutenant Whitehead tells me to back off, I'll dust you off, pat your backside, and let you go."

"Thank you, Sergeant Boggs. You, too, Southland," said Whitehead as Southland walked out of the tent and joined the trio. "Frankly, I don't know what to do with Cook. "But I do know we're not going to let him go."

Boggs and Southland watched Cook very carefully, keeping their M14s trained on him and listening to Whitehead.

Approaching Cook with great caution, Whitehead said, "Drop the pistol in front of you then back away two steps."

From the tree line, a heavy motor sound erupted. Out of the brush and over a small hill came the bulldozer. Smoke pouring from its high rising exhaust pipe, the dozer crushed everything in its way, heading directly at the four men.

"Move!" Whitehead shouted.

The small group scattered as the bulldozer sped through the small clearing. Diving out of the way of the construction vehicle, Whitehead lost sight of his own men and Cook. Turning back to look, he tripped over some rocks and fell, rolling down a slight incline.

He watched the dozer as it passed by. Sitting in the driver seat was Bradley holding the controls with one hand. In his other, he held an AK-47.

Bradley opened fire from the bulldozer's driver seat. Whitehead dove behind a small outcropping of rocks as bullets traced his path in the dirt. Bradley continued firing, chipping away at the rocks. Whitehead listened as Bradley fired again. Boggs, Whitehead said to himself. Looking from behind his cover, Whitehead watched as Bradley fired a few more rounds out the other side of the bulldozer's control compartment.

The dozer continued to pick up speed. Bradley tried to turn the machine, only to have it begin to slide to the right. With the dozer out of control, Bradley leaped from the driver's compartment. Hitting rocks and boulders, the dozer slid down the hill, the treads moving at full speed. In a tremendous crash, the vehicle fell onto its side. The sounds of hisses and screeches continued from the bottom of the hill and the smell of gasoline filled the air.

Whitehead watched as Boggs, still holding his M14, rose from the ditch on the other side of the road and began to look around. Southland was laying off to the side. Then, Whitehead saw Cook moving toward Southland. In Cook's hand was the pistol.

Pointing the gun at Southland, Cook shouted to Boggs, "Drop the rifle, sergeant, or your friend is dead. I mean it."

Whitehead froze as he watched the standoff. Boggs stood his ground for a moment then placed the weapon on the ground.

"Good boy. Now back away." Cook looked at Whitehead, the pistol still pointed at Southland. "Dave, get the carbine. Now!"

Whitehead didn't move. He didn't know what to do.

"Get it!" Cook shouted. Then he fired at Southland at point blank range, killing the sergeant instantly.

"Your other sergeant friend is next." Cook then turned the pistol toward Boggs who was staring at Southland's body.

Whitehead walked slowly over to the jeep and knelt beside it. Whitehead looked back at the body of Southland lying on the ground next to Cook. Then he looked at Cook, the man's eyes intently following Whitehead's actions. Cook seemed oblivious to everything around him now, especially Boggs who began to slowly move toward Cook.

Whitehead began to move slower, hoping to give

Boggs the time he needed to make his move. Whitehead could hear his heart pounding in his chest. The smell of the dozer's gasoline seemed stronger.

Boggs only got within twenty feet of Cook when bullets ripped up the ground in front of the sergeant. "Stay right where you are, Boggs." Bradley moved from the brush where he landed after jumping from the bulldozer. "Keep your distance," Bradley spoke as he moved between Cook and Boggs. "I'll kill you just as quick as Cook killed your buddy."

Bradley moved next to Cook pointing the AK47 at Whitehead and Boggs. "Kill them! They've already caused enough problems."

"Shut up," said Cook. Looking to Bradley, he added, "Watch Boggs. If he says a fucking word, shoot him." With that, Cook walked over to Whitehead, grabbed him, and pushed him toward the jeep. "We'll try this again. I want the carbine. You get it."

Whitehead moved to the jeep, then knelt beside it. He began to crawl under when another shot rang out. Whitehead looked back where Boggs was standing expecting to see another corpse, but the sergeant was still there. Instead, he saw Boggs over the body of Bradley on the ground. The fat man was laying on his back, his chest full of blood.

"Cook!" Whitehead turned scanning the area for Cook. Heading toward the tree line, Cook ran holding the pistol out in front of him.

Whitehead turned as he heard the sound of a bolt sliding back. Boggs held Bradley's AK-47 in his hands, raising the weapon toward the tree line and the fleeing Cook.

As Boggs' finger tightened around the trigger, a large fireball erupted as the bulldozer exploded, drowning out all sound and sending flames and metal into the air. The force of the explosion knocked Whitehead and Boggs to the ground.

The dozer continued to flame as Whitehead rose. Boggs was already on his feet.

"He's gone," said Boggs.

\*

"What happened? Who shot Bradley?" Whitehead asked as Boggs covered Southland's body with a poncho he found in the jeep.

Noise from the tree line stopped conversation as both Whitehead and Boggs grabbed their weapons. Two figures walked toward them. Both were armed.

"Don't shoot." The voice was recognizable almost immediately. It was Cohn. He was followed by a second figure, who continuously looked in every direction.

"I got here as soon as I could." Cohn dropped his M16 and pulled out his canteen. "To answer your question, Dave, my friend here shot Bradley," said Cohn between drinks of water. "You can thank him for saving your lives."

"Did you also blow-up the dozer?" asked Whitehead.

"No. But Cook got away again."

"You'll get him next."

Cohn looked around and saw the poncho. "Who's that?"

"That's Sergeant Southland. I guess you didn't get here soon enough."

"Damn," Cohn swore as he took of his cap. "Listen, Whitehead, I know you're upset about losing Southland. I've lost men, too."

"Bullshit, Cohn. This stuff is your life. It's not mine. Boggs and I are going to put Southland in the jeep and take him back to Nha Trang."

"Sorry, Lieutenant," said Cohn. "Your jeep, and

your sergeant, are coming with me.   We're going up the hill and getting Cook."

"The jeep's mine!   And Boggs works for me!" Whitehead was now standing and shouting in Cohn's face. "Fuck you and Uncle Sam.   We're done!"

"Wait a minute.   Let's ask Boggs," Cohn retorted.

Whitehead stopped and looked at Boggs.

Boggs had been quiet for much of the time. Things had moved so fast, the sergeant seemed to be at a loss.   After what seemed like forever, Boggs spoke, "Major, I work for the Lieutenant.   I do what he wants. But maybe me and Lieutenant Whitehead better talk alone."

The lieutenant and sergeant drifted off.   "Sir," said Boggs, "I don't want to go with Cohn either, but I don't feel comfortable about letting Southland's killer go."

"Shit, Sergeant, I feel so rotten about Southland.   I watched that bastard shoot him and couldn't do a thing about it."

"I feel the same way. I only knew him a few months but we got pretty close.   He was doing what he wanted. He wanted to see action.   He was always asking for a transfer.   After his mission with the Americal, he asked to go back.   It's not your fault."

Whitehead sighed   "Christ, Boggs, do you know what really bothers me?   Kneeling over Southland, I realized that I didn't even know his first name.   It was always Southland."

"He didn't like it," Boggs said, smiling.   "His given name was Elton."

"Shit, Boggs, I don't even know your first name."

"It's Herbert, but my wife calls me Buddy.   Most people just call me Sergeant."

"Are you telling me we should help Cohn?"

"Yes, sir.   I think it's better for us, and for Southland, to keep going."

They stood together, with Whitehead looking

toward Nha Trang.    Minutes passed.
    "Let's go."

## CHAPTER 29

Whitehead turned back toward the clearing. He watched as Cohn and his assistant collected the weapons and supplies they needed for their assault at the top of the hill. The two men had moved Southland's body over to the side of the clearing, covering it with a poncho. Next to Southland, Cohn also had placed Bradley's corpse.

As Whitehead and Boggs approached, Cohn turned and said, "Well, what's the story?"

"We're coming," said Whitehead.

"OK, but I need a full rundown on what's up at the top of the island."

"Besides Cook and Van Phan, there's about three or four other men, armed. The weapons are in the cave. And there's a helicopter." Whitehead took a deep breath and wiped his brow. "What do we have, Major?"

"There's us two," Cohn replied, pointing to himself and his partner, Shaw. "I have a chopper at a clearing near the far north end of the island with a few more soldiers there. Shaw here is going to let them know when we leave so they can approach the clearing up there, and we can coordinate an attack. Oh, and of course, you and Boggs, here."

"I better get the carbine," said Whitehead. "Since Cook wants it so bad, we may want to use it for bait."

"I'll get it," said Boggs, "I put it there in the first place." Boggs knelt down beside the jeep and crawled under.

"What?!" Whitehead shouted. "What made you do that?"

"You seemed real concerned about it, like it was really valuable. So I hid it when you left." Boggs passed the carbine from under the jeep and then slid out to stand up. "Sorry for the confusion."

Whitehead took the carbine from Boggs silently

watching him walk back to the jeep.

Cohn and his man worked quickly. Where the backseat had been, there was just empty space. Cohn got in the driver seat of Whitehead's jeep. Sitting on tarps in the back of the jeep, Boggs and Cohn's man had their backs to the major. With their legs hung over each side, they could watch the back and sides. Their weapons were loaded, with the safeties off. Whitehead looked at the trio, took a deep breath, then moved into the passenger seat next to Cohn. Cohn started the engine and headed for the road up the hill.

Cohn handled the jeep like an expert, shifting gears and rounding the curves with what seemed to be little effort on his part. All four men sat quietly, Boggs and Shaw in the back scanning the tree line and the road behind them. Whitehead, holding his carbine tightly, watched the road ahead.

Whitehead leaned over and shouted over the motor, "How are your men going to find us?"

"They have eyes. They'll see us."

The two men grew silent again. The road widened as they passed through a small clearing, signs of the engineers' work lining the sides of the dirt road. The forest on each side grew thicker as the jeep made its way up the mountainside. The road, with its twists and turns, became rockier. The sounds of the island muffled under the roar of the straining jeep engine.

Whitehead looked up as a new sound reached his ears. Twisting his head around, Whitehead faintly made out the sound of an approaching helicopter. He turned to his companions. Cohn concentrated on the road, the other two in the back still scanning behind and to the side. None seemed to be aware of anything more.

"I guess you were right," said Whitehead finally breaking the silence. "Your men found us."

"What?" Cohn shouted over the jeep's engine.

"Don't you hear the 'copter?" asked Whitehead.

Before Cohn could answer, a chopper came up behind the jeep flying very low, just above the trees. Both the chopper motor and the blades were loud burying the sound of the jeep. Boggs and Shaw ducked as the chopper passed over.

"Hold on!" Cohn shouted as he watched the helicopter turning to make another pass. "Those aren't my men!"

Cohn shifted gears, slamming down the accelerator as he took the next curve on what felt like two wheels. The forest became a blur of green as the jeep sped up the road, each rock sending the jeep into the air. Up ahead, Whitehead watched as the chopper completed its turn and headed back down the road toward them.

Gunfire erupted from the back seat of the jeep. Boggs and Cohn's man had shifted positions and were now facing the front of the jeep. The two men fired upon the helicopter bearing down on them, emptying their clips.

The chopper returned fire, the bullets eating up the road ahead of the jeep. The next burst caught the hood as the chopper passed over.

"Damn!" Cohn shouted as he lost control of the speeding jeep. Steam began to pour out of the bullet holes as the major quickly regained his hold on the jeep. Bucking and sputtering, the wounded vehicle began to lose power, and lose it fast. "The jeep's dying," Cohn said. "Where's the chopper?"

"It's not in our field of vision, sir," Cohn's man replied. "It must be turning around somewhere."

"No shit, Dick Tracy!" shouted Cohn. "That chopper is going to be back. It must be Van Phan's men. I told you he hates you."

Before Whitehead could protest, the chopper reappeared directly in front of the jeep. It swooped in over the jeep and hovered. With its guns out of position, the chopper hung in the air, the men inside scrambling to turn the guns on the target in the road. Cohn saw a uniformed figure lean out the door, holding something in his hand. It was small and round.

"Jesus Christ, get out of the jeep and get behind cover!" Cohn jumped from the moving jeep as he shouted his commands. "Get the fuck out of here! Move! Move!"

Whitehead rolled out of the seat as he heard the grenade drop onto the seat behind him. All four men dove away from the jeep into the ditches lining the sides of the road. Thank God for engineers, Whitehead thought as he covered his head in the ditch. With no one at the wheel, the jeep began rolling back down the hill.

The explosion was deafening. Shrapnel from the vehicle flew in every direction. Whitehead felt the metal hit him on the top of his head breaking skin. Blood poured down onto his face, his ears ringing in pain. Still lying in the ditch, he lifted his head and looked around. Whitehead picked up a few pieces and actually tried to determine if it was part of the seat or the gear shift.

Cohn shouted again, "Stay down. Lie still. They can't see us in the ditches because of the overgrowth. Don't move."

Whitehead did as he was told, but wasn't sure it was good advice. What if Van Phan's men decided to spray everything with bullets to make sure? Whitehead froze at the sound of the chopper's blades in the sky above.

Again, the sound of gunfire filled the air. Whitehead could hear the bullets rip into the road and the remnants of the jeep. He could also feel the dirt and rocks fall on him as the bullets tagged the side of the ditch he was in. As quickly as the shooting started, it stopped. Looking up, Whitehead watched as the chopper began to turn, then move quickly away from the area.

Whitehead began to wonder why the chopper left

when he heard the answer to his question down the road behind them. The calvary, he wondered as the sound of the motors grew louder. No, he laughed to himself, just the engineers.

CHAPTER 30

"I'm glad to see you're still alive.    I'm even more glad to see you took you're carbine with you."    Cohn sat down beside the sprawled Whitehead and looked at the cut on his head and the blood on his face.    "You'll heal and won't have any scars."

"Thank you for your opinion, Dr. Cohn."

"Wrong Cohn.    My brother's a doctor, Dr. Harry Cohn of Boston," Cohn said, smiling.    "When you get up, we can start moving up the hill again."    Cohn stood up and began looking at the remnants of the jeep.    It was a shell with four wheels, lying on its side.

*

The engineers had been there only about ten minutes before Lieutenant Walker was shouting.    They came with a jeep and a large truck, and a belly full of anger.

After talking briefly with Cohn, Walker became animated.    "Fuck you!" shouted the engineer Lieutenant. "You destroy my bulldozer, turnover a dead civilian, and use my camp for your crazy work.    Now, you got the balls to ask me for my jeep."    The engineer shook his head, "You must think I'm the biggest asshole in the world."

"Hold it Lieutenant," said Cohn.    "I'm a major in the US Army, a member of CID, and I'm ordering you to turn over the jeep."

"You want me to drive it for you, too?"

"Lieutenant, you're going too far," warned Cohn.

"Who's going to sign for all this destroyed equipment?    I'll be in Vietnam for 100 years paying for that dozer."

Cohn looked at Whitehead, and thought about the time being wasted, and said, "Write up a statement saying you assigned the jeep to me, and I'll sign it."

"What about you, Lieutenant Whitehead? You going to sign it, too?" asked the engineer.

"I'm just an observer. I'm like you, Lieutenant Walker. I only do what I'm told," Whitehead said without a smile or gesture.

The engineer looked at the two, and finally said, "Take the fucking jeep. Take my backhoe. Take the other dozer. Take anything you want. Just get away from my area, and don't come back."

*

It took the four men about fifteen minutes to get re-organized. Most of their time was spent watching the engineers' hook a chain to Whitehead's burned out jeep and drag it down the road to the bottom of the island. When the engineers disappeared around the bend, Cohn got behind the wheel and the four continued up the mountain road.

It took another twenty minutes to reach the hilltop. The four had grown quiet once again, each one looking in the sky now as well as the forest. Reaching a small clearing near the mouth of the road, Cohn abruptly stopped the jeep.

"What are you doing?" Whitehead asked, surprised that the major would place the jeep in such a dangerous position. They were near the cave which meant Van Phan's chopper was close by.

"We need to get a strategy."

"Okay, so what are we going to do when we get there?"

"I don't know. I don't know what we'll find. They may be gone for all we know." Cohn didn't seem to make this last statement with conviction. "C'mon," the major said as he got out of the driver's seat.

"Where are you going?"   Whitehead asked.

"We're going to take a look up there.   We can't go in without knowing exactly what we're up against.   Boggs, you and Shaw stay here.   Whitehead, you're with me."

Leaving Boggs and the CID man to guard the jeep, Cohn and Whitehead headed for the cave area on foot.   It was getting late in a day that was already very long.

Cohn finally stopped and crouched low in the elephant grass.   Whitehead remained standing.   Cohn pulled Whitehead down, saying, "Do what I do.   When I stop, you stop.   When I get down, you get down."

Whitehead nodded.

"Stay put for a second," Cohn whispered.

Whitehead watched as Cohn moved around to an area away from the trail and the road.   Finding good cover, the major inched forward, staying low.   Cohn rounded some rocks nearly entering the open area.

Whitehead raised his head slowly.   He tried to look at the cave while also trying not to lose sight of the major in the tall grass.   He saw Cook and Van Phan sitting on a couple of boulders in deep conversation.   Looking at the cave, Whitehead saw some new players.   Well armed and ready to protect the cave were Cook's three young Vietnamese guardians.   From his vantage point, he couldn't see the chopper.   It must be over behind those trees, Whitehead thought, along with more men probably.

The grass to Whitehead's left parted as Cohn crawled through, bumping into Whitehead who tripped and almost yelled.

"What'd you see?" asked Whitehead.

"Van Phan and Cook are there.   So are about six or seven others."

"I can only see three others from here.   What about the chopper?"

"Off the crest of the hill," Cohn responded.   "It's totally shut down.   The pilot had the engine compartment open and was looking inside. Where did those three kids come from? They aren't with Van Phan."

Whitehead slouched down and sat with his back to the opening. "All the way from Duc My."

"What are you talking about?" asked Cohn.

"Cook. His three playmates from Duc My are guarding the cave and his weapons." Seeing Cohn confused, he related how Cook appeared at the Special Forces camp with these three Vietnamese as his well-armed aides. Hon Tre Island seemed to be the place to meet.

\*

Cohn and Whitehead stayed behind the rocks silently watching the cave. Nothing seemed to be happening. Cook and Van Phan still sat at the cave mouth deep in conversation while the other men stood around, guns in their hands, eyes focused on their two leaders. In the sky above, the heat of the bright jungle sun beat down upon Whitehead sapping his energy away.

About ten minutes had passed when Cohn began to move.

"Let's move closer," Cohn said turning to Whitehead.

"What? Is that smart?"

"Would you rather just sit here and bake in the sun? Up where I was before, there's at least some shade," Cohn answered. "Besides, we can get a better view and maybe hear what they're talking about up there." With that, Cohn moved quickly into the underbrush. Whitehead, shaking his head, followed.

Cohn had been right. The new location, while closer to the cave, provided them with some shade, a better view, and surprisingly, more cover. The grass was higher and the shade allowed Whitehead and Cohn to sit in the shadows behind the rocks.

"You know," Cohn whispered as he pointed toward the chopper, "I think something's wrong with Van Phan's chopper. The pilot looks real concerned. Maybe we hit it with one of our rounds."

Whitehead looked over the rocks. To the side of the clearing, the pilot stood outside the chopper, its engine compartment opened. The Vietnamese repeatedly looked inside the compartment, his hands moving furiously as he worked on the chopper's engine, then raised his head shaking it in disgust.

"This may be our chance to take them." Cohn continued to watch the pilot as Whitehead laid back down on the ground behind the rocks. Cohn then slid down alongside of Whitehead. "Okay, I decided. We wait for my men and then we go in. Hit them shooting."

"Oh Christ, Cohn, you know who you're with here. I'm not a real soldier. I'm scared shitless, and you're preparing for a major assault."

"Don't worry, you've done alright so far." Cohn sat quietly looking at Whitehead. "Maybe you're right," the major said finally.

"And speaking of 'your men', where the hell are they?"

"Keep your shorts on, Whitehead. They'll be here. We just have to wait."

After another ten minutes, Whitehead was almost drifting off to sleep, when he felt Cohn stiffen. Cohn reached down and pulled Whitehead up. "Something's going on. There's a problem."

Whitehead looked over the rocks. He noticed that Van Phan's men had tensed up, their rifles now at the ready. The chopper pilot had closed the motor compartment and slipped behind the controls. Cook's three Vietnamese guards disappeared, leaving the cave seemingly unguarded.

"What's going on?" Whitehead asked, more to himself than Cohn. Looking at the mouth of the cave, he saw the answer.    Cook and Van Phan were arguing, violently.

Whitehead watched as the heated argument continued.    It seemed over as Cook turned and began walking away from the cave.    About half way, he stopped and turned around shouting, "Van Phan, you've got one more chance.    You want the arms, you can have them. But I went through alot of trouble to get them here and you're not leaving without those guns.    But I'm not letting you leave until I get my money!"

The two men resumed their battle in hushed tones as Cook once again sat across from Van Phan.    Van Phan didn't like the situation.    That was clear.    But Whitehead couldn't hear what the fat Vietnamese was saying. Whitehead turned to Cohn as he cursed himself for not being able to read lips.    From the look on Cohn's face, the major could, and he read their meaning clearly.

"What's Van Phan want?" asked Whitehead.

"I'll tell you in a minute," answered Cohn.

Cohn now dropped down.    Looking at Whitehead, he said, "C'mon, let's get back to Boggs and Shaw."

Stooping and running, the two men wove back to where they left the jeep.

At the jeep, Cohn announced, "I've got a plan."

## CHAPTER 31

"Fuck you, Cohn! I'm not doing it," Whitehead shouted as he stood next to the jeep, glaring at the major sitting in the driver's seat. "Now I know why you wanted me to come, you son of a bitch. I'm goddamned bait."

Cohn sat up in the jeep and said, "Dave, all I'm asking you to do is hold your carbine up in the air and get Cook's attention. No one's going to shoot you." Cohn said it with a perfectly straight face.

"What happens if someone does shoot me?" Whitehead paused for a second then continued before Cohn could answer. "Oh, I know, just fall down and bleed. Just the way we planned it!"

Cohn held his hand up. "No, no. As soon as you reach the center of the opening near Cook, Boggs and Shaw will come flying into the clearing with the jeep. Those guys will be so disoriented, they won't know what's happening."

"Shit!" Whitehead was mad, but more important he was scared. He turned from the jeep and began to walk away. Standing a few feet away, Boggs and Shaw remained silent.

Cohn got out of the jeep and walked after Whitehead. Grabbing the lieutenant's arm, the major said, "As soon as you hear us open fire, hit the ground."

"That's all? Hit the ground?" Whitehead looked at Cohn. "I don't believe you. What else?"

"You throw the grenade toward the chopper."

"Grenade?" Whitehead spit the word out. "Where's this grenade coming from?"

"Shaw," Cohn spoke turning to the CID man. Shaw took one of the grenades out of the small pouch they had taken with them on their trip up the mountain road and handed it to the major. Holding the grenade out in front of him, Cohn continued, "Tuck the grenade in your pant leg, near the top of your boot where the elastic holds it tight. That way, you'll be able to retrieve it easily while you're on the ground. Just reach down, get the grenade, pull the pin, and toss it toward the chopper. It only has to get close."

"And what do I do when the grenade goes off?" asked Whitehead.

"Just keep your head down, and the shrapnel will go over you."

"You know, Cohn, you're a real prick. You had this plan going on in your mind from the moment you hit the island. You know Cook wants the carbine and Van Phan wants me."

"No, you're only partly right."

"You mean the part about you being a prick," snarled Whitehead, "or the part about the plan."

"I don't care what you think of me. But the plan just came to me," said Cohn. "Remember you asked me what Van Phan said before?"

"Yeah, so what did he say to Cook."

"He said that he was only staying on the island because he wanted you, the man who killed his son. As for Cook and that carbine of yours, I don't know why he wants it."

Whitehead stood silent for a few moments, staring at Cohn then looking at Boggs and Shaw. He didn't want to tell them that Cook didn't really want the carbine, but the jade inside the weapon's stock, but now it seemed like he had no choice. If they were going to get killed, Whitehead decided, they should know why.

"Jade."

"What?" Cohn answered, caught totally off guard by this latent information. "What jade?"

"Cook doesn't want the carbine. He wants the jade inside the carbine. That's all. He doesn't want some stupid weapon."

"Jesus!"    Boggs shouted.    "Why didn't you say something earlier, you idiot!"

"I know I should have said something earlier -"

"You're damned right you should have," Boggs interrupted Whitehead.    "Southland's dead because of this little omission on your part, maybe all of us too.    I should take your head off for this shit."

"Okay, okay, Boggs.    At least he told us," Cohn said stepping between the sergeant and Whitehead. Turning to Whitehead, the major asked "Where's the jade now?"

"Here.    In the carbine.    I have it with me." Whitehead looked at Boggs.    "I didn't want any of you involved.    Cook wants it and he'll go through anybody who's in his way.    I figured the less you or Southland knew, the better."

The four men grew silent.    Boggs walked away from the jeep, cursing under his breath.    Shaw and Cohn stood next to each other near the jeep talking to each other. Shaw then took the radio and walked away to the other side of the clearing.    Whitehead stared at the carbine, the source of his problems since he came over from America. After a few moments, Whitehead looked at Cohn and spoke.

"OK, let me get this straight.    I hold the carbine high above my head.    I walk slowly into the clearing and inch my way toward the chopper, shouting to Cook and Van Phan that I want to talk."

Cohn nodded in approval.

"Then I tell them that I want the killing to stop. They can have the jade."    Whitehead continued, "When I hear the jeep and you three shooting, I hit the ground and throw the grenade."

Cohn continued to nod.

Whitehead also continued to talk, "Why do I feel like I have to throw up or wet my pants?"

"You'll do alright."

"I don't want to do alright.   I don't want to do it."
Whitehead stared at Cohn.   "Shit."

"Sir," Shaw said, returning to the jeep with the
radio.   "I just spoke with our men at the chopper.   They
haven't been able to rendezvous with us due to the engine
overheating.   They say it'll take some time to fix.   They'll
be here as soon as possible."

Cohn looked at Whitehead.   The major said just
one word.   "Damn."

*

Cohn accompanied Whitehead back to the rocks at
the edge of the clearing near the cave.   Boggs and Shaw
remained with the jeep.   They would slowly drive up the
road and move into position, then wait for Cohn's signal to
barrel into the clearing.

"Why am I agreeing to do this?"   Whitehead shook
his head as he saw Cook and Van Phan walking around
giving orders to each of their men.

"You've got to!" whispered Cohn. "We've got no
choice.   There's not much daylight left.   And without that
chopper, we're the only thing that can stop those guys."
Cohn pushed Whitehead.   "Get going."

Whitehead rose and positioned the carbine above
his head holding the weapon in his left hand.   Deep down,
he knew he was in a world of shit.   Moving out from
behind the rocks, Whitehead entered the clearing.   He
walked slowly, moving toward the chopper.   He tried to
shout Cook's name, but nothing came out until one of Van
Phan's men noticed the approaching American and fired.
The round tore a hole in the ground in front of Whitehead.

"Cook!   Hold your fire!" shouted Whitehead.
"I've got your jade."

Cook turned away from the mouth of the cave when

he heard the shot. Seeing Whitehead, he began to move toward the center of the opening, shouting, "Hold your fire."

Cook met Whitehead in the center, and grabbed the carbine. Without a word, Cook hit Whitehead with the butt of the carbine, sending the stunned Lieutenant to the ground. Whitehead tried to get up, but remembered that when he did that in the cave Bradley hit him, so he just laid there.

"I should kill you here and now, Whitehead," Cook said as he stood over the fallen lieutenant, the carbine's nozzle up against Whitehead's temple.

Damn you Cohn, Whitehead said to himself, where are you. There was no jeep, no Cohn, and more importantly, thought Whitehead, no hope. Then, before Cook carried out his threat, a voice came from the cave.

"Cook!" Van Phan shouted as he moved closer to the two men. "I told you, the American is mine. Put him in the aircraft. He will suffer for what he did to my son."

"C'mon," Cook said grabbing Whitehead by the collar.

At that moment, the jungle erupted with gunfire as Cohn began shooting from the opposite end of the clearing. Whitehead fell back down to the ground as Cook released him in favor of finding cover. From the mouth of the road, the jeep roared into the clearing, Boggs in the back firing his M14. Shaw drove the vehicle directly into the middle of the clearing hoping to scatter the Vietnamese.

But Van Phan's men responded, firing at the oncoming jeep. Whitehead saw the windshield shatter and watched as one of the front tires blew. The jeep went out of control, twisting and then going into a roll. Whitehead watched as Boggs jumped from the jeep, but Cohn's man couldn't get free.

Meanwhile, Cohn had changed position as the jeep barreled into the middle of the firefight. Cook's men, focused on the crashing jeep, were unaware as Cohn opened fire. Two fell to the earth dead, the other, bloodied and wounded, crawled back to the mouth of the cave.

The jeep continued to roll landing on its top, then skidding another twenty feet to a halt in the center of the clearing.

Whitehead looked around. All around him, Van Phan's men lay dead. He could see the two Vietnamese Cook brought with him sprawled by the cave entrance, their bodies riddled with bullet holes. The sounds of sporadic gunfire continued to fill the air. Then Whitehead also heard the chopper.

Looking at the chopper, Whitehead saw Van Phan in the cargo door. Remembering the grenade, Whitehead reached down and pulled the explosive from his pant leg. Staring at Van Phan, he tried to pull the pin. It wouldn't come out. The pin was bent.

Whitehead watched as the chopper began to rise into the air, but the pilot was having some difficulty. Smoke was coming from the rear of the aircraft. It looked as if the repairs to the chopper hadn't been completed when Cohn began the attack.

Using the edge of a rock, Whitehead straightened the end of the pin. With one final pull, the pin came out easily.

The chopper continued rising off the ground, now about fifty yards in the air. Whitehead threw the grenade and watched it stop beneath the chopper. He then hit the ground like he was told to do. The shooting continued, but Whitehead kept his head down. Cohn and Boggs were on their own.

Whitehead expected a long wait for the grenade to explode, but it seemed like it blew up almost immediately. He felt the shrapnel all around him, thinking he would get hit by some of the grenade fragments. He expected pain any minute.

Whitehead raised his head as he heard the chopper's engine groan and strain. There seemed to be more smoke coming from the aircraft as the pilot tried to continue the liftoff.

He heard Cohn shout, "Boggs, shoot at the chopper!"

Boggs' M14 barked as the bullets ripped into the chopper. The windshield shattered, sparks flew from the chopper's metal frame. Whitehead could see Van Phan screaming, his white suit bloodied.

Whitehead looked back to the edge of the clearing. Cohn, his left arm covered with blood, kept shouting orders.

"Keep firing at the chopper! Bring her down!"

Boggs emptied his clip into the cockpit. The pilot fell dead against the controls of the chopper.

The chopper lurched into the air, gaining altitude as Van Phan tried to grab the controls from the dead pilot's hand. The aircraft seemed to hover over the clearing before screaming back down to the earth.

The last of Cook's Vietnamese limped from the cave's entrance, and aimed at the pilot with his AK47. He emptied the clip into the cockpit. Whitehead watched as Van Phan took the full brunt of the AK's fire. The chopper veered out of control, fire and smoke coming from every place on the aircraft.

Whitehead watched as the chopper dipped and rose. It stopped flying and seemed to glide forward, heading directly for the cave. The young Vietnamese started to crawl back to the cave. The chopper picked up speed as it hurtled toward the cave's entrance.

"Down!" Cohn shouted.

The chopper hit the top of the cave entrance, the cockpit of the flaming aircraft literally sliding into the cave. The cave erupted into a fireball as the flaming wreckage came into contact with the weaponry Cook had placed inside the cave. Fire and debris flew out the entrance, as if every piece of explosive and ammunition in the cave exploded at once.

Whitehead flattened himself against the ground holding his ears. Rocks and pieces of the chopper rained down upon the clearing.

\*

When the dust settled, Whitehead picked himself up off the ground. His ears were still ringing from the explosion and he found that his legs were shaking. Whitehead looked at the cave and saw the inferno. Immediately, he began looking for his friends.

Boggs and Cohn emerged from behind the rocks they used as cover and walked into the opening. Cohn and Boggs held their rifles at the ready, but they found no life. No one else had survived.

"Dave!" Cohn shouted.

"I'm okay. Shaking in my combat boots, but fine. You?" Whitehead asked as the two men walked over to him. Cohn's left shoulder was covered in blood. Boggs walked with a noticeable limp.

"I'm fine," Cohn answered. "Took one to the shoulder, but it's not that bad."

"How about you, Boggs?"

"I'm fine too. I think I twisted my ankle," Boggs answered obviously embarrassed about his clumsiness.

"I have never seen anything like that in my life," Cohn said aloud as he watched the remnants of the chopper burning.

"Wait. Where's Shaw?"

"I don't know," Cohn said, looking around the clearing.

"He didn't make it. He couldn't get free when the

jeep overturned," Boggs said putting his hand on Cohn's healthy shoulder.

"Damn," Cohn cursed. "There's another I owe Cook." With that, the major walked to the overturned jeep. He gently pulled Shaw's body out of the wreckage and covered it with a shirt he had taken off the body of one of Van Phan's men.

Whitehead and Boggs walked around the perimeter checking everybody. After a few moments, Whitehead realized that everyone was not accounted for.

"Major! I can't find Cook's body," Whitehead shouted as he ran back to the major at the center of the clearing.

"What? Okay. Spread out. He has to be here." The three split up and walked around the clearing and the surrounding forest. Each came back empty-handed. In the background, both Whitehead and Cohn heard the noise of an approaching chopper. It was Cohn's men.

"Good thing we waited for them," said Whitehead.

"Shut the fuck up," Cohn shouted. "Don't say one more fucking word."

Whitehead didn't say a word. He didn't have to. They had stopped Van Phan from getting the weapons and busted the smuggling ring, but Cook got away. Again.

# EPILOGUE

Life in Vietnam was strange. The day after Hon Tre, everything seemed to return to normal. It began with a terrible breakfast of powdered eggs, stale toast, and burnt coffee in the transportation officer's mess with Norm Range. They talked only briefly about what had happened to Whitehead over on the island. When they couldn't find Cook's body, Cohn and his men took over the site ushering Whitehead and Boggs onto the chopper and back to the mainland. Cohn barely spoke to them when his men arrived other than to order Whitehead not to speak about what exactly went on at Hon Tre.

Norm had some news of his own to tell Whitehead.

"While you were over on the island, my wife went into premature labor. Right now, she's in the hospital and could give birth at any time. I really need to get back to her, but the C.O. won't give me the emergency leave."

"Sorry to hear that, Norm. Anything I could do for you?" asked Whitehead.

Before Norm could answer, the battalion adjutant came over and told Whitehead that the battalion commander wanted to see him right away.

"Dave, ask him about my emergency leave."

"Okay, Norm. I will if he's not reaming me a new asshole."

At battalion headquarters, Whitehead was sent right in to the battalion Commander. Whitehead reported and saluted.

"Lieutenant Whitehead, I just got finished talking with a Major Cohn. I haven't got the faintest idea what he was talking about, but he said you helped CID deal with a very difficult problem. He asked that, if I could, I should offer you some form of reward."

"Sir, I just want to do something about Sergeant Southland."

"Well, Lieutenant, I do, too!" The senior battalion officer seemed to be a little upset about it. "This Major Cohn gave me some details about the situation, and gave me assurances that his death was in the line of duty. He assured me that you and Boggs also served in an honorable fashion."

"Sir, I merely assisted in any way I could. Sergeants Boggs and Southland served well above the call of duty."

"Very noble, Whitehead. What if I were of a mind to raise questions about the three of you not doing your real job while you were working for Cohn. I'm not too pleased with Southland, let alone any man under my command, being killed. And don't worry about Boggs. He'll be taken care of. He's getting a promotion and at least a Bronze Star. So will Southland posthumously."

"Sir, Boggs and Southland were only doing what I asked them to do. I'm responsible for what took place."

"Whitehead, this talk all comes under the heading of bullshit. There's nothing I can do anyway. Without information, I can't even write you up for a medal. What can I do for you? Tell me."

"Send Norm Range home."

The battalion commander looked at Whitehead, and seemed to be studying him. He then rose and went out to the adjutant. The colonel spoke quietly, took some papers, and brought them back to his office area. He sat down at his desk, and read the papers. Looking up at Whitehead, the colonel signed the papers.

"Here, give these to Lieutenant Range, and then drive him to the airfield."

Whitehead saluted, and said "Thank you, sir."

\*

The trip to the airfield was uneventful and kind of

sad.    Norm had become a good friend, and helped Whitehead deal with the evils of Vietnam.

"Dave," said Norm, "What happened to the jade?"

"I don't know, Norm," responded Whitehead.    "We checked every carbine.    Nothing."    Whitehead sighed, then continued, "It all began with Cook and it probably all ended with him too.    He got it, I'm sure of it.    When he got it, I don't know."    Whitehead looked down, and finally said, "Shit, who gives a damn."

Whitehead put his hand out, and Norm shook it.

Norm said, "Thanks for everything."    He then walked to the plane.    Half way, he turned and waved.

Whitehead waved back and offered a mock salute.

The C130 took off and left Whitehead to himself.

*

Arriving back at the officers mess hall, he decided that he would let the battalion adjutant know that Norm was on his way home.

Before reaching the battalion area, he ran into Captain Dancer.    "Dave, c'mom into the office, I want to talk to you."

Once inside, Dancer got a chair for Whitehead and began a conversation dealing with the events of Hon Tre. He seemed to know a lot of the details, giving Whitehead the impression that Cohn must have briefed him.

For some reason, Whitehead didn't volunteer much information.    It seemed better to let Dancer take the lead. The twenty-minute chat came to an end when he received a telephone call.

"Sorry, Dave, but I've been waiting for this call all day.    I'll let you go, and we'll talk some more tomorrow."

Shaking hands, Whitehead left the office and moved toward the front of the building.    He nodded to the two clerks and was putting on his hat when he heard one of them speak.

"Hey, Bob, who is this Major Benson calling Captain Dancer?"

\*

Whitehead had thumbed a ride to the Nha Trang beach. Without his jeep, he would have to get used to walking again. Whitehead walked through the sand, kicking some to each side.

Ahead of him was a stone jetty that went out nearly a hundred feet into the harbor. He climbed the rock and walked along the top, almost to the end. Stopping, he looked around.

Seeing no one, he reached into his fatigue pants pocket. He gathered the stones in his right hand. Removing his hand from his pocket, Whitehead looked at the bright green stones of jade. He counted them, brushing some lint off them. He admired them, watching the sun reflecting their brilliance.

After a few minutes, he moved the stones to his left hand to free his right. One by one, Whitehead took a stone and tossed it in the South China Sea. When done, he wiped his hands on his pants and walked back to the beach.

Now it was truly over.

them speak.

"Hey, Bob, who is this Major Benson calling Captain Dancer?"

\*

Whitehead had thumbed a ride to the Nha Trang beach. Without his jeep, he would have to get used to walking again. Whitehead walked through the sand, kicking some to each side.

Ahead of him was a stone jetty that went out nearly a hundred feet into the harbor. He climbed the rock and walked along the top, almost to the end. Stopping, he looked around.

Seeing no one, he reached into his fatigue pants pocket. He gathered the stones in his right hand. Removing his hand from his pocket, Whitehead looked at the bright green stones of jade. He counted them, brushing some lint off them. He admired them, watching the sun reflecting their brilliance.

After a few minutes, he moved the stones to his left hand to free his right. One by one, Whitehead took a stone and tossed it in the South China Sea. When done, he wiped his hands on his pants and walked back to the beach.

Now it was truly over.

sad.    Norm had become a good friend, and helped Whitehead deal with the evils of Vietnam.

"Dave," said Norm, "What happened to the jade?"

"I don't know, Norm," responded Whitehead.    "We checked every carbine.    Nothing."    Whitehead sighed, then continued, "It all began with Cook and it probably all ended with him too.    He got it, I'm sure of it.    When he got it, I don't know."    Whitehead looked down, and finally said, "Shit, who gives a damn."

Whitehead put his hand out, and Norm shook it.

Norm said, "Thanks for everything."    He then walked to the plane.    Half way, he turned and waved.

Whitehead waved back and offered a mock salute.

The C130 took off and left Whitehead to himself.

*

Arriving back at the officers mess hall, he decided that he would let the battalion adjutant know that Norm was on his way home.

Before reaching the battalion area, he ran into Captain Dancer.    "Dave, c'mom into the office, I want to talk to you."

Once inside, Dancer got a chair for Whitehead and began a conversation dealing with the events of Hon Tre. He seemed to know a lot of the details, giving Whitehead the impression that Cohn must have briefed him.

For some reason, Whitehead didn't volunteer much information.    It seemed better to let Dancer take the lead. The twenty-minute chat came to an end when he received a telephone call.

"Sorry, Dave, but I've been waiting for this call all day.    I'll let you go, and we'll talk some more tomorrow."

Shaking hands, Whitehead left the office and moved toward the front of the building.    He nodded to the two clerks and was putting on his hat when he heard one of

# THE AUTHOR

David E. Weischadle is professor emeritus at Montclair State University in New Jersey. A former army officer in Vietnam, he draws as much on his experience as on his imagination. He lives with his wife in New Jersey and Massachusetts. They have two sons who are attorneys and are principals in Granary Way Media LLC, a television and radio production company in Princeton, New Jersey.

www.ingramcontent.com/pod-product-compliance
Lightning Source LLC
Chambersburg PA
CBHW071128170626
46809CB00002B/537